'Why agree to marry him in the first place if you do not like him?'

His head was thudding, and the gilded ornamentation of the room seemed to shimmer in the candlelight, but Jack found himself fascinated by the play of emotion on Lily's face. The expression of self-deprecation changed to one of surprise.

'He is a baron,' she stated, as though he had asked a very foolish question.

'Er, yes. And so…?' She still seemed puzzled. 'You must marry a baron?'

'Someone with a title, and baronets are too low down, so it had to be at least a baron.'

The room was definitely beginning to blur.

'But why?'

'So my sons will be gentlemen, of course.'

Author Note

On 10th November 1810 a certain Mrs Tottenham received a delivery of coal at her modest middle class residence in Berners Street, just off London's Oxford Street. But Mrs Tottenham had not ordered coal, nor had she ordered any of the other things that came to her door that day—musical instruments and wigs, coffins and fruit, hats and bibles. Virtually every commodity one could hope to find in the great city was delivered to poor Mrs Tottenham's door.

Nor were goods all that descended on the harassed lady—the Lord Mayor of London, the Governor of the Bank of England, a number of cabinet ministers, all attempted to fight their way through the near riot in the narrow street, all victims of the same hoaxer.

Years later Theodore Hook, a writer of comic operas, confessed to the plot, saying that he had taken a bet to make a modest house the most talked-about address in London. Mr Hook won his five guineas and a lasting notoriety—but what, I wondered, about poor Mrs Tottenham? How would it feel to be on the receiving end of this joke?

And as I wondered it occurred to me that this might be how my heroine, Lily France, a wealthy, vulgar, merchant's heiress, might meet my hero, Jack Lovell—proud, broke, and the possessor of a secret.

I enjoyed finding out how Lily and Jack resolved their differences, and whether Jack ever did persuade her to give up her passion for the Egyptian style in interior decoration, and I hope you do too.

NOT QUITE A LADY

Louise Allen

MILLS & BOON®

First published in Great Britain 2006
Paperback edition 2007
Harlequin Mills & Boon Limited,
Eton House, 18-24 Paradise Road, Richmond, Surrey TW9 1SR

© Melanie Hilton 2006

ISBN-13: 978 0 263 85152 6
ISBN-10:   0 263 85152 4

Set in Times Roman 10½ on 12¾ pt.
04-0107-87263

Printed and bound in Spain
by Litografia Rosés S.A., Barcelona

Louise Allen has been immersing herself in history, real and fictional, for as long as she can remember, and finds landscapes and places evoke powerful images of the past. Louise lives in Bedfordshire, and works as a property manager, but spends as much time as possible with her husband at the cottage they are renovating on the north Norfolk coast, or travelling abroad. Venice, Burgundy and the Greek islands are favourite atmospheric destinations.

Recent novels by the same author:

ONE NIGHT WITH A RAKE
THE EARL'S INTENDED WIFE
THE SOCIETY CATCH
A MODEL DEBUTANTE
THE MARRIAGE DEBT
MOONLIGHT AND MISTLETOE
  (in *Christmas Brides*)
THE VISCOUNT'S BETROTHAL
THE BRIDE'S SEDUCTION

Chapter One

Almack's Assembly Rooms: late March 1815

'My dear, I agree it would be laughable if it was not my own cousin involved with the creature, but as he is, I simply cannot find it in me to be amused.' The speaker's affected voice was instantly recognisable as she entered the room. Lady Angela Hardy. Behind the screen in the retiring room Lily's fingers stilled on the recalcitrant knot in her garter, then slowly curled.

'Oh, I do so understand and sympathise.' The other speaker oozed understanding. 'So vulgar—the whole family will be devastated if your suspicions are true. And that impossible hair. And the clothes! No wonder she has stayed unmarried so long.'

'With that amount of money?' The third female voice was harsher. 'I cannot agree; personally I am amazed no one has snapped her up before now, despite the grocer grandfather and the carrot curls and her age. Society is littered with gentlemen in dire need of a fortune to restore their own. Worse handicaps than red hair and vulgarity have been overlooked often enough—and at least her parents are dead.'

Lily wrenched the knot undone, then retied the garter with enough force to cut off the circulation to that leg. As she straightened, she caught a glimpse of her own reflection in the mirror and pushed a stray lock of dark auburn hair back behind her ear. It was *not* carroty. And what, precisely, was wrong with her gowns? Nothing, except that those three witches could not afford anything so fine.

Lady Angela and her two bosom bows, Miss Fenella George and Lady Caroline Blackstock, seemed in no hurry to take themselves back to the dance floor. Probably they had no partners, Lily thought unkindly, applying her eye to the join in the screen panels. From the expression on Angela's face her friends would be made to regret the remark about age; Lily, the object of their venom, might be twenty-six, but Angela was all of twenty-five and just as dangerously on the shelf.

As her father had taught her, Lily closed her eyes and thought calming thoughts. *Never let your temper master you, Lily my girl,* Papa had said so often. *We redheads are at enough of a disadvantage without making an exhibition of ourselves. Flying into a rage is bad business—keep calm and get even later.*

The door opened again, admitting a small group of young ladies, flushed from their exertions in a country dance. *No, get even now.* She would probably regret it, but she was sick and tired of playing the meek little miss, pretending that she did not hear the catty remarks about her parentage, her money or her looks.

With a twitch at her satin skirts that made the rows of fringing toss, Lily sailed out from behind the screen. Her appearance effectively silenced Angela, who froze, her mouth half-open.

'Lady Angela, Lady Caroline, Miss George.' Lily dropped a neat little bob of a curtsy. 'So edifying as always to hear your opinions, but if I might just drop a little hint, Lady Angela? I heard two of the Patronesses earlier this evening commenting on your misfortune in not receiving an offer again this Season.

'They seemed to feel that your so freely expressed views might have something to do with it. How did they describe you? Oh, yes, *the bran-faced spinster with the adder tongue.* Very unfair, I thought. After all, I am sure that the application of enough of Rowland's Kalydor Balm must improve even the most sallow complexion. It can do nothing for the tongue, of course.'

Lily smiled sweetly and swept past the giggling girls who had just come in, ignoring the livid fury on the faces of the trio she had been addressing. As the door swung shut behind her, she caught the first spluttering words from Lady Angela.

'The cat, the vulgar little cat! She'll live to regret she ever—'

The music and the babble of conversation cut off the rest of the threats as Lily made her way out into the main assembly room at Almack's. She was already feeling guilty for losing her temper; at least she had had the discretion not to name the Patroness who had uttered that damning verdict—and all of them, save Lady Jersey, were present this evening, so hopefully Angela would not guess which one was responsible.

As she made her way around the edge of the room to where she had left her chaperon, Lily glimpsed an elegant figure making his way in. *Adrian.* At last. He had been his usual offhand self when she had tentatively enquired whether he would be present this evening, and Lily had learned better than to try his patience by pressing him. That a baron was taking an interest in her was exciting enough; that the handsome, assured, thoroughly top-lofty Lord Randall seemed on the point of offering was a miracle.

The cold blue eyes swept the room haughtily before he turned and made some remark to the men who had come in with him. Who was he looking for? Her? Or for some family member—his cousin Angela, for example? And would Angela pour out the tale of how that vulgar Miss France had insulted her? Of course she would.

Lily ran the tip of her tongue between lips that seemed suddenly dry. If she let Lord Randall slip through her fingers now, then her father's ambitions, her family's future social prospects, her own carefully mapped-out destiny, would slip away too. Adrian Randall was a leader in society, for all his notorious debts and spendthrift ways, and if he spurned the 'Grocer's Granddaughter', then the other hopefuls with their pockets to let would think twice about being seen to take up what he had rejected.

Adrian was making his way towards her now, taking his time about it, greeting friends as he did so. Mindful of her chaperon's strictures and her aunt's warnings, Lily contained her impatience and waited demurely upon his pleasure. Oh, but he was handsome: slender and pale, blond and languid— a complete contrast to her blaze of dark auburn hair, her vivid green eyes and her restless energy.

He reached her side at last and she managed a start of surprise that would have deeply gratified Lady Billington, her excruciatingly expensive hired chaperon, if she had been privileged to observe it.

'My lord.' Her curtsy was another triumph of hard-learned decorum.

'Lily.' There was a spark of heat under the cool tones and he lifted her hand to his lips, letting it rest in his for just a daring fraction too long. 'You are very lovely this evening, I do not think I have ever seen your eyes sparkle quite like that.' Her heart thudded and she felt a little sick. Nerves, of course.

Aunt Herrick, totally focused on her mission to marry her niece off to a member of the aristocracy, had been quite blunt about it. *Give him what he wants, Lily—whatever he wants. This is no time to be missish. You must catch him fair and square. He's a gentleman, he'll do what's right. After all, once you are married, who is to know what went before?*

The thought of giving Adrian what he appeared to want made Lily feel quite dizzy and not a little apprehensive. She was not even sure if she *liked* him. Not that that was any bar to marriage, as her entourage of supporters assured her. Liking did not enter into it. Love most certainly did not.

She, the great-granddaughter of a hardworking carpenter, the granddaughter of an ambitious grocer and the daughter of a tea merchant—a very, very rich tea merchant—had a destiny that had been set out for her from the moment of her birth. She was to marry a lord and be the mother of English gentlemen. It was the duty she had been raised for.

Papa had even explained how fortunate it was that she was a girl, for a son would have had a much harder time breaching the walls that upper-class England set about itself.

But his protracted illness when they had been visiting tea plantations in India, her period of mourning, the long journey back to England and the necessity to find a suitable chaperon—all delayed her come-out until she had reached the impossible age of twenty-five. And now that she had just had her birthday, it was only her huge fortune that kept her in the Marriage Mart at all.

Apprehension about what she had done made her decisive; if Lord Randall reacted badly to this indiscretion, then it was hopeless in any case. 'I have to confess that I have just lost my temper and have acted most imprudently,' she declared.

'Indeed?' Adrian's azure eyes glittered with interest. 'Tell me.'

'You will be annoyed with me.'

'That might be stimulating.' His voice dropped to a purr. Lily did not quite understand what was going through his mind, but whatever it was, she blushed at the look in his eyes.

'I insulted your cousin, Lady Angela,' she blurted out, with none of the finesse she had intended to use. 'I am afraid something she said about me—'

'Say no more.' Adrian waved it away with one white, exquisite hand. 'Angela is a shrew. She needs a husband, but with that tongue she is never going to get one. She will end up on the shelf with no one to blame but herself.'

'But—'

She almost winced at the immediate flash of displeasure in the pale eyes. Adrian disliked being contradicted. 'Angela is a bore. I have an aversion to being bored.' He looked round the stuffy, crowded room. 'In fact this assembly looks utterly dull. I can think of much more interesting things to be doing.'

The heat was back in his eyes and something inside her stirred, not altogether pleasurably, in instinctive recognition. And yet, her breath was suddenly short in her throat and her heartbeat seemed to trip. It was exciting to be looked at like that, to feel wanted and desired. Lily lowered her eyelashes modestly, feeling the brush of her long diamond ear drops against her cheek reminding her of her own worth.

'More interesting? At Almack's?' Her own laugh sounded false to Lily. 'Surely not?'

'No. Not here. Come with me, Lily.' Adrian's fingers were caressing the inside of her wrist and he was standing scandalously close. She could feel the heat of his body. The strange sensation inside was becoming more disturbing now, but pleasurably so.

'Where to?'

He chuckled softly. 'I thought we should get to know each other better my dear—before we make any announcement public.'

'You mean…my lord, are you making me a declaration?'

Adrian drew her back into a curtained embrasure, letting the heavy brocade fall softly behind them, secluding them in a secret bubble amidst all the chatter and music. 'Would one be welcome, Lily? My lovely Lily…' His mouth was very close to hers now. They were almost exchanging breath.

'Yes. Yes, I think you must know it would be, my lord.' *Was it?* She would be the most arrant flirt if she had not meant the encouragement she had given Adrian Randall these past few weeks. And he was exactly what she knew it was her duty to seek: titled, fashionable and with connections through every layer of the aristocratic world.

'Then come with me now. We can…talk about things. Alone.'

'You mean you will drive me home?' It was not what he intended and she knew it. One had to play the game, Aunt had explained.

'Eventually.' Adrian smiled, his blue eyes narrowed with amusement.

'But my chaperon? Lady Billington…'

'Janey Billington will turn a very blind eye. I think she

would be most surprised and disappointed if we stayed here all evening, don't you?' He was running the back of his hand down the curve of her neck now, murmuring appreciatively at the soft touch of her skin. Lily could feel her eyes becoming heavy with a languorous need. *Can this be love? Surely I would not feel like this otherwise?*

'Very well.' It was like stepping out in the dark. Where would she land?

'Just go and tell Lady B. you've got a headache and that I'll see you home.' He took her arm and steered her out into the room again, ignoring the outraged stare of a dowager with complete insouciance. 'In fact, I will come with you.'

As they circled to the chaperons' corner, Lady Angela stepped out into their path. The patches of colour on her cheeks made Lily think of a wooden Dutch doll. 'Adrian! This bitch—'

'Been sucking lemons again, have you, Angela?' Adrian's tone was anything but playful. 'I hardly think we all want to hear your spiteful ravings. And do take care, coz, or that expression will stick.'

Their departure was a haze after that. The picture of Angela's furious face as Adrian swept Lily past her, Lady Billington's complaisant, knowing, smile, the scrupulously bland expressions of the servants fetching their cloaks—they all swirled together. And in her head Aunt Herrick's voice—*You can't afford to be nice like those aristocratic little misses. Your money is all very well, but you'll need to sweeten the pill of your birth for him. You are buying his name and you need every penny piece and then some for that.*

He helped her up into the carriage, his hand warm on her arm, his every gesture graceful and respectful. 'Home, Granger.'

The vehicle swept out into the foggy night, into St James's Square. Torches flared, light spilled from doorways into the murky damp of the evening. *Sweeten the pill.* No, surely Adrian wanted her for herself as well as for her money. Surely?

Adrian moved to sit next to her, lifting her hand in his. Lily thought he might kiss it. Instead he bent it back so that he could nuzzle the inside of her wrist where the tender flesh was exposed in the gaps between the tiny pearl buttons of her long evening gloves. His lips were hot—and seemed hotter still when he shifted her into his arms and began to kiss her neck.

Lily stiffened, then tried to make herself relax. This was the man she was going to marry, and she should not be shy of his advances. But no one had tried to make love to her before, so naturally it felt—strange.

No, it did not feel strange, she realised. It felt *horrible.* She fought down the panic and tried to slide away a little, her satin skirts slipping over the leather upholstery, adding to her sense of being off balance. Adrian was breathing heavily, his mouth not merely hot as it moved over her skin, but moist. His hands seemed to be everywhere.

In response to her wriggling, he pressed her back, down on to the seat. He was hurting her upper arm where his hand was clenched on it, but her protests were stifled by his lips and his weight as he shifted, almost on top of her.

'No!' Lily managed to get her mouth free. 'Adrian…'

His other hand was under her skirts, moving up past her garters to the bare skin of her thighs with practised ease. Lily moved convulsively, too panicked now to try argument or reason. The carriage lurched round a corner and Adrian rolled off her, cursing.

'Adrian, please do not, not here like this…'

'Oh, yes, just like this.' She caught glimpses of his face as the lights in the street outside caught the inside of the carriage in flashes. He was flushed, breathing heavily, his lips parted and an expression on his face that Lily, even in her innocence, had no trouble in interpreting. Adrian was excited by her fear, excited by the semi-public nature of the carriage with its undrawn blinds—and he was in no mood to be gainsaid.

Adrian lunged for her and Lily twisted away, but not before his hand had jerked open her cloak. 'Damn it, keep still, I am not going to hurt you.'

But he was. She had known that, assumed it was an inevitable part of losing one's virginity—but Adrian did not care, it was obvious. With a grunt of satisfaction his fingers closed on the neckline of her gown, pulling her towards him. 'Don't be such a bloody tease, Lily.' And then his mouth fastened on hers.

Lily groped wildly for some weapon, reached up to try to get some purchase on the top of the squabs, and found the check-string twisting in her fingers. With a sob of relief she pulled it. The carriage slowed and stopped.

'What the hell?' Adrian pushed himself off her and jerked down the window. 'Granger, what the devil are you about?'

Lily tore at the opposite door handle and half-jumped, half-fell into the roadway. Where was she? The thoroughfare seemed nightmarish as the fog swirled around the flambeaux and lanterns. The road itself was congested with hackneys and private coaches, men with handcarts and sedan chairs. The pavements were thronged, mostly with men, but amongst them the cream of the demi-reps in paint and feathers. Lily swung round, still grasping the door handle in an effort to keep her balance. Piccadilly—at least she knew where she was.

'Get back in here, Lily!' It was Adrian, scrambling across the seat and reaching for her. Lily took to her heels, feeling her cloak tear from her shoulders as she went. She looked back; he was jumping down from the carriage. The moment's inattention was almost fatal, the kerb tripped her and she fell headlong, only to be caught up by a tall buck.

'Well, damme, but here's a pretty thing to have fall into my arms!' His long fingers slid under her chin. 'Let me look at you, sweetheart.'

'No!' Lily tore herself free and ran on, looking for a hiding place. The fog swirled as a door swung open and she glimpsed an interior as vivid and unreal as a stage setting: Hatchett's Coffee House, the sign said. Sanctuary.

The tall man in the corner booth at the back of Hatchett's leaned forward, watching the door for long minutes after it closed, his face as expressionless as when he had shaken hands and said goodnight to his companion. Then he sat back abruptly and rubbed both hands over his face, as though to scrub away the evening's effort at diplomacy and persuasion. The wasted effort.

What did that leave now Hotchkinson had proved unwilling? He flicked through the notebook on the table beside him. A few more introductions to take up, one or two ideas still to be tried, before his money ran out and he had to return home. One hundred pounds he had allowed himself for this London venture, budgeting it as carefully as a prudent young lady making her come-out might. His expenditure was far more prosaic, but his aim was the same as hers: to catch a rich man. Only he was rapidly coming to the conclusion that what he had to offer was much less attractive.

He clicked his fingers at the waiter and ordered the house

ordinary. There were cheaper eating houses; his choice of this one had been a futile attempt to impress Hotchkinson, but now he was here he would indulge himself for once. When the man came with the food and a tankard of porter, he asked for paper and ink. This warm, noisy space was a more pleasant place to spend the evening than his room at the Green Dragon off Compton Street.

The man forked some braised gammon and greens into his mouth, then pulled forward his notebook and began to draft.

Persons desirous of investing… No, too wordy. *An attractive investment…* Only it was apparently unfashionably *unattractive.* If he was promoting a canal now, that would be another matter altogether.

He paused to tear off a hunk of bread and to glance at the advertisements in that day's *Morning Chronicle* for inspiration.

…will provide the fullest particulars at the sign of the Green Dragon…

And if this did not work? How much longer could he afford to stay in London? He flicked to the back of the book and did some rapid calculations—he would have to budget carefully unless he was prepared to travel home in the basket of the stage.

The door opened again, slamming back against a settle and sending a swirl of damp air into the warm room. He glanced up, along with most of the men in the room, then slowly lowered his quill. The person who stumbled in was not, as one might have expected, someone slightly the worse for wear, looking for a strong cup of coffee, or a meal to sober himself up.

The young woman who half-fell into the room, pushing the door shut behind her and leaning back against it, was no street walker. She was not even one of the expensive barques of frailty who flaunted themselves amongst the fashionable crowd like so many moths seeking nectar. This was a lady, as incongruous and as flustered as if she had been picked up by a whirlwind off the dance floor at Almack's and dropped into the midst of this coffee house.

She had no cloak over her gown which was, even to his eye, in the extreme height of fashion. Diamonds dripped from her ears and flashed across her bosom with the unmistakable watery fire of the real thing. Her rich auburn hair was elaborately dressed and pinned with yet more gems. He corrected his initial fancy—not so much Almack's, she seemed to have been snatched from the floor of Carlton House itself. He half-expected Prinny to stumble in after her. The other occupants of the coffee house just gawped at the vision, transfixed.

The lady stared around, green eyes wide, looked at him—and he found he was on his feet. Her dress was torn, her hair was coming down; she was in trouble. He took a step forward and she held out a hand. 'Please, sir, I beg you, hide me.'

Chapter Two

~~~~~~~~~~~~~~~~~~~~~~~~~~~~~~~~~~~~~

Why she should turn to this one man, Lily did not know, except that he was so big she felt instinctively that she would be safe with him. When he stood, and she saw his decent, unfashionable suit moulding broad shoulders, his gaze steady on her, his shock of dark hair which was so badly in need of trimming he had tied it back, she could have wept with relief at the contrast with Adrian.

'Please, sir, please hide me, Ad…he is following me.'

His gaze flickered to the neck of her gown and his lips tightened. 'He hurt you.' It was a statement and he held out his hand. 'Here. To me.' Lily let herself be pulled down on the seat next to him, sheltered by the broad cheek of the settle. The man stayed on his feet, his eyes sweeping the crowded coffee house and the fascinated customers. 'No one has come in here these five minutes past,' he said, his voice carrying across the room with no apparent effort. 'This lady is not here.'

People turned away, conversation picked up, the scene began to animate again and Lily let out a little sobbing breath. 'Thank you sir—'

'Get down.' His hand on her shoulder pressed her inexorably towards the floor as the door flung open again. Lily slid without grace between settle and table and found herself curled up tight against her rescuer's leg. There was barely room. She wrapped her arms around his calf and pressed her cheek to his knee. From her hiding place she could see Adrian's feet, his striped silk stockings, the hem of his cloak, nothing else. The room had fallen silent again, so quiet that the clatter of crockery and the raised voices from the kitchen could be heard clearly.

'A lady came in here not a moment since. Where did she go?' Lord Randall's voice was languid, arrogant—and under it Lily could detect seething rage.

She stirred, trapped, convinced that every finger in the room was pointing at the table she hid under. A big hand settled on her head and stroked as though it was reassuring a nervous cat.

'No gentry mort's come in here, sir.' The waiter sounded bored, as if he thought Adrian was yet another half-cut young buck out on the town. 'And we don't let no other kind of woman in either, should that be what you're looking for, sir. Gentlemen only, this place. If you want the other, then there's a place down the road I can—'

'No, I am not looking for a harlot, damn your impudence. Come along, someone must have seen her.' The tone was demanding and patronising. Without being able to see a single face, Lily could sense the antagonism of the patrons—Adrian could have chased Napoleon Bonaparte into Hatchett's and they would have refused to hand him over to this lordling.

'Reckon you must be mistaken, sir,' a voice said, full of mock-civility. 'Lady's given you the slip by the look of it.'

The door slammed behind Adrian, but the derisive cackle

of laughter would have reached his ears, Lily thought with satisfaction. She tried to wriggle out, but the gentle hand held
her down. 'Not yet, just in case.'

'Unlicked cub,' an elderly man at the next table observed.
'You can let her up now, sir, he's gone.'

Lily emerged and smiled shyly round at the interested
faces. 'Thank you.' She received a few grins and nods, then
the patrons went back to their own business. The entertainment was over.

The waiter came across, lifted the empty plates and whisked
a cloth over the table. 'A cup of coffee, miss? Or chocolate?'

'Chocolate, please. Oh, I have no money.' She began to tug
a ring off her little finger. 'If I leave this and send a footman
in the morning, would that be all right?'

Long fingers closed over her hand. 'Put it on my reckon-
ing. And here, that's for your acting.' A coin changed hands.

Lily turned to her rescuer and pushed her hair back from
her face. 'Thank you, sir, I do not know what I would have
done if you had not hidden me.'

His eyes were a dark grey, almost like slate under level
black brows. They seemed to look right into her mind. Lily
realised she had no clear idea of what he looked like, and
dragged her gaze away to look at his face. Wide cheekbones,
a strong nose and chin. A little on the thin side for his build
perhaps; he looked like a man who had missed a few meals
lately.

A face used to commanding men, she thought. And he was
big, especially in contrast to Adrian's languid elegance. It was
not so much his height, although he must have topped six foot,
estimating from her own five foot five, but he carried muscle
like a man who used his body hard.

Some sort of craftsman? A sailor? Yet his voice was educated and he held himself with complete assurance.

'Do you want me to send for someone?' he asked. Lily realised he had shifted so he was shielding her from most of the smoke-filled room.

'No, but perhaps you can call me a hackney carriage shortly, thank you.'

'You will be reporting him to the magistrates?' It was hardly a question.

'No! Why should I do that?'

'Attempted rape?' he suggested softly.

'Oh.' Lily found she was blushing scarlet. 'No…I mean it was not like that. Not really.'

The man did not speak, but his glance at her torn gown was eloquent.

'Lord—I mean, that gentleman, is my betrothed. We had a misunderstanding. It was my fault, I should not have gone with him alone in his carriage.'

'It was not your fault. He had no business to treat you like that. Don't let me hear you say that again.' Anger throbbed in the quiet, deep voice.

'I doubt we shall meet again,' Lily said with a touch of frost in her voice, 'so the question is academic.' She had the sudden feeling that if she did not stand up to this man she would simply acquiesce to whatever he wanted. Which was preposterous, as all he appeared to want was to protect her.

Her *froideur* made him smile, transforming his face, making him look younger. Late twenties? she wondered. 'I should introduce myself. My name is Jack Lovell.' Lily half-expected him to add something, a hesitation seemed to hang in the air, then he added, 'From Northumberland.'

'Lily France. From London.' She held out her hand and it was enveloped in his.

'What a pretty name, Miss France.'

'Thank you, Mr Lovell. You are a very long way from home. Are you on business in London?'

'I am seeking investors.' The waiter appeared and slid a cup in front of her. The fragrant steam curled up to her nostrils, comforting and blissfully ordinary.

'Investors? What for?' Lily twisted round, interested, Adrian momentarily forgotten.

'Steam engines. For a coal mine. Not a very fascinating subject for a lady, I am afraid.'

'But it is,' she protested. 'I am most interested. Are you an engineer, Mr Lovell?' That might explain the muscles.

'An amateur. I own the mine.'

'Then you will be concerned with canals as well, perhaps?' She took a sip of chocolate. 'I have investments in several canal companies, but I do not know about any canals that far north. Do you send house coals by sea to London through Newcastle, or are you supplying industries close to hand?'

Jack Lovell's expression made her smile. 'I have trustees,' she explained. 'But I like to be involved in the investments. My father was a tea merchant, not a manufacturer, so I know more about importing than manufacturing and very little about mining.' It was such a relief, she realised, to be able to speak openly about her family and their business without having to pretend they had nothing to do with the squalid pursuit of making money.

'We supply sea coal for London mainly. I want to reach more industry, but there are not the canals close enough yet.'

Lily drank her chocolate, thinking. 'Why do you need the steam engines? For pulling up loads of coal from the shafts or for pumping out water?'

'Miss France, you do know what you are talking about, do you not? It usually takes me half an hour to get to that point with a potential investor.' He smiled at her and she found herself smiling back, basking in the praise. Her trustees took it for granted that she would study her facts, and everyone else subscribed to the fiction that women had no brains to speak of. She was unused to compliments on her knowledge. 'I need them for pumping, possibly ventilation. Lifting would be a bonus.'

'Well, I have to admit you have now reached the limit of my understanding of steam engines,' she confessed. 'Tell me…'

'No, you should not be here, in this place, with a strange man. Now you have recovered a little I will call you a hackney carriage. Finish your chocolate and I will be back in a moment.'

Lily watched him thoughtfully as he made his way to the door. Mr Lovell's steam engines might be an interesting investment. She would have to find out more about it. The fact that Mr Lovell's broad shoulders and quietly dominant masculinity was making something flutter pleasantly inside her was, of course, nothing to do with the matter. She pulled the dance card off her wrist and scribbled her address on it.

'There is a clean and respectable hackney cab waiting outside.' She looked up and found he was standing by the table. 'The driver will take you home.'

Lily got up and held out the card. 'Thank you, Mr Lovell. This is my address: let me know if you need an investor for your steam engines.'

'Ma'am.' He took her elbow and showed her out and into the cab which was standing at the kerb. 'If I might venture some advice? Find a new man, one who realises you are worth waiting for.' Jack Lovell stepped back before she could do more than stretch out a hand and start a few words of thanks.

He spoke to the driver, giving the address from her card she realised, then lifted his hand in farewell.

And I cannot find him again. Lily craned out of the window, but he had vanished into the fog, back into the coffee house. She leaned against the lumpy squabs and made herself think. *Adrian. What am I going to do about Adrian?*

The illustrations in *La Belle Assemblée* were delightful this month. Lily flattened the spread pages of the journal open under the weight of her side plate and tried to divert herself by studying the walking dress. Three rows of cutwork ruffles enhanced with french knots of deep blue ribbon rose from the hemline, the cambric skirt was gathered high under the bust, contrasting with a bodice and sleeves in blue velvet with white puffs at the shoulders and cuffs. An ornate knot of velvet and lace was posed at the neck.

The shawl it was shown with was disappointingly plain and the bonnet no more than tolerable, but it had possibilities, especially in green velvet with a silk skirt. And more ruffles, of course. Lily narrowed her eyes and wondered which items from her jewel box would set it off best. The emeralds in the gold setting were the obvious choice, but there seemed to be some stuffy rule about coloured gems in the morning. Still, even with pearls, Adrian would admire it.

Lily picked up her neglected toast and bit into it thoughtfully, thankful that Aunt Herrick was breakfasting as usual in her room where she would remain for much of the day, venturing out later for a carriage drive or to go shopping.

In fact, the presence of her mother's sister was a nod to respectability. She was not a close and watchful guardian of her niece. Mildly eccentric, Anne Herrick excused her laxity with the accurate excuse that as the widow of a mill owner she would not lend her niece any countenance and could safely leave that to Lady Billington whenever Lily attended a social gathering.

But Mrs Herrick was an avid reader of all the papers and a mine of information about the glittering world into which she was devoted to propelling Lily. And, as a woman who had had no scruples about the tactics she had used to win the prosperous Mr Herrick, she was equally open minded in her schemes to entrap Lord Randall.

She seemed to have succeeded all too well. To Lily's amazement Adrian had appeared on her doorstep the morning after that shattering incident in Piccadilly and confirmed his proposal of marriage.

'But, last night…' she had stammered, realising that she had not expected to see him again.

'Lily, my darling…' He had taken her hand and pressed a chaste kiss on it, '…you must make allowances for a man in love. I should have realised how shy and innocent you are; no wonder you reacted as you did. I cannot pretend an innocence to match yours—you know that. But I have learned from this and I promise to behave from now on.'

And, to her own inner amazement, she found herself accepting his apology, accepting the engagement. It seemed the only thing to do in the face of his penitence. What would happen if she rejected him now? But he had not been in any hurry to see it puffed off in the announcement columns, which was a trifle flattening, even when he explained that it would be best to deal with 'all that boring business with settlements' first.

In other words, Lily brooded, the very large sum of money he was expecting her trustees would reveal to him as her inheritance. He would anticipate that all her assets would be his as her husband. A frown creased Lily's brow in a way that would have earned her a sharp reprimand if Lady Billington had observed it. Would Adrian be very upset when the Trust was explained to him and he discovered that things were not quite that simple? And what was he going to say when he realised just how involved Lily was with the management of her inheritance?

She realised, guiltily, that she was half-hoping he would change his mind—not that that was a course of action a gentleman could take after what had passed between them. And not one a lady could tolerate either…if a merchant's daughter who had allowed herself to be alone in a carriage at night with a man could be categorised as a lady.

Lily shook herself briskly and ordered another pot of chocolate. Each member of the family had made sacrifices in order to advance the fortunes of the Frances. Grandfather had scrimped and saved to amass the inheritance that her father had then made into a fortune. Her mother had died in India soon after childbirth, her father had weakened his health with his long hours and even longer journeys. Her duty was to capture a title and respectability at whatever cost to her finer feelings. Papa's grandsons would be gentlemen: it had been his dearest wish.

If only she could feel more enthusiastic about Adrian. She had not expected to love him, but she wished she could at least feel warmly about him. That faint glimmering of physical attraction had vanished after the incident in the carriage and had not resurfaced, even after four weeks.

Oh, dear. She had burnt her boats, she was realising that now with the benefit of hindsight. If she could be transported back, she would not have gone with him, whatever anyone else advised her—even at the cost of his proposal.

A deep, serious voice echoed in her memory. *Find your-*

self a new man... And with the memory came the inner stirring that she experienced every time she thought of those broad shoulders, the calm strength, the deep grey eyes of her rescuer.

The door opening to admit Blake and the chocolate also admitted a faint rumour of noise, which seemed to be coming from the street, despite the distance from the front door to the rear breakfast parlour.

'Blake, what on earth is that racket outside?'

'I was just coming to ask you, Miss France. Have you ordered any coals?'

'Coals?' What was the man talking about? 'Blake, Mrs Oakman orders the coals, I do not.'

'I know, ma'am. But she says she hasn't and there are three coalmen all claiming you wrote and ordered four hundredweight of best sea coal to be delivered this morning.'

'Well, I did not. There has obviously been a mistake. Send them away at once.'

'Yes, ma'am. What about the fishmongers and the milkmaids?'

'What fishmongers and milkmaids? And what is Fakenham doing, for goodness' sake?'

'Arguing with them, ma'am.' The footman was looking increasingly unhappy as the sound of the elderly butler's voice, raised in a controlled shout, reached them. 'There's the carters, too, with the root vegetables. And the pianoforte. The man with the pianoforte is none too pleased about being jostled by the coalmen, Miss France.'

The sound of the front door slamming cut off the worst of the noise. 'Ask Fakenham to come in here, please.' Lily threw down her napkin and got to her feet as her highly superior butler appeared, red-faced and spluttering. 'Fakenham, whatever is going on outside?'

'I have no idea, Miss France.' The man pulled himself together with a visible effort. 'The street is a mass of tradesmen, all, so far as I can gather, insistent that they received orders to deliver goods here or to attend upon you.'

'Well, send them away!'

'Miss France—' A heavy knocking sent him hurrying back down the hall. Lily followed, then slipped into the front drawing room and drew aside the curtains just enough to peek out.

The steps were occupied by four soberly clad men, each clutching a tall hat wreathed in black gauze. Behind them a black open vehicle displayed a magnificent coffin.

At least Fakenham's denials appeared to have some effect upon them. As one, they bowed stiffly and made their way down the steps, only to be swept up in the rush as half a dozen sturdy men jostled past the coffin brake to deposit wooden boxes on the steps.

'No! We have not ordered any Madeira wine!'

Lily stepped back, utterly confused. It was a scene of bedlam. Behind the coffin brake several post chaises were manoeuvring amidst a crowd of delivery men, none of whom seemed backward in expressing their opinions of each other's right to be there, the quality of their produce or what they thought of Fakenham's denials.

A small coterie of women battered their way through the mob, wielding hat boxes with lethal determination, and gained the front steps.

'Lily, what a racket! Is it a riot?' Her aunt's voice behind her was a shriek.

'I have no idea. But at least you can see it too—I was beginning to think I had run mad and was hallucinating.' Aunt

Herrick sank into the nearest chair, fanning herself; her satin-sheathed bosom heaved alarmingly. 'Go back upstairs, Aunt—go to one of the back bedchambers where it will be quiet.'

'It is the Revolution! We'll be murdered in our beds! Those wretched mill workers have infected the London mob with their dreadful continental ideas.'

'I doubt we are being besieged by a mob of revolutionary tradesmen armed with coal and carrots. I will send for the constables,' Lily said, tugging the bell pull with more calm than she felt. 'Blake, find Mrs Herrick's woman and see she helps her to her chamber and stays with her. Then send Percy and Smith to assist Mr Fakenham and you run round to the Marlborough Street office and request as many men as possible to come at once.'

She twitched back the curtain and winced. A man had arrived with a moth-eaten bear on a chain; it was, at least, clearing a space in the road, although the group of burly chairmen seemed prepared to dispute the ground. 'Go out of the back door and through the mews. And hurry!' she called as the footman bowed his way out.

The youngest footman staggered in. His elaborate frogged livery was dishevelled. 'Miss France, ma'am, there are three midwives and a surgeon and two dentists.'

'Tell them to go away, for goodness' sake, Percy! Does it look as though anyone here is about to give birth or needs their teeth pulling?'

'No, Miss France.' He ducked out again, only to reappear moments later. 'Miss France, there's a clerical gentleman come from the Bishop of London…'

'That is the outside of enough!' Lily marched to the front

door, beaded trimming jingling around her hems. Poor Fakenham could not be expected to deal with this.

'Sir.' The clergyman stopped his involved explanations to the butler and bowed politely, his broad-brimmed hat clutched in both hands. Her appearance seemed to have an effect on the crowd and the noise level dropped markedly as all heads turned to regard her.

'I very much regret that you have been put to inconvenience and that my Lord Bishop has been so imposed upon, but, as you can see, I appear to be the victim of some outrageous practical joke.' It had to be that, she recognised with a sense of relief. There was no other explanation for it.

As the flustered cleric plunged back into the mob, Lily scanned the crowd from her vantage point on the top step, ignoring Fakenham's agitated attempts to make her go back inside. It felt hideously exposed, and the noise was building again as the people who filled the street came to the realisation that here was the person who had—apparently—commanded their appearance. They began to push forward again. The crowd was packed out even more by figures who seemed to be nothing more than curious onlookers, drawn by the free entertainment.

'Come inside, ma'am, *please*. It will be all over the newspapers by tomorrow.'

'Oh, where are the constables?' Lily stood on tiptoe to try and see the street entrance. One tall man, dark and hatless, was making his way through the press. Not an officer, but somehow her gaze was drawn. He did not seem to be pushing or shoving, but people made way for him like a shoal of fish parting before a predator. She could not take her eyes from him. *Jack Lovell.*

Chapter Three

'Look here, miss, did you, or did you not, order these chickens?' The heated demand from the foot of the steps jerked Lily's attention back, but her heart was thudding.

'No, I did not. Now, please, go away and stop waving that poor bird at me!' She flapped her hands at the cloud of feathers that the struggling chicken was shedding. This was hopeless, but they could not leave the front door undefended and she could not abandon her staff to face the chaos either. And Jack Lovell was coming.

The slender, red-headed woman on the top step was, indeed, Miss France. He had not been surprised at the formal tone of her letter referring to his advertisement in the newspaper; she would not wish to refer to their first meeting, not in writing.

What this bear garden in the street was about he could not imagine, nor why she was exposing herself to it. It was bizarre, even by the standards of everyday life in London. And why, at ten in the morning, Miss France was dressed in a manner which suggested that, not only was she going to pay a morning call on the Prince Regent, but had donned most of the contents of her jewel box, he could not fathom. She seemed to have a lavish taste in dress, the only thing he had found about her so far that he did not admire. Other, of course, than her taste in men.

A snarl and a blast of foul breath to his left had him turn a broad shoulder and change his course slightly away from the shaggy brown beast. It seemed it truly was a bear garden. Dodging round the back of the coffin brake, he found himself at the foot of the steps.

'Miss France?'

'Yes?' She turned and he stopped abruptly, one foot on the next step. Close to, he could ignore the ornate hairstyle, the dangling earrings, the frills and furbelows. The young woman who was staring back was the one who had stumbled into the coffee shop, and his heart performed the same futile dance it had then. She looked at him with her wide green eyes—such long lashes. In daylight he realised just how lush her mouth was. Her skin was like peaches and she had the look of a deer at bay. He corrected himself: an angry deer.

'Mr Lovell—I do not know how you come to be here, but if you believe I have written to you, I can assure you it is all a mistake. Some malicious jest.'

What the devil was her household about, letting her expose herself to this mob? Two footmen, magnificently attired and well over the desirable six foot in height, flanked her butler, but none of them appeared to be able to control matters. It was doubtful that anything, short of a platoon of infantry, could.

'Miss France, you really must go back inside.' He reached the step beside her as shouts and Hibernian oaths behind him signalled that a fight had broken out amongst the chairmen.

'I cannot leave my staff....'

She has guts, he thought, seeing the way she moved protectively closer to her elderly butler. 'I will stand here with them. Have you sent for the constables?'

'Yes, some time ago. Mr Lovell, I know I should not presume upon you, but I would be so grateful for your help.' She winced as the ripe oaths and threats grew louder.

'Inside. Now.' He half-turned, shielding her body with his own as he reached for the door handle. He wanted to pick her up, bundle her indoors, protect her.

She was going, almost, but she lingered, one hand on his sleeve. 'I am so sorry about this.'

'It is hardly your—' The cobblestone came out of nowhere. He knew what it was as it struck his temple, then the world went black, the sounds ebbing into a sort of rushing as he went down. The last sensation he was aware of was the feel of fine cloth under his clutching fingers.

Lily knelt beside the sofa and tried to support Jack Lovell's lolling head while she organised her panicking household. 'Fakenham, send to the kitchen for warm water and bandages. Bring the other footmen in, close the front door and have them stand by in the hall in case anyone tries to break in—except Percy, send him for the physician.'

'Ma'am, shall I fetch your maid to you? And, er...' He gestured at the bosom of her gown. Lily spared it a glance. In falling Jack Lovell had caught at it, exposing her shift, the edge of her corset and the generous curve of the top of her right breast. It hardly seemed of importance now, with his face a mask of blood and the wound seemingly unquenchable.

Lily dragged the torn cloth up and tucked it into the edge of her stays. 'Yes, find Janet. Tell her I need salves and bandages—and some pillows. And a blanket,' she called after the butler's retreating back.

She managed to wedge Mr Lovell back against the sofa cushions, heedless of the effect on the fine striped satin. Head wounds bled a lot, she knew that, but knowing something in theory was a far cry from facing the gory reality. Lily dragged her handkerchief out of her reticule and pressed it to the wound—where had that girl got to?

'At last!' she snapped as the door banged open. 'Bring the bandages here, quickly.'

'Lily, what the devil do you think you are doing?' It was not her maid, it was Adrian.

'What does it look like? Please, give me your handkerchief. This scrap of lace is no use.'

'I will do no such thing.' He stalked over to peer at the man on the sofa, then stepped back with a grimace of disgust. 'Lily, you are covered in blood. Stop that at once.'

'And let him bleed to death?' she demanded. Oh, he was slumped so awkwardly now she could hardly get any pressure on the wound. She tugged at the broad shoulders, but he was too big for her to move. 'Jack! Jack, can you hear me?'

The man groaned and shifted slightly, letting his head fall on to her breast as she struggled to keep the handkerchief in place. The door opened. 'Janet, finally! Make me a pad with those bandages. Good, now stop cringing and help me—'

'Get out.' She was so taken aback by Adrian's curt command that for a moment Lily could only gape at him from her crouched position by the sofa. Janet gave a little squeak of alarm and scuttled out before she could call her back.

'How dare you! What right have you to order my maid—'

'I have every right, and the sooner you learn it the better, if you intend to be Lady Randall. I come here and find the house the focus of some sort of vulgar riot, I have to enter through the back door like a servant and I find my soon-to-be wife half-naked, clutching some tradesman to her bosom. Who the devil is he?'

For some reason, she was not prepared to admit she knew Jack. 'I have no idea. He came to my aid and was hurt by a flying stone. And I am not half-naked, my gown was slightly torn as he fell, that is all.'

'No idea?' His voice sneered. 'I heard you call him by name. Do you take me for a fool?'

'No, I do not. I take you for uncaring and suspicious.' Lily turned her back and managed to tie the pad of bandage around Jack's forehead. Where her hand rested on his shirtfront she could feel the heat of his body, the pulse of his heart. He felt hard and male and formidable for all his present helplessness. She wanted to wash the mask of blood away and see his face, but forced herself to concentrate on the important things.

'I think the bleeding has eased. For goodness' sake, Adrian—why are you in such a temper about this?' she tossed back over her shoulder. 'I have no idea what caused the chaos outside and I am certainly not responsible for it.'

'It is not the sort of thing that happens outside a respectable household,' he retorted. 'And why am I out of temper, you ask? Because I have just spent an hour with your trustees, and a more awkward set of old women I have never met. They tried to tell me that as your husband I would have control over only one-third of your fortune. How can they think that lying to me is going to help them stay in their position? With their fingers in the honeypot, I have no doubt.'

'Because it is true,' Lily said, fighting to keep her voice calm. She gave the bandage a final pat and stood up, keeping her hand lightly on Jack's shoulder. It seemed to give her

strength. 'Until I am thirty, or I marry, all my money is controlled by my trustees. Then I, or my husband, comes into
control of one-third. The remainder is in perpetual trust for
my children until each reaches the age of twenty-one.'

'Impossible.' Adrian was white with anger. 'That cannot be
legal.'

'I can assure you it is, my father took the very best advice.
I do not find it onerous; I sit with the trustees to make decisions.'

'You? Your father must have been insane. No woman
understands money.'

'I do. And you will not insult my father, if you please.' She
could feel her fingers tightening into the shoulder of the man
lying at her side and forced them to open. 'I am a very rich
woman. One-third of that fortune is enough for anyone.'

'It is not enough for me—I do not marry some tradesman's
daughter for *one-third* of anything.'

'Then that is easily remedied.' The words were out of her
mouth before she could think. Under the flat of her palm she
felt Jack stir and bent anxiously to look at him. A hand closed
hard on her shoulder and pulled her away.

'…your lover…' The words buzzed and faded in Jack's
ears, making no sense.

God, it hurts. He tried to lift a hand to his head, but his arm
wouldn't move. He tried to open his eyes, but they seemed to
be glued shut. Either that, or he was struck blind.

'…dare you!' A woman's voice, incredulous, yet shaking
with fury. 'I have no lover…'

'Trollop.' He heard her gasp at the flat insult. 'You get the
taste for it in my arms, then you pick up with some lusty
tradesman…pretending you're so shy…' The colours swirling

behind his blinded eyes intensified; he was losing consciousness. He fought against it—she needed him.

'I hardly think that after your groping, any woman would be in haste to repeat the experience! Unless possibly in the hope that it would not prove quite so repellent with someone else.' Jack felt his lips quirk involuntarily at the frank vehemence of her opinion, then stiffened as he heard her give a gasp of pain. *The bastard was manhandling her.*

Somehow he got his feet on to the floor, then struggled to stand, lurching like a drunk, rubbing at his crusted eyes in an effort to see. Blood, that must be it. He managed to get them half-open, the room swaying madly about him, furniture and figures blurred.

'Get your hands off her.' His voice cracked; he had no idea if he was whispering or shouting. The pain in his head was like an axe blade, cleaving his skull. He was going to lose consciousness in a moment, the blackness at the edge of his vision was closing in.

'Adrian, stop it!' Her voice was familiar, lovely, even tightened with fear and anger. *Lily, that was it…* The male figure came towards him, pushing the girl away roughly. *Bastard.* He raised his fists against flashes of burning agony in his shoulders. Another fist was coming towards him. He tried to focus, dodge; something hit him on the point of the jaw and the darkness claimed him again.

So, this was death. It must be. There was no pain, yet he could not move, his eyes would not open. He was laid out straight on something soft and yielding, his arms by his side. Vaguely he recalled a blow to his head. Last time he had been hit on the head the awakening had been all too vividly physical: darkness, wrenching pain, the taste of coal dust in his mouth and nose, the crushing weight of a pit prop across his shoulders. No, this time he must be dead.

Heaven or hell? That was the important question. Jack dragged his lids apart. A background of deep lapis blue boded well; no leaping flames, at any rate. Between him and the light there was a figure, blurred and wavering. It leaned closer. A woman. 'Angel,' he murmured.

As if trying to hear, the angel leaned closer still. An oval face, lush lips, great green eyes, a cloud of burnished amber-red hair. Simple desire lanced through his body and he blinked. Was he supposed to feel that if he was dead? His loins tightened. 'Angel?'

She leaned even closer. Now he could feel her breath on his face. No, not an angel, not with that face nor with the emotions he could sense behind it. A temptress? He was prepared to be tempted…

His arm could move after all, clumsily. He encircled her shoulder, pulling her down. His lips found hers. *Oh, they were sweet.* She tasted of fruit and smelt, deliciously, of roses. His mouth moved, sampling the softness, the warmth, the innocence of her hesitant response. Not a temptress then. He was kissing an angel—he'd be damned. Worth it, though… His eyes closed and he slipped back into darkness.

Lily felt the consciousness leave him again as the heavy arm pinning her to his chest slid away. Yet she did not move, other than to push herself up a little so she could study his face.

Jack Lovell. She knew no more about him than his name, that he owned a mine, that he was chivalrous, courageous— and kissed like the devil. Which ought to be impossible, considering the wound on his head and the amount of blood he had lost.

Her hand spread, feeling the muscle strapping his chest under the thin linen of his shirt. When he had gone down under Adrian's cowardly blow he was still struggling, fighting to raise himself on one arm. She remembered a print of the *Dying Gaul,* unyielding even in defeat, and shivered; she had never been close to a man so strong, so *male* in such an obvious way.

When she had turned from furiously flinging open the door and ordering Adrian out, Jack's fingers were still locked in the pile of the carpet as though he was trying to drag himself up. It had taken four footmen to get him upstairs and into the best spare chamber; even unconscious and battered, he dominated the ornate room like a wild animal let loose in a formal salon.

A knock on the door sent her scrambling back to stand demurely by the bed. 'Doctor Ord, I am so relieved to see you. Did you have much trouble making your way through the crowd outside?'

The fashionable practitioner put his case down with precision on the bedside table and bowed. 'Miss France. No, no trouble once I had convinced the constable that I was indeed expected and not another victim of this deplorable hoax. Your footman explained a little on the way back. Outrageous, ma'am. It must be investigated. Now then, what do we have here?'

'A gentleman who was knocked out by a thrown cobblestone while attempting to help me.'

'Hmm.' The doctor bent over the unconscious figure, running his fingers through the thick hair. 'How did he fall? Did he hit his head on the ground?'

'I do not think so. He fell heavily on the steps, though; I suspect he may have bruised his back badly.' Dr Ord tipped Jack's head and bent to study the bruise on his chin. 'There was a fight,' Lily improvised.

'I see. Well, off you go, Miss France, this is no place for an unmarried lady. If you can send me in a footman—no, make it two—that would be helpful.'

Lily retreated to her sitting room and tried to order her thoughts. What had caused that mêlée? Even now, well into the afternoon, there were still people outside, constables barring the way to her front door, raised voices.

It was a practical joke, certainly. No mistake could account for it. Who disliked her so much that they would go to so much trouble? A name came easily to mind, now she was thinking calmly: Lady Angela Hardy. And she had certainly succeeded if her intention had been to cause Lily the greatest possible amount of trouble and public embarrassment. In fact, she had succeeded beyond her wildest hopes and had ensured that her cousin was no longer involved with the despised Miss France.

'Lily dear?' Aunt Herrick peered round the door. 'Have they all gone?'

'Almost. But I think we should stay inside today.'

'But what was it? I really cannot understand. Had they all mistaken the address?'

'I believe it was a malicious trick by Lady Angela Hardy,' Lily said grimly. 'I upset her a month ago at Almack's.'

'Oh, dear.' Mrs Herrick frowned. 'You must make it up with her as soon as possible. Lord Randall will be most displeased when he finds out that you have quarrelled with a close relative of his.'

'It is rather too late for that: I have broken off the engagement.'

'You have *what?* But, Lily…'

'Adrian was angry when he found how my money has been left in trust and he was upset because of the uproar outside—which he seems to blame me for. He behaved very badly, so I broke it off.' Saying it out loud brought nothing but a wave of relief. She should never have let herself become entangled with him, never let herself be persuaded that it was right to buy a husband and a title when she did not even feel liking for the man himself.

It was dawning on her that Papa and her family might be wrong and that her instincts were all too correct. It felt like treason—could it be true? No, surely not. Papa had always been right.

'But, Lily—whatever will people say?'

Lily got slowly to her feet, staring at her aunt's appalled face. Fear roiled through her stomach; it was worse than what people might say about the hoax or the simple breaking of her engagement. She had let Adrian compromise her. For one error of judgment she could be ruined and Adrian, furious with her, would no doubt do nothing to protect her good name.

'Miss France, Dr Ord asks if you will join him.'

'The doctor!'

'Aunt, please, it is merely that a gentleman was injured in the street. None of our household is hurt. I will just go and speak to the doctor, there is nothing to be concerned about.'

Leaving Aunt Herrick lamenting behind her, Lily followed Blake back to the guest room. Thinking about her ruined reputation would just have to wait. Jack Lowell was lying quite still, his head bandaged and his shoulders bare above more strips of linen encircling his chest.

'His skull is not fractured,' the doctor said immediately on seeing her anxious face. 'In fact, it must be as hard as rock to have withstood that blow. His back is a mass of bruises; he will have hit the steps as he fell.'

He began to pack his case. 'But your man's no stranger to injuries. I would be a little careful, Miss France. It is hard to guess what his background is. He has got more scars than the average soldier, but not bullet or sabre wounds. His back has been damaged before, but not, I am happy to say, as a result of flogging. He is well fed and fit and muscled like a navvy. If his knuckles were scarred differently I would guess at a prize-fighter, but, although he has worked hard with his hands, they are well kept. I cannot make him out—and I do not like puzzles.

'There is nothing to be done for him but to wait until he comes round, then give him plenty to drink—that cordial on the table there is for his headache—and keep him resting. Call me if there is any bleeding from nose or ears or if, when he regains consciousness, his vision is blurred.'

Doctor Ord bowed his way out, escorted by Blake, leaving Lily gazing dubiously at her guest. She was still standing there, wondering how long it would take Angela Hardy and Adrian between them to spread the news of her disgrace and the hilarious tale of her discomfiture, when his eyelids flickered and she found herself looking directly into a pair of dark grey eyes.

Chapter Four

'**W**here am I?' *Not the most original of opening lines,* Jack told himself, focusing on the magnificently dressed figure in front of him. He should recognise her; flashes of memory—of an angry aristocrat, a crowded coffee shop, of crowds, a bear, his schooldays and, improbably, of an angel—tried to force their way through the headache that was an almost physical presence in his skull.

He shifted his gaze, but not his throbbing head, found himself staring at a sphinx—of all things— and hastily looked back at the young woman. The *beautiful* young woman, now he could see past the ornately piled hair, the frills and flounces and the jewellery.

'You are in my house in Chandler Street, sir.' She moved closer, forcing him to refocus painfully. 'You were injured coming to my aid outside—do you not recall?'

'Some sort of riot? I came because you wrote…Miss…?' He frowned with the effort of recall. 'Have I met you before?' For some reason she seemed to be blushing.

'France. Lily France. You came to my aid a month ago in Piccadilly—can you remember that? As for this—it was a hoax, someone was playing a malicious trick on me. A fight broke out and you were hit by a cobblestone. The doctor says you bruised your back badly on the steps as you fell.' Which no doubt accounted for the fact that he felt as though he'd been flogged. But why, if he had fallen on his back, did his jaw ache? Jack raised a hand and prodded it, wincing.

'Did someone land me a right hook at the same time?'

Now what had he said to make her blush even deeper? 'I am afraid so. My…the man to whom I was betrothed hit you.'

'What the hell—sorry—for? Miss France, please will you not sit down? I can focus better on the level and for some reason I keep seeing sphinxes when I look up.'

She came and sat by the bed in a rustle of silk that whispered *money* to a man who had three sisters. 'That's because the room is decorated with a gilded frieze of them,' she said, pride evident in her voice. 'This room is in the Egyptian style, you know, quite the height of fashion.'

Jack risked a glance around and repressed a shudder. And quite the worst of taste. 'Why did he hit me?' he asked again. Shreds of memory were coming back: a woman's gasp of pain, a sneering voice. Fog.

'Because he was angry with me for having you brought into the house, and he mistook the situation—but he was angry in any case. I broke our engagement, he raised his voice and you—somehow—managed to get to your feet. You were trying to protect me, which was very gallant of you. But you could hardly see I imagine, what with all the blood, and Adrian took advantage of that and hit you. The coward,' she finished, vehemently.

'Adrian?'

'Lord Randall.'

Well, that explained some of the memories. It seemed that Randall was still picking on those smaller or weaker than himself—undersized boys, women, injured men. Strange that neither of them had recognised the other in the coffee house, even after sixteen years. That evening in Hatchett's was coming back now. 'It took you rather a long time to get rid of him.'

'Four weeks,' she agreed ruefully. 'I should have listened to my own feelings and not done what everyone else said was right.'

'Why agree to marry him in the first place if you do not like him?' His head was thudding and the gilded ornamentation of the room seemed to shimmer in the candlelight, but Jack found himself fascinated by the play of emotion on Lily's face. Her expression of self-deprecation changed to one of surprise.

'He is a baron,' she stated as though he had asked a very foolish question.

'Er, yes. And so…?' She still seemed puzzled. 'You must marry a baron?'

'Someone with a title, and baronets are too low down, so it had to be at least a baron.'

The room was definitely beginning to blur and he could feel his eyelids drooping. 'But why?'

'So my sons will be gentlemen, of course.'

Lily saw Jack had lapsed into unconsciousness again and sat watching him blankly for a while. In the space of a day she had lost her betrothed, and very probably her reputation, and had gained one decidedly large and disturbing house guest. She doubted that Aunt Herrick would consider it a very good bargain.

Had she really let him kiss her? Try as she might, she could hardly dismiss that as being due to the shocks of the day. And yet she had felt unable to resist. The sensations that strange caress had evoked were far more powerful than Adrian's hot embraces had been. At least Jack Lovell showed no sign of recalling it. Thank goodness.

And what to do with Mr Lovell? She could not send him back to his lodgings in the state he was in. But what if someone was waiting for him? She should have thought of that and asked him for his direction, rather than discussing her motives for wanting to marry Adrian.

Lily eyed his coat, which was looking considerably the worse for wear as it hung over the back of a chair. She could hardly search his pockets. But if someone was expecting him back they would be anxious by now. Tentatively she patted the coat, noting that it was at least two seasons out of style and, although well enough made, was certainly not by a London tailor. Something hard and flat in the inside breast pocket seemed promising and she fished out a notebook.

Scrupulously trying not to read anything, Lily flicked through the pages. Early on there was a list of inns with a mark against at least six of them. Not helpful. Then halfway through, the draft of an advertisement: *…at the sign of the Green Dragon.* Sliding the book back, she picked up the pile of clothes and tiptoed out.

Two hours later, Lily regarded the still figure anxiously across the small table she had ordered to be set up for her dinner. Doctor Ord's strictures made her uneasy about leaving Mr Lovell to the care of one of the housemaids, as she had explained to her aunt. Mrs Herrick inspected the bandaged figure with a shudder, but pronounced it safe for her niece to be alone in the same room, provided she left the door ajar.

The soup in the bowl in front of her smelled delicious. Lily dipped in her spoon and began to sip, wondering what tomorrow would bring. Recriminations from her relatives over the end of her engagement, that was for sure. Aunt was probably on about the sixth outraged letter even now. And gossip to face wherever she went. Gossip about the hoax and just as much about Adrian. Would he behave like a gentleman and tell people that it was an amicable mutual decision? Somehow she doubted it.

'Soupe de Cressy.' The voice was so unexpected that Lily dropped her bread roll.

'I had quite forgotten you were there,' she apologised. 'Oh no, you should not move.' But he was already hauling himself up painfully against the pillows. 'Here, let me put another one behind you.' That was intimately close, she realised as she wedged a bolster down behind the broad shoulders.

Now that Jack Lovell was sitting up she was all too aware that, except for the bandages, he was naked. Her hand stilled, an inch from the skin of his shoulder. She had never felt the slightest temptation to touch Adrian, although she had admired his beauty. Why now did she want to run her hands over the scarred brown body of this man? His hair, released from the cord that had confined it, touched his shoulders. It was deeply unfashionable when severe crops were all the rage, yet profoundly masculine in its thick vigour.

Lily straightened up, hastily. 'There. How do you feel? Would you like some soup?'

He caught her wrist in his hand as she turned for the bell pull. 'Thank you, I would welcome that. However, I cannot get up while you are having your own dinner.'

The long hard fingers encircled her wrist easily. Lily was not used to regarding herself as particularly slender, and certainly not fragile, but the grip made her feel both. She glanced down, her mouth dry, and he released her.

'You are certainly not going to get out of bed this evening, Mr Lovell.' She tugged the bell and retreated to her table.

'Miss France, I insist.'

Blake appeared and they spoke at once.

'Please fetch me my clothes…'

'A bowl of soup, some bread and some wine for Mr Lovell.'

'Miss France? The clothes the gentleman was wearing today are being cleaned.' The footman turned towards the bed. 'Mr Fakenham has set Percy to unpacking and pressing your other things, sir. He has instructed him to act as your valet while you are with us, sir.'

The dark grey eyes did not show much gratitude for this arrangement. Lily intervened. 'Mr Lovell's supper, please, Blake. At once.' The footman effaced himself.

'What other things, precisely, Miss France?'

'Your luggage from the Green Dragon. I thought it best to have it removed and your account settled. They know where you are in case there are any replies to your advertisement,' she added hastily when the dark brows drew together.

'And how did you discover my direction?'

'From your notebook. I had to check, I had no idea if anyone would be waiting for you, expecting you back. And I did not read anything, I only skimmed through to find some clue as to your lodgings. Now, please rest. I am going to eat my soup before it gets cold.'

'I cannot stay here.'

'Why not, for goodness' sake?' Lily put down her soup spoon impatiently. 'You have had a very nasty blow to the head, the doctor says you must rest, and this is much better for you than staying in that cheap inn.'

'You are a single lady and I am not in need of charity.' For some reason he seemed to be becoming positively annoyed.

'I did not suggest that you were; you may certainly refund me whatever Percy expended at the Green Dragon. But if you think I am going to allow someone who has come to my aid not once, but twice, to nurse a bad head wound in some third-rate hostelry, you may think again, Mr Lovell.'

They glared at each other. 'Miss France, you are in enough trouble with that business this morning, and ending your engagement to Lord Randall, without harbouring a down-at-heel mine owner in your bedroom.'

'Who is to know?' Lily shrugged. 'And this is the spare bedroom, not mine, and you are not down at heel. Your hair may need cutting and your clothes are thoroughly out of fashion, but your boots are admirable.'

The grey eyes narrowed dangerously at this sweeping assessment, but much to Lily's surprise he laughed. 'I like to get my priorities right. Do you always get your own way, Miss France?'

'I try to,' Lily confessed. 'I do not see the point of being extremely rich if one does not get the benefit from it.'

'That is certainly frank! But money does not buy you everything.' His smile was wry and Lily stiffened. Was he criticising her?

'Most things it does,' she retorted.

'But not obedience from those who are financially independent of you—and I am. Please ring for your footman and my clothes, Miss France.'

'No! I am not asking for your *obedience,* you exasperating man—just for you to show some common sense and do as the doctor orders!'

'I will get up anyway.' Jack gripped the edge of the bedclothes and sat up straighter.

'You cannot—you haven't got any clothes on.'

'That is your problem, Miss France. Not mine.' Jack Lovell tossed back the coverlet and blankets and tugged the sheet free where it had been tucked in. 'Now, ma'am—am I going to have to find where my luggage is by myself, or are you going to ring for it?'

He was bluffing, he had to be. He would never do it. 'No.'

'Very well.' Before Lily's horrified gaze Jack swung his legs out of bed, swathed the sheet around himself toga-fashion and stood up. The effect was ostensibly decent—he was certainly better covered than most Classical statues that she had seen—but the impact of bare legs, one exposed shoulder and most of his chest suggested all too vividly the nakedness that the sheet concealed.

'*Mr Lovell.* Get back to bed!'

The door opened to reveal Blake with a loaded tray. He stopped dead at the sight of the apparition facing him, then stepped forward hastily as someone behind him must have pushed. Aunt Herrick bustled past him, glanced round, saw Jack and let out a piercing scream. Blake dropped the tray, showering all of them with *Soupe de Cressy* and claret as Percy shot into the room, alarm on his face.

'Are you all right, ma'am?' He stared around wildly, then gawped at the near-naked man dominating the bedchamber.

'No, I am not all right!' Mrs Herrick waved a frantic hand at Jack. 'This…*brute* was trying to assault my niece—send for the constables!'

Lily, torn between laughter and horror, pressed her hands over her mouth as Jack took a hasty step forward. 'Madam, I assure you my intention—'

He could not have untucked all of the sheet from under the mattress. With his long stride it caught at the back with a jerk, pulled from his grip and fell to the floor. Lily stared, realised what she was doing, and clapped her hands over her eyes. With a gasp Aunt Herrick slid to the floor in a dead faint. Blake, kneeling amidst the wreckage of the supper tray, let out one startled expletive and was silent.

For a moment the tableau was frozen, then Lily, keeping her back to the bed, hurried to her aunt's side. Mrs Herrick had subsided safely on to the thick pile of the carpet and was moaning, apparently more in shock and outrage than from any bruises.

'Mr Lovell, please go back to bed *this minute*. Percy, fetch Mrs Herrick's woman, and my maid, and then help Blake clear this up.' She waited a moment. 'Mr Lovell, are you decent?'

'Yes, ma'am.' He sounded chastened. *Good. So he should be, the reprobate!*

Still on her knees, Lily turned slowly round and regarded the dishevelled bed and its occupant, now decidedly paler than before he had got up. He looked at her with rueful apology, and somewhere, at the back of those expressive grey eyes, wicked amusement.

This was dreadful. Lily bit her lip. Aunt would have fits when she came round, the carpet with its special border of golden crocodiles and papyrus foliage was going to have to be cleaned and Blake's be-frogged livery was covered in claret. It was also very, very funny. Coming on top of a day packed with horrible surprises, it was too much. She turned away, tried to control herself and failed utterly. With a gasp she sank back on her heels, buried her face in her handkerchief and wept with laughter.

'Miss France—Lily! I am sorry…*hell,* I did not mean to make you cry.'

'Don't you dare get up again,' she threatened, raising her flushed face from the linen. 'It is so unfair—you create havoc and then you make me laugh. Oh Maria, Janet, help Mrs Herrick to her room—she fainted, but she does not appear to be hurt. That's right—' she turned to the footmen who were sponging the soup off the carpet '—do the best you can and we will have to look at it again tomorrow when the light is better. And fetch Mr Lovell another supper tray, please.

'Not that you deserve it,' she scolded, approaching the bed and wrenching the coverings straight as the footmen hurried out. Lecturing him was the only defence she could find to hide the shock and embarrassment—and fascination—of seeing his naked body. 'Now, will you promise me you will stay there?'

'Will you finish your supper up here?' Jack was managing to sound reasonably contrite; Lily did not trust him one inch.

'Certainly not. Aunt would never allow it after what she has just seen. I mean…' *Oh, Lord, that could have been better put!* 'I mean, she thought you were unconscious. Please do not be difficult.'

Without thinking she put out one hand imploringly and Jack caught it in his and raised it to his lips. 'I apologise Lily. I would apologise to your aunt too if I did not think it would set her off again. But I can stay for one night only.' He released his grip and Lily thrust her hand safely behind her back. 'And thank you. I am sorry if I seem ungrateful, but I am not used to accepting favours, and I am not good at being told what to do.'

'I had noticed,' Lily remarked with a smile as she closed the door behind her and left Mr Lovell alone with his crumpled sheets and a strong smell of claret.

Aunt Herrick was propped up on the *chaise-longue* in her chamber, smelling bottle in one hand, fan in another, while Janet and Maria hovered with cordials and pillows. To Lily's surprise she waved them away when she saw her niece. 'Leave us, off you go. Well.' She eyed Lily's flushed face with a knowing eye. 'And just what have you brought home, miss?'

'I have not brought him home,' Lily protested, perching on the end of the *chaise*. 'He was knocked out on our doorstep—what was I supposed to do with him? Leave him to bleed to death outside the front door?'

'He is a well-built young man, that I'll say for him.' The older woman chuckled at Lily's blush. 'What is he?'

'He owns a mine in Northumberland and he is looking for investors for steam pumps for it.'

'Oh. Trade. Then he's no use to us.'

'Aunt!'

'Well? You have lost your baron, young lady—what are you going to find to replace him with?'

'Not Mr Lovell, that is for sure,' Lily retorted, resolutely ignoring a disturbing mental image of muscular thighs and narrow hips. 'Infuriating man.'

'Handsome, though, so long as you aren't looking for the languid elegant type. He would turn out quite well with a good suit of clothes and his hair cut. Pity he's not got a title.'

'I like his hair,' Lily said without thinking. 'Not that that is anything to do with anything, so stop teasing me, Aunt, please. I really do not know what I am to do. Today's events will be all over town by tomorrow, so even if it were not for Lord Randall, everyone would be talking about me.'

'Laugh about the hoax and say *you* broke it off with *him*, who's to know any better? Put on your best new dress and your diamonds and find another lord.'

'It is not as simple as that,' Lily confessed, twirling the bullion fringe on the *chaise* between restless fingers. 'About a month ago I let Adrian drive me back from Almack's and he…he tried to make love to me in the carriage and I repulsed him and ran away. And Mr Lovell rescued me. But I was alone with Adrian, and then I was in this coffee house on Piccadilly with Jack, even though nothing happened. And sooner or later Adrian is going to realise that the man he hit today was the one who told him I was not in the coffee house, and—'

'He will put two and two together and make twenty-seven,' Aunt Herrick finished for her. 'I do not pretend to understand half of this tale, but if Lord Randall chooses to be spiteful then you're in trouble, Lily, my child.'

'I know.' Lily's fingers had twisted the bullion fringe into a knot. She released it and watched it spring back into its own intricate twirls. 'I think I am probably ruined.'

Chapter Five

Lily spent a restless night. Fretting about Adrian and her reputation was fruitless, she decided at about one in the morning. Either she was ruined or she wasn't and there did not seem to be very much to be done about it, unless Lady Billington had any good ideas. And as Lily was paying Jane Billington a very favourable retainer for her services, it would be in her interests to think of something as soon as possible.

More immediate was what to do about Jack Lovell, even now sleeping in her best guest room. The *prudent* answer, she supposed, giving up on sleep and plumping the cushions behind her into a more comfortable heap, was to do nothing. He would return to the Green Dragon, to his search for investors, and eventually to his distant mine. Lily gazed into the gloom of her bedroom, dissatisfied.

The *practical* answer was to find some way of investing in the mine herself. That would reward Mr Lovell for his gallantry, add something new and interesting to her portfolio and be a satisfying gesture of defiance towards Adrian, whether he knew of it or not. There was also the consideration that Mr

Lovell, when not being as stubborn as a mule, was undeniably attractive company.

But how to keep contact with an intelligent, independent man who had every intention of shaking the dust of your doorstep from his excellent boots at the earliest opportunity? A smile slowly curled Lily's lips. *Oh, yes, now that's* an idea. All she had to do was to deal with him first thing before he had a chance to bully Percy into fetching his clothes. With a pleasurable shiver Lily slid down under the covers. She did so enjoy organising things to her own satisfaction.

Jack surfaced from sleep and lay very still. The room was restfully dim, with heavy draperies keeping out the morning sunlight, but his head threatened to fall off his shoulders if he moved suddenly and his body ached like the devil. He shut his eyes again with relief.

Someone was moving quietly around the room. Jack cracked open one lid; the young footman—Percy, that was it—was padding around the room, reaching for the curtains. Jack braced himself for the flood of light and rolled over. His head remained attached. Just.

'Good morning, sir.'

'Good morning, Percy.' Jack hauled himself up, tried not to wince and looked around. The sphinxes, palm trees and other Egyptian ornamentation was as lurid in the morning light as he recalled. The Prince Regent would love this room, although even he—surely?—would draw the line at a *chaise-longue* supported on six rearing gilt crocodiles and apparently upholstered with leopard skin.

'I will bring your breakfast at once sir.'

'Just coffee and some hot water—I will get up.'

'No, sir, begging your pardon, sir. Miss Lily said you are

to stay in bed sir.' Jack narrowed his eyes at the man and the footman backed away. 'Just until the doctor's been, sir.'

'Coffee, hot water, clothes. Now.'

There was a tap on the door and Lily came in. Jack snatched at the edge of the sheets and yanked them up to chin level, recalled that after yesterday's fiasco it was a futile gesture, and tried not to glare. The satin bedcover was in a leopardskin print to match the *chaise.* He repressed a shudder.

'Good morning, Miss France. I am having some trouble communicating with your footman.'

'Percy will do as I tell him, Mr Lovell.' She was quite exasperatingly calm. 'Fetch Mr Lovell's breakfast, Percy.'

'Miss France, I cannot stay here.'

'Of course you cannot.' She smiled at him and Jack sat up straighter, raising his knees sharply in attempt to disguise the effect she was having on him. *Hell's teeth, woman! Have you no idea what a smile like that could do?* He pulled himself together with an effort. *No, of course you do not.* 'Just as soon as Dr Ord has been to see you and says you may move, you may have your clothes and your luggage.'

'Thank you.' Now he had a doctor's bill to pay—and by the cut of the good doctor's togs, that would not be cheap— and another inn room to find. And investors to woo while looking like the sort of man who got into brawls in the street.

'I have an idea about where you might stay.' Miss France perched neatly on the *chaise,* her skirts swirling around the jaws of one rearing reptile, the bright blue silk arguing nastily with the upholstery.

'Probably the Green Dragon will still have a room available,' he said indifferently. *Her eyes are the same colour as the dragon's scales on the inn sign, a complicated mix that seems to change with the light.*

'I have had a better idea. Why pay good money out from your budget, which I am sure will be put to better use entertaining your investors, when you can stay here?'

'We have just agreed that I must move.'

'To the bottom of the garden.' She beamed at him, obviously delighted with whatever hare-brained scheme she was hatching. 'The previous owner was an amateur artist and he had the long attic over the carriage house in the mews converted into a studio. You can stay there.'

'No.'

'Why not?' Those green cat's eyes slitted as she watched him and her full lower lip pouted. Miss France was not used to having her will thwarted, obviously. What would it be like to bite that swelling fullness? Just a very gentle nip…

'It would not be proper, and, as I believe we have agreed before, I will not accept charity.'

'You will not be in the house, so where is the impropriety? And if you insist, I will charge you bed and board, exactly what you would have paid at the Green Dragon. Mrs Oakman will cook your meals.' He shook his head and she glared at him with an exasperated irritation that matched his own. 'You are a very stubborn man, Jack Lovell.'

'And you, Miss France, are a very managing woman.'

Endearingly, she shrugged. 'Yes, of course. I am used to getting my own way. It does help to be very rich.' She cocked her head on one side. 'Please? I dislike not being able to say thank you to people who have helped me.'

Of course he should say no. It was preposterous and probably improper, bottom of the garden or not. Lily opened her eyes wide and smiled at him. 'I have had the room cleaned and made ready for you. The footmen have worked so hard this morning…'

Preposterous, improper and impossible. Jack fought down the headache that was intent on kicking its way through his temple and took a breath. 'Yes.' *What have I just said?* 'Yes, thank you.'

Lily whisked out of the door before he had a chance to change his mind. Her voice drifted back through the opening. 'Now remember, Percy. No clothes for Mr Lovell until the doctor says so.' There was a pause and the sound of the footman whispering. 'And I do not care what excuse he comes up with, not even if the house is on fire.'

Damned managing, bossy, infuriating, vulgar, brass-faced…

'Your breakfast, sir.' Percy placed a heavy tray squarely and painfully in Jack's lap. 'Did you say something, sir?'

'I was merely grinding my teeth.' Castration by breakfast tray. That at least was one path to continence. 'Thank you. Please will you fetch me the portfolio that is with my luggage? I give you my word it does not contain so much as one neckcloth.'

The faintest tremor of a smile passed over the young footman's face. 'Very good, sir.'

By the time Dr Ord was ushered in, Jack had demolished a substantial breakfast of eggs, ham and Braughing sausage and was scribbling annotations in the margins of a report to the Royal Society on a new type of valve for steam pumps. His headache had subsided from penetrating to merely pounding and he had regained his temper.

'Good day, Mr Lovell.' Doctor Ord placed his case on the table and advanced on Jack, giving him ample opportunity to notice his fashionable suit of clothes and the handsome signet on his left hand. *A very large doctor's bill indeed.* 'And how are you feeling this morning?'

'Stiff in the back. I have an evil headache and a sore jaw, but other than that I am perfectly fine and I would be deeply obliged to you, sir, if you would prevail upon Miss France to have my clothes returned to me so I can get out of bed.'

'Tsk, tsk. Well, I am sure you know best, but I suggest you submit to an examination; Miss France will no doubt be most disappointed if I do not stay for a reasonable length of time.'

'I will be paying your bill,' Jack pointed out with some difficulty as the doctor manipulated his jaw.

'Of course. But Miss France will still expect the most thorough treatment for her guest. No bleeding anywhere? No? Excellent. Vision blurred? How many fingers am I holding up? Good, good. Bend forward so I can see your back. Tsk, tsk. Shall we remove the bandages? I applied them more to prevent Miss France glimpsing the extent of the bruising than for any other reason; it looks most alarming, but no doubt you are used to that.'

'You have noticed some scars? I imagine you will have cautioned Miss France about me as a result?' Jack said it amiably and the doctor responded in kind.

'I did. I have known Miss France for many years and have a concern for her welfare.'

'I own a coal mine. I have been involved in a few accidents, and in the collapse of a gallery that caused most of the more dramatic marks on my back.'

'Well, you have a hard head, sir. I see no problem with you getting up, provided you take things easy and rest.' The doctor glanced at the pile of paper on the bed. 'And do less reading.'

'I will promise anything if you will tell the young man on guard outside my door to bring me my breeches.'

* * *

Getting washed, shaved and dressed was more of an ordeal than Jack would have admitted. Somehow the prospect of taking things easy for a day or so was less onerous than it had seemed when he was trapped in his bed.

At last Percy hefted his portmanteaux and led the way out of the bedchamber. Braced for further Egyptian assaults on his nerves, Jack found himself blinking in what he assumed was supposed to be a passage in an Indian palace. The stuccoed arches and inlaid marble gave way abruptly to gilded Classical columns as the corridor opened out on to the landing. He stopped to study the junction between the two, trying to decide whether such a clash of styles could possibly be deliberate.

Percy put down the bags and came back. 'Are you all right, sir? Not feeling dizzy?'

Yes was the honest answer, but not because of the state of his head. 'I was just interested in the different styles of decoration,' he said mildly.

'Yes, sir. Miss France got as far as here with this—Indian it is, or Mr Fakenham says, Chinese—and then when they reached the landing she changed her mind and said it all had to be redone like that with columns and things.' He lowered his voice, 'And there are all the statues, in the nude, sir! But Mrs Herrick said she wouldn't have them in the house, however much Miss France said they were art so it didn't count, them not having so much as a fig leaf on, and they're all in the stables, wrapped up.'

Savouring the thought of the ranks of modestly draped nymphs and gods filling the stables, Jack followed Percy down the sweep of the double staircase. A middle-aged woman in pelisse and bonnet was just drawing off her gloves at the foot. For a moment Jack failed to recognise her, then she glanced up and he remembered her all too well. Quite what did one say to a respectable matron before whom you had, however inadvertently, revealed all?

'Good morning, ma'am.'

'Good morning, Mr Lovell. Dressed at last, I see.'

'Yes, ma'am.' Could that possibly be a satirical glint in her eyes?

'Percy, wait over there.' She waited until the young man was out of earshot, then smiled. Jack did not make the mistake of interpreting it as a warm gesture. 'Mr Lovell. I may faint when confronted by strange young men in a state of undress, but I am not a conventional chaperon. In fact, I am a very poor one by any usual standards; I leave all that to Lady Billington. I am a vulgar woman, Mr Lovell, the daughter of a master weaver and the wife of a mill owner, and I would do my niece no favours in society by being seen with her.'

He opened his mouth to make some demur, but she waved him into silence. 'I love my niece, who is an intelligent, headstrong girl. At the moment she is also a very hurt and fragile one—and believe me, sir, should another man do anything to upset her further he would find that I can still recall how to use a pair of nap-cutting shears, even if they are a bit rusty.' The chilly smile did not waver. 'Good day, Mr Lovell.'

Fighting the instinctive urge to place his hands protectively over his groin, Jack followed Percy out into the back garden and down the path to a gate in the wall. Gradually a grin spread over his face; vulgar Lily and her aunt might be, but they were refreshingly willing to say exactly what they thought. He decided he could grow to like it.

* * *

'What are you doing?' Lily demanded. The footmen looked guilty, Jack had that expression she was beginning to recognise. Determined, he would no doubt describe it as. Or resolute. Mulish, stubborn and pig-headed were the politest of her words for it. 'This is a lovely carpet. It is a very masculine carpet. It usually lies in the study and all my trustees consider it most handsome. Why are you having it rolled up? And what is wrong with those lamps?'

'It is indeed a magnificent carpet,' Jack agreed. 'Far too fine for me; I would be forgetting and walking on it in my boots half the time. Or dropping my breakfast. I am not used to such splendour, Miss France.'

Lily pushed the rolled-up carpet open with her foot. Jack hooked a toe under the edge and flipped it back. The footmen sat on their heels and both gazed tactfully out of the window with the air of men who wished they were anywhere else but where they were.

She glared at Jack across their heads. He was standing there with his arms crossed, one foot on the end of the roll, showing every sign of being prepared to wait there all day if need be. Brangling in front of the servants was out of the question. She would have to give way with good grace. She just wished he did not look like a *sahib* who had shot a tiger and was posing with his foot on its head—it made her want to giggle.

'Take those lamps and fetch some plain branched candlesticks,' she said tightly to the men, 'and bring the old carpet that we took out of the housekeeper's room for Mr Lovell's approval.'

Lily waited until she could see them in the garden before she swung back to confront him. She found her arms were crossed, her hands gripping her elbows as though to hold in her irritation. Nobody thwarted what she, Lily France, wanted: not in her own house!

'It is nothing to do with your boots, is it? You find my taste vulgar and will not live with it, even for a week or so.' She kicked the roll hard so that it shot from under his foot and opened up to reveal ornate medallions on a dark red ground. 'You see? Lovely. It is copied from Roman wall paintings.'

'My taste runs to plainer, older things,' Jack admitted with a shrug. 'It all depends what you are used to, and what you can afford. You can afford to indulge your taste to buy the very latest and finest. That is your right. I believe I have the right to worry that I will spill ink on it and tread dirt into it. I had no wish to trouble you personally in the matter.'

'You are very tactful,' Lily retorted bitterly. 'But I know what you are thinking. They all say it, mostly behind my back: I have no old things that I have inherited, so that makes me inferior. I have to buy my silver and my furniture *new*, which seems to be some sort of crime against good taste. Why should I have to put up with old-fashioned, faded, worn, shabby things just because they *are* old?'

Before, she had just found this attitude inexplicable, too foolish for it to hurt. Now, believing she saw the same sort of rejection in Jack's expression, she wanted to cry. And who was he to judge? He might sound like a gentleman, but society would be just as harsh to the mine owner, however careful his schooling, as they were to the merchant's daughter. More so; she had money, he did not.

'They must have to buy new things some time,' she muttered. 'Every thousand years or so things must wear out or get broken.'

Jack snorted with laughter and dropped to one knee to re-roll the carpet. 'Much more frequently than that, Lily. Do you think all these titled families came over with the Conqueror? Virtually none of them did. Most of them began their climb up the ladder in Henry's reign—all those lovely monastic lands to buy their place at court with. Then there was another lot ennobled after the Restoration. I'll bet they were all scrambling to buy the latest in wall hangings and silver then.'

'Truly?' Lily stood and regarded his bent head as Jack tied the cords round the roll.

'Truly.' He looked up and grinned and her heart did a foolish little stutter. 'It is just inverted snobbery. Sometime we will sit down with the *Peerage* and look up the dates of the titles of the people who annoy you most and have a satisfying sneer.' He got to his feet with a wince, which reminded her that his back must still be painful. 'May I have an old carpet? Please? Not because I am a snob, but because I dearly like to behave like a slovenly bachelor when I have the chance.'

'Very well.' She turned away. His smile, when he chose to deploy it, was dangerously unsettling and highly seductive. 'Does your back hurt very much? The doctor did not leave anything for it, but I am sure we have something in the stillroom…'

'It is stiff, that is all. I am not getting enough exercise to work out the bruising.'

'I will send Percy for arnica.'

'He is doing very well with my boots, but I do not think that having my back rubbed with lotions by Percy is going to be a very healing experience. Now if you were to do it, I am sure there would be a great improvement.'

'If you think it would help,' Lily began dubiously. *What would Aunt Herrick say?* Then she saw the teasing glint in his eyes. 'You are teasing me! You deserve to be black and blue. Now, I am going shopping and you must rest.'

'You do not mind going out, after yesterday?'

'Yes, I do mind,' Lily admitted. 'But it is that or run away and hide and I will not do that. Tonight is Lady Troughton's reception. I shall go and wear my newest gown and my second-best *parure* of diamonds.'

'Well done.' The approval in Jack's smile sent her down the stairs and into the garden with a warm glow. It lasted up to the point when she tied her bonnet ribbons in a large bow under one ear and picked up her parasol. What would happen if she met anyone who had heard about the broken engagement or the near riot outside her house? What if Adrian was already telling the polite world that she was ruined?

Chapter Six

The shopping expedition passed off without incident. Lily bought six pairs of silk stockings, an ell of wickedly expensive Swiss lace and a pair of the indecent new pantalettes. Putting such a garment on seemed impossibly daring; on the other hand, they might be just the thing should she ever wish to thoroughly scandalise anyone.

'They are so *long*,' she explained to Lady Billington as they set out in the carriage that evening for Lady Troughton's reception. 'It would not be like showing one's petticoat; if anyone caught a glimpse, they would know they were encasing my *legs!*'

'Most improper,' her chaperon agreed. 'But pantalettes are the least of your problems, Lily! That riot outside the house yesterday is all over town and there is the most vulgar speculation as to why it occurred. Some people are saying that you have so much money that you ordered things without thought and the resultant traffic jam was all honest tradesmen attempting to deliver. All nonsense, as I have been telling people, but say what you will, they love a good story.

'But that pales into insignificance when one considers your

engagement. What were you doing that made Lord Randall break it off?'

'Nothing! And I broke it off, not him. He was furious because of the hoax, and because he had discovered how much of my money would still be in trust even after I marry. And then he found Ja…Mr Lovell in the salon on the sofa and made insulting accusations and I told him I no longer wished to marry him and threw him out.'

'Indeed? You should have at least kept your temper long enough to have agreed a mutually acceptable notice to the papers and not left it to him.'

'What? There is something already?'

'The notice of the engagement between Adrian, Lord Randall and Miss France, etc. etc. was inserted in error and no such engagement exists,' Lady Billington quoted from memory.

'But…but that makes it sound as though I put it in to entrap him and now Adrian is denying it!' In the darkness of the carriage Lily could feel her face flame. 'The beast!'

'I am not at all sure that appearing tonight is a good thing,' Lady Billington said. 'We are almost there. Possibly we should leave it until things die down a little.'

'Oh no, we do not!' Lily said grimly. 'I am not letting Adrian get away with this.'

At the head of the stairs Lady Troughton was greeting her guests with beaming affability—until her gaze lighted on Lily, when it became positively frosted. 'Miss France. I had not expected to see you after…after what has just occurred.'

'You refer to that horrid hoax someone played upon me? But to renege on my promise after I had accepted your kind invitation would never do.' Lily knew her smile was brittle, but somehow she maintained it. 'Can you imagine anyone being so spiteful that they would go to so much trouble as that hoax involved? Jealousy is a terrible thing,' she added piously. Out of the corner of her eye she saw Lady Angela approach. 'One can only assume that the person concerned has a sad life and nothing better to fill it.'

She tilted her head to include Adrian's cousin in her smile, then followed her chaperon into the great reception hall. 'She heard me,' she observed with satisfaction.

The room was already full. A string quartet was playing light incidental music and on the dais a pianoforte had been set up in anticipation of the evening's promised treat, a performance by Signora Angelina Tendesci, direct from Italy.

Lily felt her tense shoulders relax as she saw friends, the Cunningham girls and their mama. Themselves only one generation removed from trade, the Cunninghams had proved far less snobbish than many in society and Lily had come to enjoy the sprightly chatter of the two sisters.

She made her way towards them. Mrs Cunningham turned, Lily saw her eyes widen, then she simply cut her, turning away without a flicker of recognition and ushering her daughters in front of her. Hurt, Lily stepped back, found herself face to face with old Lady Wilton and was subjected to a long stare through the dowager's lorgnette before she resumed her conversation with her neighbour.

To Lily's shocked gaze the entire room seemed to be full of people drawing their skirts away or turning their backs on her. It had never happened before. When she first came out one or two people had turned up their noses at the merchant's daughter, and she had constantly heard whispers and jibes about her money and her taste, but her wealth had ensured that virtually every door was open to her.

I am refining too much on the reaction of one or two snobs, she tried to convince herself. *I am imagining that the others are whispering about me. I just need to compose myself a little and when I come back it will all be quite all right...*

There was a loggia off the reception room. Lily made her way over to it, slipped through the door and found herself alone in the long, stone-flagged passage with windows overlooking the garden. Lamps burned in alcoves and chairs and little tables stood about for later on when people needed a refuge from the overheated room. Now it was mercifully empty.

As she took a steadying breath the doors behind her opened and she found Lord Dovercourt at her side. He had always proved an amiable dance partner, but, involved with Adrian, she had never paid him much attention.

'Good evening, my lord.'

'Miss France. You are not quite well? I saw you slip away and was concerned.'

'Merely a slight headache. I thought to nip it in the bud with a little quiet and cool.' He seemed to be standing very close. Lily began to stroll away down the loggia.

'Allow me to offer my arm.' There was no way of refusing without appearing rude, so Lily let him tuck her hand into the crook of his elbow and walked with him further away from the door. 'I am so sorry to hear that your engagement to Lord Randall has been broken. What poor judgement on his part!'

'It was mutual, my lord,' Lily responded stiffly. 'We discovered we were mistaken in thinking we might suit.' They were at the end. Now they could turn and walk back. It must be her imagination, but Lord Dovercourt appeared to be pressing her hand very tightly against his side.

'He's a fool, then, to give up on a handsome girl like you. And your handsome fortune too, eh?' His chuckle was coarse and Lily stiffened.

'I am sure you mean well, my lord, but the tone of your conversation—'

'Don't get on your high horse with me, Lily my pretty. Vulgar little fillies like you can't afford to take that line if they want to find themselves a lord. And that is what you want, isn't it?'

'How dare you!' Lily tried to tug her hand free and found herself pulled back against his chest.

'Stop being so coy, you silly little jade. Do you think you are going to find a husband from the *ton* now? I suppose you could at that, with all your money. Someone—me, for instance—might be willing to take Randall's leavings.'

Lily jerked back her hand and tried to slap him, but he buried his face in her neck and began to kiss her with wet lips. It was even worse than Adrian's advances. Nauseated, Lily lifted her knee and brought it home hard in his groin, watching with satisfaction as Dovercourt fell back, groaning and clutching himself.

'I neither know, not care, what you might be willing to take, my lord,' she informed him. 'But *I* am not willing to take the leavings of every drab and whore in London.'

Buoyed up with the satisfaction of seeing him incapable of answering, let alone standing up to follow her, Lily swept down the loggia and came slap up against a woman who stepped out of the shadows to intercept her.

'That was silly, Lily.' Lady Angela giggled at the puerile rhyme. 'Silly Lily,' she repeated. 'You are making too many enemies—give up and go away. Move to an unfashionable watering place, like Bath. You'll find some broken-down, poxed old lord there who will marry you. He'll die soon enough and you'll have that precious title you are so desperate to purchase. He won't give you children, but then, that will keep your tradesman taint out of good bloodlines.'

Only the greatest effort at self-control she had ever managed kept Lily from slapping the sneering face. 'Better perhaps to make some old man's last years happy and then be a very rich dowager than to dwindle into a sour old maid as you will, Angela dear,' she retorted. 'I doubt if I will ever be so desperate that I will have to entertain myself by forging hundreds of letters to tradesmen just to score a trivial point.'

The expression that flashed across Lady Angela's face was enough to convince Lily that she was, indeed, the hoaxer— and that, if she had ever doubted it, she had an enemy for life.

Before the other woman could retaliate, or Lord Dovercourt recover himself, Lily slipped out of the door and back into the crowded room. Lady Billington was with the chaperons and, heads together with Mrs Westworth, did not notice her charge until Lily gave her skirts an urgent tug.

'Lady Billington!'

'Lily? My goodness, you look a complete romp—what have you been doing?'

'Fighting off Lord Dovercourt,' Lily whispered back. 'Lady Billington, please may we go? I feel positively sick.'

With a murmured excuse about migraines, Lady Billington steered Lily towards the door. Mercifully Lady Troughton had just mounted the dais to introduce Signora Tendesci and all heads were turned to watch.

'What on earth have you been about?' Lady Billington scolded as their carriage finally rolled away from the Troughtons' front door.

'Nothing! The beastly man cornered me in the loggia and slobbered all over my neck and made the most disgusting suggestions—until I...I freed myself.'

'It is worse than I thought,' her companion pronounced.

'Even the least stuffy of the other chaperons are tutting about the scene outside your house, and they do not seem to know what to make of the end of your engagement. The only mercy appears to be that no one has heard anything to suggest actual impropriety.

'There is nothing for it—you must take a house at one of the watering places and retire there for several months until all the fuss dies down and society finds something else to chatter about. Then perhaps you can reappear at Brighton during the summer.'

'But I will seem to be running away, as though I have something to hide, or be ashamed of. And none of it is my fault—other than being foolish enough to trust that man in the first place.' Lily stared mutinously at the drawn blinds of the carriage.

'The woman is always at fault,' Lady Billington said cynically. 'Better a strategic retreat than be seen to be forced out.'

Jack pushed the slipping bandage up for perhaps the sixth time that evening. His head ached. He leaned back in his chair, pulled the bandage off his head and untied the leather thong that held his hair back. 'That's better.' He got up, stretched and strolled across to look at himself in the incongruously large Venetian mirror that hung at one end of the room.

To have his hair cut while he was in London—or not? He was inclined against it, simply out of a stubborn instinct not to join the herd and follow fashion. Jack lifted the candlestick in one hand and pushed back the hair from his temple with the other. The area around the wound was spectacularly bruised now, a palate of purple, red and yellow—and the cut itself would leave a scar.

Fortunate I have no beauty to lose. Not like that pretty boy

Randall. Jack grinned at his reflection and went to tidy up his papers. He had things as well organised as he could hope for now, except for factoring in whatever he could learn about the new atmospheric pumps. He had updated his costings, re-drawn his maps, learned from the comments of the potential investors who had rejected him so far. An early night, then to-morrow make contact with the remaining names on his list and see how many would be prepared to give him appoint-ments.

And how many of the great and the good—and the less great, but wealthy—would be willing to spare some time to plain Mr Lovell and his schemes? Was he right to follow his instincts, and his pride, and try to sell this on its merits alone or should he come clean and use what might be a weapon if only his pride would stomach it?

Jack straightened and went over to the window, blowing out the candle as he went. Below, in the garden, someone was moving about—he could hear the crunch of gravel underfoot. A housebreaker? They carried no lantern, but they seemed to be making no attempt to hide themselves either. Then, as his eyes accustomed themselves to the gloom outside, he saw it was a woman, her long cloak brushing the ground behind her as she paced up and down.

Mrs Herrick? No, this figure moved with a youthful grace. Lily, then. But she should be frittering the evening away at that reception or dance or rout or whatever it was she said she was attending. Still, he shrugged, it was her garden, she could do what she wanted in it. Jack half-turned, then looked back. Something indefinable about the pacing figure said unhappi-ness to him. Unhappiness and indecision.

He should leave her to her private thoughts. Then he re-called how his sisters sometimes welcomed his shoulder to cry on when they would not share their troubles with anyone else, even with their mama. She could always tell him to go away if she did not want his company. Pulling on his coat, he opened the door and went softly down the staircase to the garden. He paused in the shadow of the wall, not wanting to alarm her, certain he had made no noise, but she swung round, the heavy cloak swirling around her and the sudden flash of white skirts showing beneath it like sea foam in moonlight. Then she was still again, a dark column amidst the shadows of the arbour. 'Jack?'

'Yes. I did not mean to startle you. I wondered if perhaps something was wrong.'

Lily laughed shortly. 'You might say so.'

'The party was not a success?' he persisted, coming closer, still uncertain whether she welcomed his presence or not.

'I was…I was snubbed. Some people I thought were old friends cut me dead. I had a horrible encounter with Lady Angela and…and when I went out into the loggia to be alone someone followed me and tried to kiss me and made disgusting suggestions. He implied that Adrian and I had…had…' She spun round until her back was to Jack and her voice was muffled as she added vehemently, 'And we have not!'

'Oh, Lily.' He took a long stride forward and caught her in his arms, turning her so she was held against him. 'Of course you didn't.'

'Yes, but I almost did, that is why I feel so *smirched!*' She bent back her head so she could look up into his face. The moonlight caught her and he could see the unshed tears glimmering in her eyes. 'I thought I ought to—Aunt said I ought to do it in order to *catch* him, and I almost did. How I could ever have contemplated it, even for a minute…'

'But you didn't,' Jack repeated. 'That is all that matters.'

'I ran away and you rescued me.' That seemed to provoke more sadness than comfort; there was an unmistakeable sniff from the region of his third shirt button. Acting on instinct, ignoring the voice of caution that was telling him firmly to find her a handkerchief and send her back inside to her aunt's care, Jack caught Lily up in his arms and carried her into the arbour to where a wooden bench curved under the tangle of climbing roses.

Lily found herself set down on Jack's knees and held firmly against his chest. 'Now, here is a handkerchief. Blow your nose and tell me all about it.'

'No. I do not want to.' It was a very large handkerchief. Lily blew her nose with more force than elegance and sat up. Jack's arm stayed round her and she made no effort to free herself.

'Tell me. It will all sound much better when you say it out loud instead of it churning round and round inside your head.'

'All right.' Lily began reluctantly, but Jack's very stillness, the concentration with which he was listening to her, gave her confidence. Finally, she reached the end of her account. 'And then I used my knee and, well, he stopped.'

'I should imagine he did. What is his name?'

'Lord Dovercourt. Why?'

'Because I shall add him to the list, along with Lord Randall, of *gentlemen* who need to be taught how to treat ladies.'

'But you cannot call them out! That is what you mean, isn't it? Not teaching them some other way.'

'By lying in wait with a knife, possibly? I am not a footpad, Lily. Why can't I call them out?'

'Because they would not accept a challenge from someone who isn't a gentle—' *Oh, Lord! How tactless!* 'I mean…'

'Who isn't a gentleman? Perhaps. But somehow they need dealing with.'

'You cannot fight them.' Lily took hold of his coat lapels and gave them a shake. 'Be sensible. What if you kill them?'

'Which is likely.' *Arrogant man!* They were all alike. She wished she had the strength to give him a really hard shake.

'Then you will be hanged and a lot of good that will do your coal mine.'

'True.' There was a laugh in his voice and for some reason she felt quite odd inside. Not miserable any more, but certainly not calm either. Very strange indeed. What was he thinking?

'Jack?'

'Yes, Lily, my lovely?' It was almost what Dovercourt had called her. It was certainly just as improper coming from Jack, but the words made the warm glow inside burn even warmer. She could feel the colour heating her cheeks.

Lily leaned back a little, trying to see his face in the moonlight. 'Your bandage! What have you done with it?' She put up a hand, her fingers almost, but not quite, touching the wound. Even in the faint light it looked dreadful. Jack bent his head a little and the raw silk of his hair flowed over her fingers, caressed the back of her hand.

'Jack?' *What am I asking? He seems to know.* He bent over her. There was a long moment of perfect stillness, then his lips found hers and he was kissing her.

He had kissed her the other day when he had no idea who she was or where he was, but this was quite different. Jack Lovell knew exactly what he was doing this time and shockingly so it seemed, did she. Her body arched against his, trusting. Her lips softened under his, giving. His was not at all like Adrian's mouth had felt. Jack seemed quite content to explore, angling his lips across hers, shifting and teasing. It appeared that he wanted to taste, not to take.

Lily felt her mouth following his, learning from his. He did not try to do that revolting thing Adrian had done with his tongue. So wet and disgusting and... *Oh!* It wasn't disgusting at all, not when Jack did it. Her lips parted, she opened to him and found she could taste too. Coffee, and a hint of brandy, Jack. Just Jack.

She was sinking until she felt as if she were part of him, and it was so right. So perfect. Then he stopped.

'Lily?' Blinking, she opened her eyes. 'I am sorry. I should not have done that.'

'Why? Was I doing it wrong? It was very nice.' A sudden horrid thought struck her. Perhaps he had not believed what she had said about Adrian. 'Just because I...because just now, we... It doesn't mean I let Adrian.'

'Lily, my sweet, I know. You have no need to tell me.' Lily found herself on her feet, being pushed gently but inexorably towards the house. 'Lily—'

'Lily? Are you out there?' It was Aunt Herrick.

'I am coming, Aunt,' she called and turned back. The garden was empty. He was gone.

'Hell.' Jack wrenched off his dressing gown, balled it up and threw it into a far corner. 'Hell.' He sat down, yanked off his right boot and hurled it after the dressing gown; it landed with a more satisfying thud, to be followed by the left one. 'What am I doing?'

The answer, as the rest of his clothing was tossed onto the chair, was all too obvious: he was very attracted to Miss Lily France. Worse, he was acting on his fantasies. Irritably he climbed into bed and set himself to ignore the demanding ache in his loins. In fact, he was not sure that lust was all it was. Worrying.

Why Lily France of all women? She was rich, spoilt, obsessed with shopping and social climbing and had wincingly bad taste in everything from interior decoration to men.

She was also beautiful, brave, loyal, bright—when her brain was not addled thinking about titled husbands—and in need of a defender. And kissing her was heaven and hell all in one innocent bundle.

Whereas I need an investor who can afford to take a robust attitude to risk—which rules out a woman. And I need an encounter with Adrian Randall like I need a hole in the head. Another *hole in the head,* he corrected himself. *And I most certainly do not need a romantic entanglement with a woman. Any woman.*

So, borrowing money from Lily was out of the question. Wasting time thinking about Lily was out of the question. Making both Randall and the bastard who had insulted her this evening pay would have to wait until he had some plan to achieve it without, as Lily very reasonably pointed out, ending up on the scaffold.

He had a duty to protect any woman who came into his orbit and who needed his assistance, but that was as far as it went. At home he had four women who were his responsibility, a mine, and an entire village whose livelihood depended on that mine. If he failed, he supposed he could always sell up and retreat to the farm, and the family would become yeomen farmers once again. There were worse things; it was how they had begun.

But that was no help to the two hundred souls whose fortunes were inextricably tied to the mine. The men and lads who worked down it, their families, the small shopkeepers and tradesmen who supplied them.

Was he going to go home having failed because he was becoming obsessed with a merchant's red-headed heiress? No. Jack slid down under the blankets, smiling rather grimly as he realised that sobering thoughts and resolutions had had not the slightest impact on his state of more than uncomfortable arousal.

'What have you been about, child?' Aunt Herrick marched into Lily's bedchamber in her niece's wake and shut the door firmly in Janet's face. 'Lady Billington said tonight was a disaster.'

'It was.' Lily shrugged. It was hard to keep any sort of mental balance. The soirée had been a nightmare, the last few minutes in the garden with Jack had been a dream. Except surely good dreams did not leave your heart hammering and your mouth dry and the most improper feelings turning your insides to jelly.

'Lady Billington says the only thing to be done is to retreat to the country and try again in the summer. Now, where can we go? She suggests Brighton, which means we ought to think about renting something as soon as possible or all the best places will be reserved.' Mrs Herrick's brow was furrowed in thought. 'And what do we tell people?'

Lily let her cloak fall to the floor and sat down. An hour ago she had been ready to follow her chaperon's advice and run away. Now she was not so sure. She was unused to not getting what she wanted. Of course Jack was right and there *were* things money would not buy. But as well as money she had a brain, and pride and—Jack. Not that she was quite certain how he would contribute to her reinstatement in polite society, but there was an idea stirring at the back of her mind.

'Not yet,' she said slowly, thinking as she spoke. 'Not until I try something tomorrow, and not until after Lady Frensham's dance.'

Chapter Seven

The next day Jack breakfasted early, applied a plaster to his temple and set out on a round of visits. Two possible investors who had sent cautiously encouraging responses to his letters and Sir James Arbuthnot, considered to be one of the authorities on steam power in the south of England, promised a full day, especially for a man intending to walk and not waste his blunt on hackney carriages. And besides, an early start meant there was no risk of running into Lily.

Not that the thought of an encounter with Lily was unwelcome—the reverse, in fact, which was what worried him. Jack shifted his portfolio from left hand to right and crossed Oxford Street, flicking a coin to the crossing sweeper as he went. He should never have kissed her. Worse, he was beginning to believe that the earlier kiss, the one he had convinced himself was a feverish dream, had been real.

Under normal circumstances any young lady twice kissed by a man would have considerable justification for expecting an offer. Jack passed the end of Berners Street, dodging a coal cart, a sedan chair and almost getting his boots splashed with milk from the buckets suspended from the pretty seller's yoke. 'Cup of milk, sir? Yours for a penny and a kiss, sir.' She fluttered her lashes at him and Jack grinned back.

The smile faded as he strode on towards Bloomsbury. But these were not normal circumstances. The young lady in question could buy him out twenty times over. At least. Just how rich was she? What Lily France wanted was not kisses, but a title and a place in society. She might be surprised by what Jack Lovell could offer her, but a place in London society was not included. In any case, if he fell to one knee and offered her marriage in return for having compromised her, she would laugh in his face. Thank goodness.

It was a long day, and a mixed one. Sir James had offered encouragement, confirmation that his ideas were not as outlandish as he feared, and some useful papers to read. But no suggestions for investors.

His two prospects might have been reading from the same script. They were dubious about his projections for the growth of demand for heating coals in London; personally, they preferred to concentrate on the markets in the Midland factories. But the canals did not exist to get the coal to them and they treated Jack's suggestion that steam power might eventually be harnessed to a network of tramways reaching far out into the country as fantasy. They agreed that it was so used in one or two localities in Wales—but only close to the mines. Steam locomotion was the province of dreamers and visionaries, not down-to-earth businessmen, they explained with a patronising tolerance that set his teeth on edge.

He was beginning to get heartily sick of keeping his tongue between his teeth. He was used to action, to making his own decisions and not to waiting on other people's convenience or pandering to their opinion. London made his skin itch. He wanted to tear off his starched neckcloth, tie a red spotted Belcher handkerchief round his neck instead, and go and work off his frustration by wielding a pick alongside the men.

By the time he reached Chandler Street he was, as he admitted to himself, as cross as a bear with a sore head and within an ames' ace of packing his bags and going home. His mood was not improved by finding the street outside the house a scene of activity, although this time it was orderly and respectable.

A groom on foot was holding the reins of a grey gelding that made his mouth water with envy. A second man waited alongside, mounted on a respectable bay cover hack, and Lily's maid was poised on the steps, a whip and gloves in her hands.

Other than crossing to the other side and striding past, he had little choice but to slow down and acknowledge the staff. In any event, one close look at the gelding brought him to a standstill. 'Is this Miss France's?'

'Aye, sir.' The head groom was respectful, although what he thought of Jack's status, given his lodging over the carriage house, Jack could not tell. 'Her agent bought it for Miss Lily at Tattersalls last week.' As though recognising the attention, the grey tossed its head and rolled an eye at Jack.

'Something of a handful?'

'Miss Lily's a good rider, sir, she likes them with a bit of spirit. This one's not got any harm in him.'

'Admiring Spindrift, Mr Lovell? I am bound for Rotten Row.' It was Lily, pulling on her gloves and smiling at him from the top step. If she felt any awkwardness after yesterday evening, it did not show. She probably regarded it as a trivial incident or was too innocent for it to cause her any anxiety.

Not that he could concentrate on her face—he was too struck by her riding habit. A deep sea green, it was form fitting up to her bust where the plain fabric was laced and ornamented by row after row of military frogging. There was a pert little jacket made without fastenings, which served only to emphasise her curves. The sleeves were cut and frogged, the shoulders of the jacket bore epaulettes and the train of the habit swept over her arm.

To top it off, she wore an outrageous hat, modelled vaguely on a shako. But no soldier ever wore anything as frivolous as this concoction with its cockade of French lace and its plume of ostrich feathers.

The whole outfit was ostentatious, showy and extreme and Jack realised, quite against his expectation, that she looked magnificent in it. He found that his mouth was open and shut it hastily. Lily was regarding him with a twinkle in her eye and he saw that she, too, knew just what effect she was having and what a figure she would cut as she rode her eye-catching horse in Hyde Park at the height of the fashionable hour. It was a declaration of war on her part.

No wonder I love her. The thought came into his mind unbidden and he fought to control the shock and his expression. *No! Impossible...*

Now what is the matter with the man? Lily buttoned her second glove, took her whip from Janet and came down the remainder of the steps. Jack had looked quite pleased to see her, not at all embarrassed after yesterday evening, which she was afraid he might be. Now he was looking positively stony. Perhaps he had seen her own feelings reflected in her face and that had annoyed him. Perhaps he was afraid she would expect something of him after that kiss.

Drat. She had thought she could manage matters so they

could remain friends, despite the fact that her heart was thudding at the sight of him and her mind whirling with the thought that perhaps he might kiss her again. And she had thought for a moment that he understood why she was wearing her outrageous new habit. But, no, doubtless he saw only that it was ostentatious and, in his eyes, vulgar.

'What do you think of my horse?' she persisted, determined now to get a response from him other than disapproval and a blank face. And Jack Lovell, once he assumed that flinty expression, looked every bit as forbidding as she imagined his blighted northern crags to be.

'Very fine. I was admiring him—and coveting him for my eldest sister, Caroline. She is an accomplished rider.'

Approval for something at last! 'I am exceedingly pleased with him.' Lily ran her hand down the horse's neck, then let Peters give her a leg up into the saddle. He sidled and she let him for a moment before bringing him back up to the bit; she was well aware she made a striking figure on the grey. 'My agent had a tussle to secure him; he had to pay a good round sum in the end.' *There I go again...mentioning money.* Lily could have kicked herself.

And then she could have kicked Jack, who merely looked down his nose and remarked, 'In this case, a purchase where money *does* buy quality, Miss France. Have a pleasant ride.'

In other words, most of my other purchases are not *quality I suppose, Mr High and Mighty Lovell?* she fumed as she trotted off towards Park Lane. *I just do not know why I love the wretched man.*

'Miss France?' Lily stared round wildly and found she had reined in right in the middle of Park Lane, almost causing a collision involving a landau, a chaise and two curricles. She pulled herself together and arrived at the Stanhope Gate flustered and dazed, conscious that only Spindrift's good manners had got her out of a nasty scrape.

'Are you all right, Miss France? Shall we go back?'

'What? Oh, yes, I am quite all right, thank you Peters. I just realised something, it was a bit of a shock. Come along, I want to join the promenade along Rotten Row.'

All right? Will I ever be all right again? I am in love with him. But I cannot be in love with him. He is a mine owner, and any minute he may lose that mine. He isn't even merchant class as I am, however well he speaks. He isn't rich; he doesn't even seem to be comfortably off. Papa would have been furious, everyone would be. No title, no place in society. He would never ask me to marry him anyway, he despises my taste and my money…

'Miss France!'

'What? Oh, yes, Peters, thank you, I see her. Lady Farringdon, good afternoon.' She exchanged bows with a matron in a landau; now, had she not heard all the scandal, or was she prepared to give Miss France the benefit of the doubt?

Oh, goodness, there was Lady Jersey. She had not counted on meeting one of the Patronesses of Almack's, which was foolish, given the fashionable throng who flocked to the Park of an afternoon. All of a sudden her defiance in wearing her new habit, let alone riding out with only a groom, seemed very ill judged.

Lily considered turning tail and bolting. It had seemed such a good idea, to be seen in the Park at the height of the fashionable promenade. She could demonstrate that she had nothing to be ashamed of, she would find out, once and for all, whether there was anyone she could rely upon, and she could perhaps convey her side of the story to a few influential ladies.

Now, completely overset by her thoughts about Jack, all her poise deserted her and she could only stare helplessly as Lady Jersey's carriage approached.

'Miss France! What a surprise.'

Could a large enough hole open up to swallow her and horse together? No, apparently not.

'Lady Jersey, ma'am.'

'I was just talking about you. The things I have been hearing! Now come and join me and tell me all about it.'

With a sensation of walking into the lion's den, Lily signalled to Peters to come and help her down. Lady Jersey was a notorious gossip with enormous influence. If she decided to be amused by Lily's predicament, all might be saved. If she decided it was a vulgar bore, the situation was irretrievable.

'What a *striking* habit, Miss France.' *Oh, no, she hates it…*

Jack spread the post he had collected from the Green Dragon out in front of him. A letter from home, full of news from his sisters, sensible enquiries about his well being from Mama. No indication there of what she must be worrying about, with him gone so long. He made no secret with her of the state of affairs; she had seen the family fortunes crash during his father's lifetime and knew exactly how things stood.

A long budget of news from William Sykes, his colliery manager, most of it indifferent, culminating with the intelligence that virtually every metal tire on the wagons needed replacing and enclosing the blacksmith's estimate. And, gallingly, a cheerful letter from a neighbour with the encouraging information that the market for domestic coals at the Newcastle docks was buoyant and now was the moment to sink further shafts, as he himself planned.

'Good for you, Roper,' Jack muttered, trying to feel cheerful for his friend. No, enough was enough. He would give it one more week, one more advertisement and then go home and fight this thing on the spot. A long way away from Lily France and those great green eyes. A broken heart was only another sort of pain, after all.

'Jack?'

'I did not hear you.' She was standing in the open doorway at the head of the stairs, still dressed for riding, her cheeks flushed, her eyes sparkling. Jack got to his feet and stood with the table between them. It felt safer. 'Did you have a pleasant ride?'

'It was wonderful!' She came in, closed the door behind her and pulled off her hat. A mass of chestnut hair tumbled free and she pushed it back with an exclamation of annoyance. Jack felt his whole body tense, his mouth dry. He had never seen that glory unbound before. His hands curled with the need to fix themselves in the shining mass, pull her to him, bury his face in it. He felt his body sway and stepped back away from the table, deeper into the shadows.

'I forgot we just bundled it up.' She was running her fingers through it now; the fragrance from it reached him, even across the room. Jasmine? 'I saw Lady Jersey in the Park.'

'The Patroness? But is that good?'

'It might not have been—I was a mass of nerves when she called me over. But, Jack, it is all right! She asked me to join her in her carriage and we drove the length of the Row and she was so amiable, you would not believe.

'And she admired my habit and told me I was bold but original. Then she wanted to know all about the scene outside the house, and laughed when I told her—and said, *Now, I wonder who might have been behind* that *Miss France?* in such a knowing way that I am sure she suspects Lady Angela, whom I know she dislikes. And then she wanted to know about Adrian.'

'What did you tell her? She has the reputation as a shocking gossip, has she not?' *Damn it, I just want to go over there and take you in my arms and...*

'Dreadful—but I think that is all to the good—provided she is on one's side and believes she has all the inside news. I was very careful not to say anything horrid about Adrian, just to imply that we both realised we would not suit. Then I said that despite it being perfectly amicable someone was spreading nasty rumours about it and she looked very knowing and said she would soon put people right about *that*. So I think it will be a storm in a teacup—I am so thankful I caught her on a day when she was inclined to be understanding.'

If I tell her I love her, will she be shocked? Or laugh? Or if I go over there and make love to her and then tell her—can I make her love me? And then what? 'Good news indeed,' he agreed drily. 'I suspect she enjoys meddling, setting people on end. Perhaps someone she is at outs with has criticised you, so she decides to take your part?'

'Probably,' Lily agreed, drifting into the room and beginning to turn over the pile of prints and drawings that were on one end of the table. 'Are these all steam pumps?'

'No, not all, there are maps of the coal field, some cross-sections of rock formations, that sort of thing.' He stayed back in the shadows, burningly conscious of the hardness of his body, of his need to touch her.

'Oh, what is this?' A print, stuck to the underside of another, drifted free as she lifted it and fluttered to the floor. Jack took one long stride forward and caught it, his fingers over the caption at the bottom. It brought them face to face as he straightened up.

'Let me see.' Lily craned to look at the print, a foursquare castle in the antique style with massive towers at each corner. 'Where is that? It is very picturesque.'

'Hardly that,' Jack said. 'It is simply a castle near the mine.' There was something in his voice that made her look sharply at him, but she could read neither his face nor the tone. It seemed to her that perhaps his head was paining him, for the skin over those strong cheekbones looked tight and his eyes were shadowed. She wanted to run her fingertips over his face, caress away that tension, but something in his face held her back. 'It has changed since this print was made. That tower at the right at the back has collapsed—in my grandfather's day one of our tunnels ran under it and the thing caved in.'

'Oh, my goodness!' Lily stared at him aghast. 'But how dreadful! What happened? Was there a claim against your family?' *No wonder Jack has no money.*

'The shock carried the old earl off with some kind of apoplectic fit. His son decided not to rebuild. There was no monetary claim as such, but we lost access to a large area of high-quality coal.'

Lily opened her mouth to demand all the details, then closed it again firmly. If nothing else, loving Jack was teaching her tact. He pushed the print to the bottom of the pile, allowing her a partial glimpse of the title as he did so. ...*erton Castle.*

She should leave now she had told him her news. Aunt Herrick would certainly say so. Defiantly Lily went and curled up in one of the big leather chairs she had ordered set up on either side of the closed stove. 'Jack, do come and sit down. It's giving me a crick in the neck talking to you when you are standing right over there.'

It seemed to her that he hesitated before he came across

and sat opposite her. 'I am glad to hear your good news, but you should go now.'

'Oh, you are as bad as Aunt Herrick,' she grumbled, tucking her skirts snugly around her ankles. 'Don't be so stuffy. I want to ask you something.'

'Yes?' he said warily.

Lily chuckled. 'That was not very gallant. You should have sounded eager to assist me.'

'I never know what you are about to say or do. I have not known you long, Lily, just long enough to be cautious.' He was smiling too, but there was a constraint behind it that she did not understand. 'What do you wish to ask?'

'If you will please act as my escort tomorrow night to Lady Frensham's dance. It is not a ball, more of a rout party with dancing.'

'No.'

The rejection was so immediate that Lily blinked. 'But I have not explained—oh, you are worried about not having an evening suit of clothes, but I am sure one of the fashionable tailors can outfit you in a trice, and naturally I would pay for it as I am asking you to oblige me.'

'No.' Jack crossed one leg over the other, sat back in the chair and looked as unmovable as a granite boulder.

'Why not?' she demanded.

'If you feel I am under an obligation in return for my food and shelter, beyond the amount for my lodgings which I am paying to Mrs Oakman—'

'You are what?' Lily uncurled her legs and sat up straight.

'You said that you would charge me what I was paying to the Green Dragon. I am giving it to your housekeeper.'

'But…that was not what I meant, you exasperating man!

I meant that I would take it out of whatever I and the trustees decide to invest with you.'

'I dislike being in debt.' Jack spoke calmly, but his eyes were the hard flint colour she had learned to recognise as a sign of anger.

'We will talk about that later.' Lily was not used to backing down from an argument, far less losing one. 'I would like you to come with me because I would feel more comfortable with a male escort.'

'Or that you wish to demonstrate that you can muster one? Will Lord Randall be there?'

'I have no idea whether he will or not. I would simply like to show that I am not moping around, pining for him.'

'I am sure you can adequately demonstrate that without my assistance. Buy a new gown, perhaps? I am sure the crown jewels of some minor duchy must be available at a price?'

'I will not dignify that with an answer,' Lily retorted. 'You are just set upon being disobliging for some reason.' *How is it possible to be head over heels in love with a man who makes you want to throw the fire irons at him?*

'I am busy.'

They sat in silence, Lily fuming, Jack watching her from beneath hooded lids. 'Please?'

'No.'

'I will pay you for your time.'

'What?' Jack sat up abruptly. 'I'll be damned if you do! There are names for men who hire themselves out to ladies, and none of them apply to me.'

'Oh for goodness' sake, Jack! You are as prickly as a hedgehog! I want your escort to a social event, not your…your… *body,* you conceited man.' And that was as brassy a lie as she was likely to come out with in many a long year, she recognised as soon as she said it.

'Very well.' The mobile mouth quirked into a smile. Lily narrowed her eyes suspiciously and tried not to recall what those lips had felt like on hers. 'One hundred guineas.'

'How much? That is outrageous!' Jack shrugged, still smiling. Obviously he thought she would stop at nothing to get what she wanted and was prepared to call her bluff. Lily bounced to her feet in an affronted swirl of skirts. 'Out of the question. Since you are so disobliging, I will go without you.'

She marched towards the door, forgetting the long skirts of her riding habit, and tripped over her own feet, somewhat spoiling the effect of her exit. She paused at the head of the stairs, chin up. 'And minor duchies do not have crown jewels.'

'Schleswig-Holstein,' a mocking voice called after her. Lily slammed the door and retreated with as much dignity as she could muster.

'Aunt!' Mrs Herrick was sitting in the smallest salon with her feet up on a footstool and a novel in her hand, dozing.

'Wha…? What, dear? Do not bounce so, Lily.'

'Where, or what, is Schleswig-Holstein?'

'Goodness, how would I know! Germany, I should think. Look it up on the globes in the study, dear. Why do you want to know?'

'Just something Mr Lovell said.'

'Discussing geography?' Mrs Herrick asked vaguely, picking up her novel and pushing her cap straight. 'That is nice, dear.'

Chapter Eight

Lily approached Lady Frensham's party with some trepidation, not helped by a pessimistic Lady Billington prophesying doom throughout the short carriage journey.

'I can place no reliance upon Sally Jersey remembering from one day to the next what she has promised,' she remarked waspishly. 'She is as changeable as spring weather and as empty headed as a pea goose. She has probably been sympathising with all of Randall's friends and family and saying what a close escape he had. This will be worse than Lady Troughton's; you should have retired to the country as I advised.'

But Lady Frensham was, if not effusive, perfectly pleasant, and although Lily received some frankly curious stares, no one cut her except Mrs Cunningham, who pretended, somewhat unconvincingly, that she had not seen her.

'Knows she made a mistake and does not know how to deal with it,' Lady Billington opined. 'The woman still smells of the shop—stop bristling, Lily, the whole point of our efforts are to make sure that *you* do not!—and she has no confidence, which is why she behaves so. Do not regard her.'

So Lily did not. The evening seemed likely to be pleasant enough, although it would have been nice to have a man with her—Lily still felt vulnerable. What if there were others like Lord Dovercourt who thought she would be so desperate that she would allow any liberties in her pursuit of a title?

And she missed Jack. To have quarrelled with him hurt, although she still could not understand just why that last encounter had seemed so difficult, so charged. Loving him, she felt as though his slightest look touched her bare skin, his smiles kissed her. And his anger burned like a brand.

The major domo was still announcing guests, his loud voice almost muffled by the volume of conversation. Lily looked round, puzzled, from an exchange about the weather with Miss Monroe and her beau. 'Who did he just announce?'

'I am sorry, Miss France, I did not hear. Were you expecting someone?'

'No, no one.' Shaking her head, Lily made herself concentrate. Miss Monroe was teasing Lieutenant Forrest to organise a picnic party and was begging Lily's support in convincing him that the weather would hold. She would have to learn to pull herself together if she was going to cope when Jack left London; she could not go on imagining she heard his name when he was not there.

'Miss France?'

With a gasp Lily turned. Jack was standing just behind her in an immaculate evening suit, his hair rigorously pulled back and tied with a narrow velvet ribbon, his head wound discreetly concealed by a black plaster, which gave him a rakish air.

'Mr Lovell!'

'You are annoyed with me,' he said smoothly with an apologetic glance towards her companions. 'I promised to escort Miss France and was then held up at the last minute,' he explained. Lily smiled weakly and took Jack's proffered arm, letting him steer her to a bench in an alcove.

'What are you doing here! Miss Monroe must have been wondering why on earth I reacted like that.'

'Which is why I gave a reason for you to be annoyed with me.'

'I am still annoyed with you.' At least, if he thought that, she had an excuse for her pink cheeks. Her pulse was hammering. 'Where did you get that suit of clothes?'

'Out of pawn.'

'They are very fine, and really quite modish,' Lily observed, attempting to keep the rallying note in her voice.

'Thank you. I thought them a necessity for London and then realised almost immediately that the money would be of more use, so I popped them.'

'Popped?'

'Pawned. I can see you have never had to make the acquaintance of your friendly local pawnbroker, Lily!'

'But had you the money to redeem them?' she worried.

'I risked it on the expectation of your hundred guineas.'

'You know perfectly well we never agreed that,' she retorted. 'How much was it?'

'I am not going to tell you, and I can afford it.' He was watching her with a smile in his eyes that seemed almost affectionate. 'I was teasing you, Lily. You bristle so charmingly. Now that I am here, how do you want me to act? Shall I flirt with you?' *Oh, yes, please…* 'Or do you want me to stand beside you looking possessive?' *Even better.*

'Oh…just pretend to flirt—a little,' she added hastily. 'And frighten off unsuitable men.'

'How will I know them to be unsuitable? Will they come

with labels? *Titled, amiable, gentlemanly behaviour* or *Merely a baronet, amorous rogue.*'

Lily smothered a laugh, suddenly at her ease with him again. 'I will signal to you if I need rescuing,' she promised. 'Now come and let me introduce you to some of the other guests.'

Jack is perfect at this, she thought as they circulated. *He seems to have put on a society gloss along with the clothes. Where has he learned it? Or perhaps he is simply very observant and a good actor.*

She watched him chatting easily to a group of officers and the thought came to her, that of all the civilian men in the room, he was the one who could best stand comparison with the bearing and air of command that sat so easily on the senior officers.

He is strong, and he is confident and he is...beautiful. Lily swallowed as a wave of pure longing swept over her. She unfurled her fan and took refuge behind it in the hope of hiding her blushes. He made her feel so wanton, it was outrageous.

In the hope of regaining some composure, Lily turned away and went to exchange smiling insults with Miss Shillington, an adder-tongued young woman who—for some reason, Lily found amusing—whereas most of her critics merely made her furious.

'My dear Miss France! What a stunning gown! How brave of you to venture out with quite such a weight of beaded trimming; a marvel that you can move at all.'

'I have the advantage of height to carry it off.' She smiled at Miss Shillington, a good five inches shorter than she. 'And what an unusual colour your gown is. So challenging to the complexion!'

'I am fortunate that I have not a hint of red in either my

hair or my skin,' Miss Shillington riposted. 'It is simple for me to maintain a ladylike pallor at all times, whatever colour I wear.'

Refreshed by their encounter, the two curtsied and passed on. Lily was still smiling when the orchestra struck up for the dancing to begin and she found, much to her surprise, that her hand was being solicited for a flattering number of dances.

'But not the waltzes,' a voice at her shoulder said as she was consulting her dance card in response to a pressing enquiry by Lord Wolverton. 'You recall you have promised me two waltzes, Miss France?'

'*One* waltz, Mr Lovell,' she said with mock reproof, while the temptation to demand that he dance all of them with her beat at her self-control.

'The last, then.'

'Very well.' She pencilled it in, conscious that her hand was shaking, and was whisked away by Lord Wolverton into the quadrille.

Concentrating on her steps, maintaining a easy flow of conversation, all helped keep her mind off Jack, although she was aware that he was not dancing, simply standing with one shoulder propped indolently against a pillar, watching her. Which was highly gratifying.

She accepted the escort of Captain Eden to supper, enjoyed a blameless flirtation with him, then noticed that Jack had escorted in one of the Miss Wilsons and seemed totally engrossed in her. Perhaps he just did not dance, which did not bode well for a romantic last waltz.

By the time he came to claim her hand she did not know how to feel. 'You *can* dance, can you not?' she hissed as he led her on to the floor. 'Only you have sat everything out, and I wondered…'

Jack's brow furrowed as he took her in his arms. 'I have been watching,' he said with a note of anxiety in his deep voice. 'It seems easy enough.'

'Jack!' The music started. There was no escape now without dragging him off the floor, or fleeing. Which was worse? To do that and cause speculation about why, or be a laughing stock as they stumbled around the room?

Then she realised they were moving, that Jack was dancing with perfect competence and that the beast was smiling at her with eyes brimming with laughter. 'You horrid man! You let me think—'

'It was irresistible, Lily. You should have seen your face. What do you think we do in the north? Paint ourselves with woad and dance round camp fires? Or do you think the fashions have stuck in the last century and the most à la mode dance we have heard of is the minuet?'

'Woad, of course.' She was smiling back now, moving within his guiding arms as though she had always danced with him. For a big man he had grace, even if he did not venture any of the more daring turns that made the chaperons tut in disapproval. He certainly had the strength and the confidence to command the floor.

But more than that, the way he held her, the way he looked at her, made her feel both safe and terrified all at the same time. Lily did not realise that the music had stopped until she found that they were standing still in each others' arms, their eyes locked. The rest of the couples were beginning to leave the floor.

'I think we had better move,' Jack remarked, turning and leading her off. 'Or do you think if we wait they will strike up an encore?'

Blushing, Lily let him take her off the floor. 'That is quite

my favourite dance tune,' she improvised in a frantic attempt
to explain her behaviour. 'Really, it is quite mesmerising, is
it not?'

'You are quite mesmerising,' Jack murmured in her ear.

'I—'

'Lily dear, I think it is about time we took our leave, do
you not?' It was Lady Billington, her eyes speculative as they
moved from one face to another.

'Yes, of course. Mr Lovell, would you accompany us?' Her
chaperon did not know where Jack was living, nor, Lily realised, who he was, other than that he was injured during the
riot outside the house.

'Of course.'

Lily could see in the light that flickered into the carriage
interior that Lady Billington was dozing—or 'resting her
eyes', as Mrs Herrick always called it. What was Jack thinking about? She could not read his face in the gloom, but he
was staring out of the window. Was he regretting that
strangely intense dance? Or had it been only she who had felt
the tension and the magic?

Lady Billington came to herself with a start as the carriage pulled up at the steps of the Chandler Street house.

Jack jumped down to assist Lily, then declined as Lady
Billington graciously offered to take him to his door. 'Thank
you, ma'am, but I would rather see Miss France safely inside.'

They said goodnight to the chaperon and stood looking
after the carriage as it rounded the corner. 'Is anyone awake?'
Jack eyed the front of the house with some misgiving. There
was a faint glimmer through the fanlight, but no other signs
of life.

'I have a key.' Lily produced it, her awkwardness disappearing at the expression on Jack's face as he looked from the weighty metal object to her little evening reticule. 'I left it in the carriage,' she explained with a smile, handing it to him. 'I always tell the staff to go to bed when I am not sure what time I will get in. I do not see why they should have to sit up and waste their time, simply to open the door to me.'

'Your maid too?' She nodded. 'An original attitude in London society, I should imagine.' He opened the door and stood aside for Lily to enter. 'What about the bolts?'

'I can manage those. Do come in.' For a moment she thought he would refuse. 'You can go through the garden door, there is no point in walking right round to the mews.'

The house seemed eerily quiet. It was strange that she had never noticed it before. They stood together in the hall while Lily lit a branch of candles from the single lantern that had been left burning there. The door to the small salon stood open as it always did when she had been out. A light supper was laid out on the table.

'I am just going to have a glass of lemonade, perhaps a biscuit. Will you join me?' Jack hesitated and Lily found she was holding her breath. What was he thinking? She wished she had the courage to reach out and touch him, as though by doing so she could read his mind. 'The decanters are out and the brandy is very fine, I am assured by my wine merchant.' Would he make some comment about the price of it and shatter the moment?

'Thank you, that would be pleasant. Unless you are tired?'

Lily led the way into the room, touching fire to candles until there was an intimate, warm light that glowed against the old panelling that she had not yet had replaced. Looking round at it, she suddenly realised what Jack meant about the comfort of old things. 'Shall I leave this panelling? I was going to have it ripped out, but, seeing it in this light, it is so lovely.'

'It would be a shame. It is very fine.'

Lily nodded. 'I will leave it. No, thank you—' Jack was lifting the jug of lemonade to pour for her '—I will try the brandy.'

'Are you sure?' He unstopped the decanter, sniffed and gave an appreciative whistle. 'I will pour you a little. I suggest you inhale only, this is powerful—and wonderful.'

Lily took the proffered glass, kicked off her kid slippers and went to curl up in one of the big wing chairs. 'Oh! The aroma is delightful.' She took a cautious sip, coughed and pulled a face. 'Is it supposed to taste like this?'

Jack laughed as she took another sip. 'An acquired taste, I suppose.' They sat in silence for several minutes. More out of nerves than anything Lily took another mouthful of brandy. It burned all the way down to her stomach. Strange, hot, uncomfortable, yet wonderful. It was like the feelings that ran through her body when she looked at Jack, when he touched her.

He took the chair opposite, crossed his legs and gently swung his foot to and fro while he watched the play of light on the deep amber liquid in his glass. 'It matches your hair.'

'No, surely not.' Lily held up her own glass, frowning. 'I have red hair.'

'You do not. Your hair is gold and brown, conker and brandy, mahogany and copper. To say your hair is only red is to say fire is only red.'

Lily pulled at the curl which lay on her shoulder and tried to squint at it in the candlelight. It was hopeless. Impatient, she pulled out the jewelled comb that held her topknot of curls in place and tugged. A mass of hair fell down with a heavy, silken slither, showering pearl-topped pins as it did so. She shook her head until it massed around her shoulders and got up.

'Does it really match?' She perched on the arm of Jack's chair, took a handful of hair and brought it close to his brandy glass. 'Look and see.'

'I am looking.' His voice was husky and it seemed to her that his hand shook slightly as he raised it to catch the fall of her hair. 'Oh, God, Lily, your hair—'

He must have put down his glass, for he was lifting the weight of her hair in both hands, burying his face in it, and somehow she was no longer sitting on the arm of the chair but in his lap, his arms around her.

And then they were sliding, out of the chair, down on to the carpet, at once hard and soft underneath her, the pile prickling where it met her bare shoulders, yielding just a little where his weight pinned her down.

'Lily.' It was a question, a statement. It was a demand she did not understand.

'Yes,' she answered firmly. 'Oh, yes, Jack.'

She thought she knew his mouth now, the feel of his lips on hers, the demands he would make, the sweetness he would give her. It seemed she knew nothing at all. Perhaps it was the candlelight, perhaps the flame of brandy, perhaps it was the love she felt for him.

She could hear a soft mewing sound, then realised it was coming from her own throat as his mouth angled and moved on hers. One hand held her head, moving her so he could plunder her mouth at will, yet she felt no desire to struggle or resist him.

The other caressed downwards, over the swell of her breast as she arched under it, his palm cupping her for one aching moment. Her body was alive, filled with new sensations, new heat, new aching and wanting. She moved restlessly against him as his roving hand moulded her waist, her hip. Downwards.

And all the time the drugging caress never left her mouth. His tongue filled her, tormented her, teased with bold plunging, then tantalising withdrawal. She found she could match him in bravery, in demanding, her teeth nipping at the fullness of her lower lip.

Then the air was cool on her legs and she realised his hand was sliding up over her silk-sheathed calf, up past her garter, up to the warm softness of her bare thigh. He moved higher, confident in his mastery of her as if knowing she could no more resist him than take to the air. It should have been embarrassing, she should have been shy. All Lily knew was that she needed him to touch her—somewhere. *There.*

'Jack!' She knew she cried out, felt his kiss swallow the sound as his knowing, skilful fingers tangled in the hot, moist curls, sank into her, found a place that made her sob with need for him to touch it, sob with an exquisite anguish when he did.

'Sweetheart.' His face was buried in her neck as he strained her against him, giving her the anchor she needed to hold on to as the blackness behind her lids turned to flame and sparks and her body shattered and spiralled down into peace.

Chapter Nine

How much longer could he keep her here in his arms like this? Not long, not safely. Jack rested his cheek on Lily's head and closed his eyes. Against his body hers was warm and soft. He could feel her heart beating and her breath tickled his neck. He thought the scent of her skin would never leave his memory.

'Lily.'

'Mmm?' Jack felt her lips move against the front of his shirt and fought down the need to seek them out again with his own.

'Time you were in bed.'

'Mmm?' This time there was a decidedly mischievous note in her voice.

'Your own bed, by yourself,' he added firmly, wondering which of them was most in need of the reproof.

'Jack?' Her voice was muffled. 'Jack, don't you want to…to…?'

'No.' *Yes, oh, God, so much. Yes.*

'I don't think I understand. You did not—I mean, I know what happens when a man lies with a woman, and that was not it.' *Ah, that's my Lily. Questions and more questions until you get to the bottom of things!*

'It is one of the things that can happen. One of many things.'

'Oh.' There was a hint of worry behind the monosyllable. Jack pushed the weight of her hair back from her face in an attempt to see her face, but Lily burrowed against him. 'Am I still—'

'A virgin? Yes.'

'Oh.' He could almost feel her thinking. 'Good. I think.'

'Definitely good.' He had to tell himself that. And assuredly he would be thankful for it in the morning, if his body ever stopped screaming at him for release. He reached down and smoothed her skirts back over her legs, trying not to look at the naked whiteness of her thighs, the elegant curve of her calves.

There was a sigh so deep he thought it stirred the hairs on his chest, despite his buttoned shirt. Lily uncurled herself and sat up, hairpins falling to the floor as she did so. In the firelight her eyes glinted, but he could not read the emotions in them. 'We had better find all of these before the housemaid does,' she remarked prosaically, sweeping her hand across the carpet.

Jack sat back on his heels and began to search too. 'What about your maid? Will you have to wake her to unlace your gown?'

'Yes.' Lily frowned at the handful of pins. 'I wonder if there are any more of these. Janet will just think I have let down my own hair, especially if I take off my jewels as well.' She swept her hand across the woollen pile again and their fingers touched. Lily moved her hand until they intertwined. 'Jack, I am sorry.'

Hell. Guilt hit him in the belly. The last thing he wanted was for her to feel ashamed of what had just happened.

'I should not have behaved like that when you are too much the gentleman to take advantage of me.' She bit her lip and looked him in the face. 'I know perfectly well what would have happened if you had been Adrian.'

He closed his fingers hard around hers. 'You did nothing wrong, other than to trust me. The blame is mine. It will not happen again.'

'I will always trust you.' She got to her feet, her hand still clasped in his, and he stood too. 'Give me those pins. We had better see how the back door is secured.'

Lily hopped down off the stool, gave the garden door a last shake and went back to the salon for one final check. All seemed orderly and innocuous. The fire was smouldering safely behind the fire screen, the brandy glass was back on the tray, and one pearl pin glinted on the carpet. She stooped and picked it up.

What a strange, wonderful, evening. Lily picked up the branch of candles and shut the door. She had behaved with complete impropriety, she knew that. Inside she felt warm with the knowledge that she had been right to trust Jack, and guilty to think she had taken more, far more, than she had given. And yet, he had seemed content. Perhaps he was simply so much more secure in himself than Adrian was that he did not have to take in order to be happy. Perhaps, this time at least, simply making her happy was enough. And she *was* happy, happy with a bone-deep physical contentment that overwhelmed all her mental anxieties.

How many women fell in love and found out too late that they could not rely on the man, as she knew she could upon

Jack? Then, as she reached her chamber, reality rolled back out of the rosy mist she inhabited. What had just passed between her and Jack was all that there could be. He would go back to his mine, far away. She would continue with her social whirl until she found a titled husband whom she could tolerate, and thus fulfil her duty.

Lily sat down in front of her dressing-table mirror and began to unhook her earrings and unfasten her necklace. The pearls slid over her skin in a sensual whisper as the double rope uncoiled. Could she ever be touched by a man again without remembering Jack's caress, the way his hard hands were so gentle on her body?

'Miss Lily?' She jumped. Janet emerged from the dressing room, pulling her wrapper tight and yawning. 'You should have called me, Miss Lily.'

'I thought I might be able to manage without disturbing you.' Lily stood up and let the maid begin to unhook the fastenings of her gown. A hair pin fell out. 'I made a complete mull of taking down my hair,' she confessed. 'I was fiddling with it in the salon just now and it all came tumbling down. I have probably shed pins over half the house.'

'Never mind, Miss Lily,' Janet said comfortably, lifting the heavy silk skirts over Lily's head. She set the gown down and rapidly counted the pile of pins Lily had put on the dressing table. 'Ten, and the one I've just picked up. That makes eleven. There ought to be twelve. I'll warn the parlour maids. That's a pretty set, we don't want to lose one of them.'

Lily tossed aside her chemise and petticoats and dragged on her nightgown. She had never felt bashful about undressing with Janet in the room. Now she was so conscious of her own body that she felt sure she must be one rosy blush from head to toe. Should she still throb and tingle like that in places she had hardly been aware of before—and would certainly never have considered it modest to have thought about? And yet Jack had caressed her there, brought her the most delicious pleasure with a touch, and she had felt not the slightest glimmering of shame.

'Will there be anything else, Miss Lily?' The maid shook out the undergarments and draped the gown over her arm.

'No, thank you Janet. Just snuff out the candles as you go, please.'

On the landing the clock struck a quarter-hour. Quarter past two? How long had she and Jack stayed together in the salon, locked into that private dream world? Lily snuggled down under the covers and thought about Jack. Was he too trying to sleep, or sitting up working on those complex plans and calculations that littered his work table? Or perhaps he had gone straight out again, to find an obliging Cyprian and take his pleasure with her. She stiffened at the thought of the betrayal, then forced herself to be fair. Why should he not? He was a grown man, and, unlike her, had no tie of affection to prevent him. For Jack, taking another woman would be no betrayal at all.

Lily was heavy-eyed at breakfast, toying with her toast and earning a sharp enquiry from her aunt about what she had been up to the night before to put dark circles under her eyes.

'I danced too much, that is all. And then when I got home I was too restless to sleep, so I sat up in the salon for a while.' She flicked open the pages of the *Morning Post,* pretending an interest she did not feel in a report of a debate on trade in the House of Commons.

'And Mr Lovell escorted you?' Now how did Aunt know that?

'I invited him to, but he had to join me there, in the end.'

'You are blushing, miss! Did he kiss you?'

'Aunt! Lady Billington was with me.'

'He's not the man I think he is if he let that sharp-nosed creature stop him kissing a girl if he wanted to. Well?'

'Yes,' Lily admitted baldly.

'Enjoy it?'

Lily stared at her relative, saw the twinkle in her eyes and smiled back. 'Yes.' What would Aunt say if she knew the truth about just how far those kisses had gone?

'Stop blushing, child. You'd be unnatural if you didn't like it, a handsome young man like that. Just take care it doesn't go too far—it is one thing having a warm flirtation, quite another finding yourself leg-shackled to an unsuitable man.'

'Is he so unsuitable?' Lily flipped the paper to the back page without looking up.

'Of course he is! Your duty, Lily, my dear, is to marry a gentleman. A *titled* gentleman. That's what your papa was working for all those years, the notion that his grandsons would be titled gentlemen.'

Not for the first time the treacherous thought crept into Lily's mind that perhaps Papa would have been content just for her to be happy, then she resolutely dismissed it. It was her duty to advance the family.

With the idea of distracting Mrs Herrick, she scanned the third page of the paper for some gossip, but as the majority of the sheet was taken up with the report of a *crim.con* case in Hereford, which she strongly suspected she was not supposed to read, and a depressing account of the starvation in the Scilly Isles, Lily turned to the back page.

'Is the advertisement for Dr Jordan's Cordial Balm of Rakasiri in today's paper?' Mrs Herrick enquired. 'I meant to tear it out the other day, for it sounds just the thing for Cousin Alison's rheumatic gout, and then I forgot and the girl had used it to light the fire with.'

'I'll see.' Lily ran a finger down the column. A furniture auction, a cellar of wines for sale, novelty piping bullfinches, several notes to creditors… 'Yes, here it is. Do you really think it suitable? He also says it is an infallible cure for distressed bowels and for warming the chilled bodily fluids.' Lily grinned, 'Actually, that sounds as though it would be highly efficacious for Alison—I cannot think of anyone chillier.' She was still smiling as she read the rest of the advertisement, and her eye moved down to the one below.

Gentlemen desirous of obtaining a favourable opportunity for investment in a productive coal mine producing the finest grade of coal for the London market are invited to make themselves known to Mr Lovell, at the sign of the Green Dragon…

'Lily? Whatever is the matter?'

'Nothing, nothing at all. I was so foolish as to read all the horrid symptoms in this advertisement, which I should not have done while I was eating. I will copy the address and details down for you, shall I?'

So, Jack was not waiting for her trustees to meet. Either he did not believe they would approve of her investing in the mine, or he had scruples about her doing so. And somehow, after last night, she felt certain those scruples would have hardened into resolve. *Well, I can be quite as stubborn as you, Jack Lovell.*

'If you like, I will write to Dr Jordan and purchase some of this cordial balm.' Lily stood up, the paper folded in her hand. 'I have some correspondence to take care of this morning.'

The order for the cordial balm was soon written. Lily pulled forward another sheet of notepaper and began to write.

Dear Uncle Frederick, I know that the trustees are not due to meet for another week. However, knowing that you are still in London, I wonder if I might prevail on you to call this afternoon to discuss a new type of investment in which I am interested. I trust that Aunt and all the family continue well. I am, as ever, your affectionate niece, Lily.

The six trustees had remained in town after the last meeting in order to attend the funeral of a business acquaintance; with any luck they would all have decided to stay on.

The thought of taking a walk in the garden and just, quite casually, dropping in to see Jack was very tempting. Lily looked wistfully out of the window, then resolutely pulled a pile of papers and correspondence towards her. He would believe she was pursuing him, or reproaching him. Either was unthinkable.

She had her head in her hands, trying to make sense of an involved letter from France & France's principal agent in India, when a tap on the door made her look up.

'Jack! Please come in.' Her mind was so full of the complexities of the combined effect of a unusually severe wet season coupled with an improvement in transport for the tea down from the hills, that for a moment she forgot to feel any awkwardness at seeing Jack again in broad daylight. Then she remembered the previous night and blushed to her toes.

Jack, however, seemed more than capable of keeping his countenance. Lily swallowed and tried to follow his example.

'Am I interrupting? You seem very busy.' Could she refer to last night? No, perhaps better not if he didn't.

Lily pushed the agent's letter across the desk. 'There is

good news from Bombay, and bad news, and Mr Cummings, who is otherwise an excellent agent, rambles so much it is difficult to tell whether the end result is going to be a scarcity of good tea, a glut of poor tea or neither.'

'But surely you do not need to concern yourself with this?' Jack picked up the letter and read it. 'Do you not have people to take care of this for you?' He re-read the middle section. 'Monsoon? Rates for coolies? Do you understand these issues?'

'About as clearly as you understand one of your diagrams of coal seams and faults. Do you think all I did with my fortune was to spend it?'

He hesitated for just a moment, then grinned. 'Yes.'

'So did Adrian. Papa raised me in the business as he would a son. He knew I would have to rely on agents and on my trustees to transact affairs, so he thought it was important that I would know when I was given good advice, or when someone was trying to cheat me. I was in India with him when he died—that is why I made such a late come-out.'

'I am impressed.'

'Thank you.' She waved a hand at the ledgers on the shelves and the paperwork in front of her. 'You see, I have to work at it. I research other investments as well, so I can discuss them with my trustees. It would be helpful if you could explain more about your mine and what it is you hope to achieve before the next trustees' meeting.'

'The paperwork is not yet ready.'

Lily lowered her eyes so Jack could not read the irritation in them. Why was he too proud to approach *her* trustees when he would happily advertise in a newspaper? Because she was a woman? Because he had made love to her? Well, if he was too proud, then she would simply have to trick him for his own good.

'Are you on your way out?' He was holding his hat and gloves in his hand.

'Yes. I have learned of a manufactory to the east of the City that is employing a new design of steam pump and I was going to visit it.'

'Oh. So you will be out all day?'

'Yes. I have told Mrs Oakman—or perhaps you wished me to accompany you to an At Home this afternoon?' He assumed an expression of spurious willingness.

'Certainly not, Mr Lovell.' Lily kept her lips pursed in an effort not to smile. 'Your rates are far too expensive for me to hire your escort more than once a week.'

'Ma'am.' He bowed, making no attempt to hide his own amusement. 'I hope your work prospers.'

Lily waited until the front door closed, then ran into the front room and twitched aside the curtain—Jack was striding down the road towards Oxford Street. She watched until she saw him hail a hackney carriage at the end of the road and then whirled round. How long had she got? Safely, probably two hours.

She snatched up pen and paper as she passed the study and hurried down the garden path to the door up to the studio. As she hoped, it was unlocked and the table was covered with neat piles of notes and diagrams. She stood for a minute fixing their positions in her mind before she risked touching them.

Her cousin Tobias had explained to her how, as a lawyer, he 'got up' a brief so as to be able to present a case powerfully in court. Now she had two hours to study Jack's proposals so that she could argue them in front of her trustees. Lily found a clear area of table and lifted the first piece of paper from its pile with great care. Jack would never know she had been there—not until the trustees had made their decision.

Jack stayed out all day, giving Lily time to creep nervously into the studio twice more to check that she had left everything exactly as she had found it. He was still out when she kissed her Uncle Frederick goodbye after extracting his promise that there would be an extraordinary meeting of the trustees the next afternoon to consider her mysterious proposal.

'You aren't usually totty-headed, my girl. Coal mines, indeed!' Her great-uncle peered at her suspiciously from under beetling grey eyebrows. He was past seventy, a canny old merchant who ruled his own silk importing company—and his three adult sons—with a rod of iron. He did not approve of women meddling in business, although he was prepared to admit that Lily was less foolish than most of her sex. Always provided she paid attention to what her male advisers told her, of course.

'And I am not being so now,' she assured him affectionately. 'I believe you will be very interested in this opportunity. After all, you did say only the other month that we ought to think about diversifying into canals.'

'Canals are a very different matter to coal mines, child.'

'I know, dearest Uncle Frederick. One is horizontal, the other vertical.' He snorted at her frivolity, but patted her cheek.

'Modern girls! I do not know what the world is coming to.'

She was sure he was still grumbling away as his carriage bore him off back to Brown's Hotel, which sombre establishment always enjoyed his austere patronage.

But grumble as he might, he would be sure to appreciate the merits of Jack's mine and the prospect of rich seams of coal, just waiting to be exploited. If there was one thing her trustees understood, it was the importance of having a market for your goods, and London would never cease to devour thousands of tons of coal every year.

The lack of canals in the area was a problem, she could understand that now she had thought about the problems of hauling such a bulky and heavy product. But among Jack's notes had been some ideas about steam locomotion. Lily was not at all sure she understood how that worked, it all sounded very dangerous, but Jack seemed excited about it. Once she had persuaded the trustees to let her invest in the mine, it would be an easy next step to venture into this new world of iron and steam.

And if Jack became rich and successful and covered northern England in these new steam tramways… Lily was still sitting in the blue salon, her chin cupped in her hand, dreaming of herself on the arm of the newly ennobled Lord Lovell of Somewhere, wealthy and influential industrialist, when one of the maids came in to draw the curtains.

'Are you all right, Miss France?'

'What? Oh, I am sorry, Katy. I did not hear you come in.'

'Only you were sighing, Miss France, all gusty-like, and I wondered if you were feeling quite right.'

'Just daydreaming, Katy. Just daydreaming.' Lily stood up, realising it was time to go and change for dinner. *But what a daydream! Papa would approve, and how much better to marry a man who had reached the heights through his own efforts than one of these frivolous aristocrats who had wasted their inheritance.*

It was a long step from securing an investment in Jack's mine to seeing him ennobled, of course. Lily bit her lip, a little daunted at the prospect. He would probably have to go into politics as well, to gain the influence needed. Would Jack want to do that? Papa always said that one should aim high, but then, he had never come across the stubborn Mr Lovell. For the first time in her life, Lily realised, she was coming up against a will that was a match for hers. And this time, it was not a matter of money being lost if she did not succeed, but her chance of love and happiness.

Chapter Ten

Lily kept well away from the studio that evening and the next morning, although she turned her chair around at her desk so that she could glance up at Jack's windows as she worked on her notes for the afternoon's meeting. She had to get her trustees briefed, and in a positive frame of mind, before Jack appeared, for she had not the slightest confidence that he would agree to meet them. If she had to trick him, then she should prepare the ground as much as possible first.

Percy carried off a note, asking Mr Lovell if he would care to take tea with Miss France at three that afternoon. 'If he should ask, say that you believe Mrs Herrick will be there. And do not mention that my trustees are meeting this afternoon.'

'Yes, Miss France.' Puzzled, but obedient, Percy took the note and returned ten minutes later to report that Mr Lovell would be glad to accept. 'I think he is intending to leave soon, Miss France.'

Lily's stomach sank with a sickening lurch. 'Why? What has he said?'

'He asked me to get his portmanteaux sent over. And he

has started bundling up all those papers and tying them together.'

The door closed behind the footman, leaving the room in
silence. Lily realised her vision was blurred. Furious with herself, she dragged the back of her hand across her eyes. 'Do
not be so feeble, Lily France! You haven't lost him yet—time
and enough to cry when you do.'

Jack glanced at the clock, put down his pen and regarded
his inky fingers wryly. He seemed to have spent more time
lately with a pen in his hand than he had since he left school.

Time to wash and make himself respectable to take tea
with Lily. Time to thank her for her hospitality and to explain
that he was taking the stage from the Bull and Mouth at St
Martin-le-Grand tomorrow afternoon. And time to acknowledge to himself that what he was taking away from London
was not money, but a great deal of information, new ideas and
fresh resolve. And what he was leaving behind was the
woman he had come to love improbably, impossibly and, he
very much feared, irrevocably.

Like Lily, he had a duty to marry, to have heirs. And now,
leaving Lily, he knew that whoever he did eventually wed, it
was not going to be someone he loved. He had always imagined, when he thought about it at all, that he would find someone, fall in love and marry her. Foolishly romantic, many
would say, for a man in his position. Now, marriage had become another act of duty to put alongside all the others. The
ache of missing Lily was simply another pain to be borne; he
knew how to cope with physical pain. Would emotional pain
be any different?

He washed, tied back his hair, put on a clean shirt and took
pains with his neckcloth while he rehearsed small talk for the

tea table in his mind. The weather, things that he had seen in London that seemed worthy of comment, the virtues of Lily's new horse, the presents he had purchased for his mother and sisters. That would tide over a polite three-quarters of an hour comfortably.

Lily would be upset that he was leaving, he knew that. She had decided she was going to solve his problems because she always *was* able to solve anything that simply required the application of money. She was not going to like being thwarted in that. She regarded him as a friend, he thought, as he shook out his coat and pulled it on. What she made of his lovemaking he was not certain, for she had shown no embarrassment or shyness afterwards. Nor did she seem to expect him to make love to her again, so, with her characteristic practicality, she had no doubt put it down to experience—and out of her mind.

The memory of Lily, quivering and responsive in his arms, the sweet heat of her mouth on his, the innocent passion, struck him with desire so violent it was like a blow. *God, I want her. I love her and I want her.* How had he managed to keep that under control the other night? How was he going to be able to sit with her and her aunt, politely discussing commonplaces when all he wanted was to drag her off to bed and make love to her until they were both exhausted?

One thing was certain, he was not going anywhere until he had got both his body and his imagination under control.

As a result, the clocks had finished chiming three before Jack entered the house through the garden door and his mind was busy memorising the towns on the stagecoach route back to Newcastle, the most unerotic activity he could think of on the spur of the moment, other than stripping off and throwing himself in the horse trough.

'Good afternoon, sir.' Fakenham was his usual imperturbable self.

Hoddesdon, Ware, Puckeridge. 'Good afternoon, Fakenham.' *Royston...no, Buntingford, Royston...*

'Miss France is in the library, sir.' *Odd place to take tea...Huntingdon, Norman Cross...*

'Mr Lovell, ma'am.'

...Stamford. 'Good afternoon.' *Gran...* There was no sight of the tea table, nor of Mrs Herrick. Lily was certainly there, seated at the foot of a long stretch of mahogany around which were grouped six men, all soberly suited, all of more than middle age. At the head a vigorous septuagenarian with beetling grey brows glowered at him.

'You'll be Lovell.'

What the devil is going on? 'You have the advantage of me, sir.'

'I am Frederick Conroy, Miss France is my great-niece and these are my fellow trustees in her affairs.'

Jack shot Lily one hard glance, saw her smile fade, and turned back to her great-uncle. 'Then I appear to have intruded upon a private meeting. My apologies, Mr Conroy. Good day, gentlemen, Miss France.'

'Not so fast, young man. We understood you are seeking investors for your coal mine.'

'Yes, sir, for steam pumps. However, I hardly see how that need concern you.'

'My niece is interested in investing.'

'I, however, have not sought Miss France's involvement.' The anger was an almost physical presence possessing him. Jack trampled it down. *Damn the woman and her passion for paying for things. What was this for? Payment for his injuries, or for his escort the other evening—or for his lovemaking?*

'Well, we have heard all about it now, so you might as well come in, sit down and discuss it.' The old man was regarding him with shrewd eyes. Jack could almost feel him pricing his clothes, assessing his mood, calculating his worth. 'Come along, sir! Or do you tell us we have met for nothing?'

Jack took the proffered chair, his temper under a tight rein. He could sense Lily's eyes on him and kept his own steady on Conroy. 'Your meeting was not at my instigation, sir. I do not consider my proposition a suitable investment for Miss France.'

The older man gave a sharp bark of laughter. 'Miss France begs to differ. And if you do not agree with her, Mr Lovell, how is it that you have discussed it in such detail that she is able to recite chapter and verse to us? I had no idea my niece was so well acquainted with the uses of steam power or the mechanics of coal mining.'

'I—' Jack did look at Lily then. He knew her well enough now to know when she was hiding something, and behind the expression of calm attention on her face he could read guilt and discomfort. He had not talked in detail to Lily about the mine, but he had left all his papers out in an unlocked room.

'Nor had I expected to find her with quite such a grasp of the different grades of coal and their uses or so very knowledgeable about optimum depths of mine shafts and the laws of diminishing return as applied to the length of—what is the term?—ah, yes, galleries.'

'Miss France has indulged me by listening to me thinking out loud about various problems. I should not have bored her with them and I am amazed that Miss France should have troubled to recall any of the details.' He kept his eyes on her as he spoke and watched the colour rise betrayingly in her cheeks. She could read him too, knew he was furiously angry with her.

'My niece constantly surprises us all.' The old man chuckled as he said it, but Jack could hear both indulgence and a strong will behind the words. Mr Conroy would allow his niece her whim this far, but he would not agree to her parting with a penny piece unless he and his fellow trustees were satisfied.

Every instinct was telling him to get up and walk out. But to do so would be to humiliate Lily in front of these men whose respect was important to her. He wanted to shake her, to demand to know what the devil she thought she was about, but that could wait.

'Let me introduce you to my fellow trustees,' Mr Conroy began with the air of a man calling the meeting to order, 'and then, despite my niece's excellent summation of the facts, we have a great many questions to ask you.'

Half an hour later Jack knew he had lost them. They were intelligent, hard, practical men, all of them, but they were merchants and traders, not engineers or mine owners. If he had been asking them to invest in a canal, or steam pumps in a manufactory, or possibly even in mines in the Midlands, then he might well have convinced them. But Northumberland was too far away, they could see all the problems very clearly and the solutions were outside their experience. And on the subject of steam locomotion, which for some reason Lily appeared to have been lecturing them about, they were frankly sceptical.

Lily had sat silent until then, her guilty blush faded until she was pallid, her hands locked together on the table as her green eyes followed the argument and questions around the table. But when Mr Shillington, the attorney, remarked that steam power for coaches was a fantasy, she intervened, passionately.

'It is the future, not a fantasy. You only have to read the articles—'

'Yes, yes, Miss France. It might work very well on some short tramways in Wales, but for long distances? Or even on the roads, as I believe some of these fanatics would have us believe? Madness! Why, the things would be exploding and frightening the horses, and people would go mad with the speed.'

'But there is a steam engine in Newcastle called the Puffing Billy—'

'They break the rails—I have heard all about it. And in any case, you are not proposing spending Miss France's money on these *locomotives,* are you Mr Lovell?'

'No sir. I require static engines that can run pumps, provide ventilation and lift coal.'

Mr Conroy looked down at his notes, then round at his fellow trustees. 'Do we need to ask Mr Lovell to retire while we discuss this, gentlemen? No?' His faded blue eyes looked round the table. 'Well?' One after another the grizzled heads shook; the only words spoken were Lily's.

'No! Of course we have to discuss it! You cannot simply dismiss this out of hand.'

Jack got to his feet. 'You have given me a very patient hearing. I will not impose longer on your time. Good day, gentlemen. Miss France.'

'Jack!'

He shut the door firmly, realising that his hands were shaking with anger. He nodded curtly at Fakenham, who was waiting in the hall, and strode out through the garden door, carefully refraining from slamming it behind him.

The restraint lasted as long as it took him to reach the studio. The slam of that door rattled the glass in the windows, and the nearest portmanteau, kicked with the full force of his feelings, flew down the length of the room to knock over a chair with a satisfying thud.

Jack counted out money for Mrs Oakman, a tip for Percy, and began to pack his portfolio with the papers from the table. How had she managed to study them without him noticing they had been disturbed? The thought of the deliberate care it must have taken made him angrier still. If she had just asked him, he would have told her he did not wish to meet her trustees, that it was not a suitable investment for her.

He lifted a stack of notes and found one long, reddish brown hair curling over his fingers. Not so very careful after all. He brushed it off, then picked it up again. It was as live and vibrant as Lily herself, curling round his fingers as she had twined herself around his heart. Impatient with himself for his weakness, Jack pulled out his note book, dropped the hair between two pages and thrust it back into his pocket as the door slowly opened behind him.

'Jack?'

He swung round and saw the misery on her face and a strange mixture of exasperation and love cut through the anger. 'Jack, I am so sorry they said no. I obviously mishandled it, I did not prepare well enough…'

'You are sorry *you* mishandled it?' Lily could always be relied upon, it seemed, to infuriate him afresh. 'Lily, *if* I had wanted to approach your trustees it would have been up to me to present my proposition to them. I did not wish to approach them, so your intervention was quite unnecessary. You wasted their time, you have put yourself to no little trouble to no purpose and, I have to say, I do not appreciate having my private papers ransacked.'

'I did not ransack them!' She was instantly indignant. 'I put them back exactly how I had found them.'

'Lily, they are my *private* papers.'

'If there had been anything personal, of course I would not have read it.'

She still did not understand what he was angry about—he could see the bafflement on her face. 'Lily, I realise that I am so poor that you do not consider it of any more account than you would scrutinising your servants' wages, but I do not relish having my personal finances investigated and the results discussed with a number of persons unknown to me.'

'Oh, you are so wretchedly starched up about this!' she flared at him, not at all repentant. 'Why cannot you ask my trustees for money when you will happily advertise to all and sundry in the newspapers?'

'It is risky. It is not an investment for a woman.'

'But you do not need much; it is a trifle as far as I am concerned. I could lose it all and it would not matter.'

'It would matter to me, and it is not a trifle for me.' He tried again. Somehow he had to get her out of his room before the feelings that were battering at him won and he did what he was aching to do and took her in his arms, kissed her until she could only whimper, and told her that he could not take her money because he loved her. How could he make her understand? 'Lily, this is futile. Even if I would borrow money from you, your trustees will not allow it, so there is nothing more to be said.' He half-turned away from her as he added quietly, 'Not that this is about money.'

Lily stared at him, baffled, hurt and wounded that Jack was angry with her for trying to help him, glimpsing through the fog of anger that was swirling about them that she had badly misjudged his reactions. But what was it about, if it was not about money?

'Jack—' She held out a hand and he moved abruptly. 'Please do not do that. Please do not hate me.'

'Hate you?' He took two jerky strides then, fetching up with one hand on the mantelshelf, his back to her. 'I do not hate you.'

'Good,' she said shakily, looking at the figure in front of her, wondering how she could ever have thought any other man handsome, how she could ever have contemplated living with anyone less intelligent, less virile, less interesting.

'Lily, I do not think we speak the same language. I do not think we even inhabit the same country sometimes. We do not understand each other and we are hurting each other as a result. I am leaving London tomorrow.'

What does he mean? Lily shook her head in frustration. *Of course we speak the same language! It is just pride, that is all. But Adrian Randall, a man with a barony, a man consumed with pride in his name and his status—he had had no qualms about marrying me. Marriage? Was that it?*

'Jack.' She stepped forward and put her hand on his arm. It was rigid. 'Jack…'

'Lily, please go away.'

'No. I think I see. You need to be master, I understand that. You need to be in control of…of everything. Well, marry me then, and you will control one-third of my fortune.'

'*Marry you?*' He turned then and Lily took a step backwards, suddenly afraid of what she had done. 'You want to marry a title, do you not?'

'I am sure you will have one,' she stammered, too aghast at the anger in Jack's eyes to think what she was saying. 'You will be a great man, I know it. I can see it all, the mine will be

a success, you will stand for Parliament, build steam rail-
ways…'

'And be knighted?' he enquired, his voice so chill she shivered. 'But that will not do, will it, Lily? If I recall, nothing
but a baron will do for you. Still, I hear say that Prinny is in
need of funds, perhaps you can buy me a title.

'And what do I have to do in return? Provide one little coal
mine for you to play with? Oh, yes, and father your children.
And pleasure you in bed, *Lady Lovell?* That, at least, will not
be a hardship.'

Recalling her daydream, Lily felt her face burn with
shame. *Lady Lovell.* Jack was so angry—could she tell him
she loved him? That he did not understand?

'Is this what you want for your money, Miss France?' His
hand on her wrist was like iron, but Lily did not try to resist
as Jack pulled her into his arms.

'Yes,' was all she could manage before his mouth crushed
down on hers. *Not money, just love, Jack. Please understand,
just love…*

He had aroused and pleasured her before; now, angry and
demanding, he excited her almost beyond bearing. Lily strained
against the hard body, revelling in the sensation of being mas-
tered, ready to match him wherever he took her. She was not
afraid of him, despite the anger she could almost taste; if she
said *no,* she knew he would leave her. Everything she said was
wrong, she could not find the words to reach him or the understanding to comprehend him, but in this thing at least, despite
her ignorance and her innocence, they could communicate.

He was claiming and taking, his tongue invading in a way
that flooded her with an almost unbearable longing. The room
seemed to be moving, then she realised he had lifted her,
shouldered aside the screen across the bed and laid her down.

Through the thin silk of her afternoon gown his hand
burned on her breast and she arched into it, the nipple hard
and aching. Then her skin was exposed to the air, to the rough
heat of his palm and he bent his head to take her in his mouth,
sending wild sensation lancing through her belly.

Lily writhed beneath him, her hands frantic to touch him
as he touched her, pulling at his neckcloth, tearing at shirt buttons until her fingertips met skin, yanking at the linen until
she could flatten her palm on the springing curls of his chest.

Instinctively she shifted beneath his weight, adjusting her
body to the length and weight of his and suddenly aware of
the strength of his arousal and where this was leading. And,
she realised, she did not care what the consequences were, despite the ripple of fear that ran through her at the thought of
joining with that much maleness. She loved Jack—this was the
one thing she could give him that had nothing to do with
money.

His lips trailed upwards, up her throat, to her temple, to
kiss her closed lids. And his hands were no longer restraining her, but lifting her to hold her against his chest as he sat
up.

'Oh, God, Lily. My cursed temper.'

'Jack?' She wriggled in his hold.

'Just sit still, please, while I still have some control left.'
His voice sounded muffled, she could feel the warmth of his
breath in her hair. Then she was sitting by herself on the bed
and he was pulling the screen back to shield her.

'Is your gown torn?'

Shaken, Lily glanced down, her fingers fumbling with buttons. 'No, not torn. Jack—'

'Lily, for once in your life, just listen. I am going down to
the stable yard now and I will not come back until you have

gone. There is a brush near the mirror and a cloak over the back of the chair if your gown is too crushed.'

'But Jack, what is wrong? I *wanted* you to make love to me.' Through the crack in the screen she could see him stripping off his torn shirt. The sight of his naked torso took the breath from her lungs.

'For heaven's sake, woman—accept this is the one thing you know nothing about! This is not the price of tea, or the weather in India or import duties at the docks or the latest fashion in bonnets! I should never have touched you, never have kissed you. I am no better than that lout Randall or his friend Dovercourt.'

'Yes, you are,' she cried, her hand on the screen. 'I *wanted* you to make love to me. You stopped even though you did not have to.'

'You have no idea. None. I am leaving today.'

Lily stood, listening to the sound of his feet on the stairs down into the carriage shed. *I am going to be sick.* The storm of arousal was still washing through her body as though she had drunk too much, and her knees were trembling. She pressed her face to the small window overlooking the mews and saw Jack stride towards the pump, gesturing to one of the grooms to work it. He bent his whole upper body under the cold gush of water and she shuddered in sympathy at the thought of the temperature.

As though to wash me away. What can I do? He will not take my money, he will not take my body and he will not take my hand. For the first time in her life Lily could see no way through, no answers, no plan that would make things right. Her money was no use to her now. There were not even tears; she felt as though she would never cry again, that there was nothing left inside her but a hollow shell. She turned from the window and swept the cloak around her, pulling up the hood. What would the staff think?

Lily turned back at the sounds of bustle in the mews—her trustees must be going, their carriages called for. If she went now, while Fakenham and the footmen were busy in the hall, she could slip in unnoticed. She looked round the room, trying to print the memory of Jack's presence on her mind. His neckcloth lay at her feet where she had tossed it. She picked it up and hurried for the back stairs.

Chapter Eleven

Jack shook off the worst of the water and accepted a piece of towelling from the bemused groom to rub himself dry with. What the man thought of a gentleman suddenly appearing in the middle of the afternoon and sticking his head under the pump he was too well trained to betray. Jack made a business of rubbing his hair to kill time, then went back up the stairs to the door into the studio. All was quiet inside. Had Lily gone?

Best to give her time and not to risk a meeting. It was hard to accept he would never see her again. He sat down on the top step, leaned his back against the scratched panels and stared down into the dusty congestion of the coach shed. What had happened to them that things had come to this?

He shook his head. He knew what was wrong with *him*—love, a guilty conscience, wounded pride, worry and the sick after-effects of losing his temper, which was normally on a very tight rein indeed. Oh, yes, and probably the most painful case of desire he could ever remember.

But Lily—what had led her to make that astounding offer? Marriage! It was as perverse an idea as he could imagine. Had she had him investigated and now knew more about him than he had told her? No, surely not, she would hardly have had time for one thing, and for another, he did not think that Lily France was the woman to hold back if she discovered she had been deceived.

The room behind him was still silent. Jack got to his feet and opened the door on to emptiness. There was the scent of rosewater in the air, a crumpled handkerchief on the floor, two long red hairs on his pillow. The sheets were tangled, the blankets were on the floor. He added the hairs to the one already in his pocketbook and folded the handkerchief in with his own, pulled on a clean shirt, straightened the bed and rang for Percy. Then he sat down at the table and began to write.

St Martin-le-Grand was almost solid with traffic as the hackney carriage dropped Jack off outside the Bull and Mouth. A great wagon, its hoops bare, and looking more like the ribcage of a huge dead beast than anything else, blocked the centre of the road, while all around smaller vehicles jostled for position. The noise was immense, bludgeoning his brain, which already seemed bruised with thinking.

Jack wondered how any of the stages ever got out of the Bull and Mouth, let alone the mails from the General Post Office, just along the street. He paid the driver his shilling and a tip, glancing up as he did so at the vast dome of St Paul's, dominating the skyline at the end of the street as though a gargantuan hot air balloon was rising into the air.

A pot boy came to take his bags, and, with a last glance at the looming cathedral, Jack followed him into the yard of the inn. When he had arrived in London it had been late evening and he had been too tired to stand and gaze at the famous yard, the three tiers of galleries rising up, with all manner of folk hanging over the rails to watch the scene in the yard below. As good as a play any day of the week, he had heard said about the yard of the Bull and Mouth.

'You wanting a ticket for the stage, guv'nor?' The pot boy was standing impatiently, loaded with bags.

'No, I have a ticket for tomorrow evening. I need a room for tonight.'

'Right you are, guv'nor, follow me.' The lad led the way in through a door marked Coffee Room, threading through the noisy mass of people drinking, demanding coffee, snatching a bite of pie or pasty, talking at the top of their voices and creating chaos with their bags and umbrellas. Jack almost tripped over a parrot cage, was sworn at by its occupant and glared at by the elderly lady it belonged to. He spared a fleeting sympathetic thought for the occupants of the coach on which they were travelling and caught up with the pot boy.

'Here you are, guv'nor.' The lad dumped Jack's bags unceremoniously at a hatch in the wall, took the proffered coin with a grin of thanks and wriggled back into the crowd.

As he had not booked, Jack had expected to find himself in a garret, and was pleasantly surprised to discover that, although he was up on the third floor, the room was clean and comfortable enough and the noise less than he had feared. He would have settled for the garret to get away from Chandler Street, and the constant comings and goings in the yard below were at least a colourful distraction. He leaned his elbows on the rail outside his room and watched, unwilling to go back into relative silence where he would have no escape from his thoughts.

What would Mrs Herrick make of his carefully penned apology for leaving without thanking her in person? And what would Lily make of his even more carefully composed note to her? He had taken pains to ensure that it was so innocuous that she could screw it up and throw it into the wastepaper basket.

Dear Miss France, please accept my thanks for the hospitality you have shown me and the care of your staff. Circumstances compel my return home as a matter of urgency and prevent my taking my personal leave of you and expressing my feelings as I would wish. I remain, your humble servant etc. etc.

'Etcetera,' he murmured to himself.

'I beg your pardon, sir—did you address me?' The young woman who had paused beside him, one lace-mittened hand resting daintily on the rail, opened blue eyes wide and smiled. Jack straightened and removed his hat. Inside, something very basic responded to the invitation in that mock-innocent gaze and to the complete contrast with the last young woman he had been this close to. There was no need to wonder just what this female's occupation was, and little doubt that she was most accomplished at it.

Behind her the door to his room stood ajar. She moved her head coquettishly, the blonde curls peeping from under her bonnet flirting with the movement. What she offered was a straightforward monetary transaction, and suddenly that seemed a refreshingly straightforward answer to a gnawing need both to slake the ache that still possessed him and to banish the vision of a pair of wide green eyes, dark with hurt.

'A dreadful crush, is it not? Might I offer you some refreshment?' He gestured towards the door.

'Oh, I am sure you can, sir.' She just touched the tip of her tongue to her lower lip as she spoke and turned towards his chamber with a practised, inviting, swing of her hips.

* * *

Lily sat at her dressing table, the contents of her jewellery case spread out before her, her aching eyes dazzled with the reflection in the glass. Diamonds dripped from her ears and caressed her neck in a waterfall of light. She lifted her hands to her lips and rings flashed fire and bracelets seemed to pulse with flame in time with her heartbeat. In her hair diamond clips and pins trembled and sparkled like candles on a river at night.

'Miss Lily?' Janet sounded almost scared, as she had ever since Lily had swept in, thrown an old black cloak on the floor and demanded that it, and the gown she was wearing, should be burned. 'Are you all right, Miss Lily? Have you a fever? Should I call Mrs Herrick?'

'No. Be quiet, please, Janet, you are making my head ache. I am trying to decide what to wear to the Duchess of Old-bury's ball in two days' time.'

'With the new ballgown, Miss Lily?' The maid's voice was eager; of all the gowns Lily had ever bought, this one was the most wonderful in her eyes. 'Shall I bring it out?'

'Yes, do that.' Lily swivelled on her stool to watch as Janet opened a press and reverently lifted out a mass of fabric swathed in white linen sheets. Inside the linen was silver paper, then tissue, and under it all the gown. The sheath of white satin was overlaid with gauze, heavy with silver beads and silver embroidery, floss edged the hem like a cloud of swansdown and the bodice was low-cut to the point of daring and heavy with crystals.

'I will try it on.' Lily stood patiently, welcoming the pounding headache that filled her skull to the point of preventing thought. The correct undergarments were found, the stockings and the slippers, and finally the weight of the gown slid over her head.

'Oh, Miss Lily!' Janet stood back and looked at the column of sparkling white and silver that was her mistress. 'You look like something out of a fairy tale, a diamond princess.'

'Yes,' Lily agreed, lifting her hands to her aching head. 'All I need now is my prince.' And she turned her back on the maid before she could see the tears running down her face like moving diamonds. 'Send for Madame Hortense, there are changes I wish to have made.'

Four hours after he had arrived at the Bull and Mouth, Jack poured another bumper of rum into his glass, sat back against the settle and contemplated getting very drunk indeed. The drinking house—one could hardly call it an inn, that had too respectable a sound—was hot, almost bursting at the seams, and full of the most extraordinary mixture of people.

Draymen rubbed shoulders with flash coves, bruisers with top-of-the-trees sportsmen. There were more than a few black faces, seemingly representing a range of occupations from respectable tradesmen to down-at-heel servants, and someone was trying to set up a cock fight in the corner, with a number of top-lofty Corinthians already laying bets.

Only the women seemed to be of one uniform class. Jack smiled grimly and took a swig of his rum. Three hours ago he had paid off the little ladybird who had propositioned him at the inn—and he was as damnably unsatisfied now as he had been when he had met her.

Lily had as good as emasculated him, there was no other word for it. Not physically, oh, no. His body had been more than willing, damn it, and yet, his mind would not let him do it. To take another woman like that would have been to betray Lily.

He could not have done it to save his life and, as a result, he was out of pocket by several guineas he could ill afford, his *amour propre* was at rock bottom and his body was furiously at odds with his brain. There seemed to be only one answer: to get blind drunk and to hell with all women.

The pot boy at the Bull and Mouth had sent him here, with a knowing grin. 'Want a bit of the low life, guv'nor? I can tell you just the place. All the toffs go there when they want to slum it, you'll enjoy it, see if you don't.'

Jack snapped his fingers at the serving girl and watched sardonically as she winked back at him, adjusting her already perilously low bodice even lower before she brought him a fresh bottle. He would forswear all women, become a monk...

'Damme, but she's a tasty little bit, never mind her parentage.' The drawling voice from the settle, set back to back with his own, jarred on Jack's nerves. Some bloody aristocrat, out slumming. He smiled at himself for his own hypocritical thoughts, and let his head fall back against the greasy wood. 'And those pert little titties, and those big green eyes, all topped off with a fortune that would make a man drool, that's what I call temptation.'

'I heard Randall's had her already. He'll be at the Oldbury ball, night after next, what's the betting he'll take her back?' Another voice, lascivious.

'Not he. And so what if he has had her? So what? For the money she has, I'd take Lily France if she'd been tupped by the whole of the *Peerage* and the House of Commons after them. And she's got spirit too, I've got the bruised balls to show for it. But she won't be so fast with her knee next time, little—'

'Lord Dovercourt, I presume?' The rum seemed to have drained out of Jack's bloodstream as rapidly as it had entered it. He felt stone-cold sober and angry enough to kill. The young man sprawled at the table goggled up at him as though he had appeared through a trap door in the floor, like the Devil in a melodrama.

'Who the hell are you?'

'My name is Lovell and I take exception to you bandying a lady's name around in those terms. If you give me your word you will not repeat it again, I may— No, what the hell, I am going to beat the living daylights out of you anyway.' Jack reached out, took Dovercourt by the neckcloth and hauled him to his feet. 'I cannot begin to tell you how much pleasure this is going to give me,' he remarked conversationally, making a fist with his right and fetching his protesting victim a square punch to the jaw.

It lifted Dovercourt off his feet and sent him sliding across the table, taking with him his companions' tankards and the dish of oysters the landlord had only just placed on the table. Jack found himself confronted by two new opponents, both with porter and oyster juice on their flash suits, both pot valiant with drink and indignation. 'Come on, then.' He raised both fists, suddenly happier than he had been since he got to London. 'Which of you wants to be first?'

The fight was spectacular, bloody, and rapidly spread to encompass virtually every male occupant of the Cat and Bottle, two pairs of fighting cocks, a brace of pit bull terriers, the landlady with a stout staff and three of the serving girls who had a private score to settle.

Twenty glorious minutes later Jack found himself out on the street, his arm around the shoulder of the man with the pit bull terriers and his shirt covered in blood. 'You hurt, my boy?' the dog owner demanded. 'By old Harry, we raised a fair breeze in there. Look at the state of you now. Do you need a doctor?'

Jack looked down. 'No, not much of that's mine, I thank you.' Several victims of the brawl staggered out, assisted by the landlady's stout arm and a mouthful of eye-wateringly bad language. One of the black tradesmen grinned at Jack.

'You can fight, guv'nor. Thought of taking it up professional-like?'

'No.' Jack shook his head. 'No, that was personal.'

'Well, come on then, lad, let's be finding another touting ken.' The dog owner whistled up his animals and slapped Jack on the back. 'What do you say? Shall we make a batch of it? Night's not old yet.'

'Not for me.' Jack shook his head and wondered if all his teeth were still with him. 'If you can give me a steer back to the Bull and Mouth, I'd take it kindly.'

He strolled back in the direction the man indicated, taking his bearings from the looming mass of St Paul's in the distance and whistling softly between bruised lips as he went.

Well, that was Dovercourt dealt with. It had been fretting at the back of his mind that he was walking away from those two. But what to do about Randall? It was too much to hope that he would find him slumming in some backstreet boozing ken, and, now he knew for certain that Randall was slandering Lily's good name, something had to be done about it.

Jack found he was twisting the worn gold signet ring on his left hand. Anything that had been engraved on it was long gone, so it was safe to wear. He glanced down at it. *Why not? You are leaving town after all. But not yet, not for another two nights. Coach tickets can be changed.*

Chapter Twelve

'My dear Lily! What have you done with yourself?' Mrs Herrick stared at her niece as she came into the room where Lady Billington was waiting to collect her for the Duchess of Oldbury's ball. 'Your hair! And surely that is not the gown you ordered—and where are all your jewels?'

Lily stood just inside the doorway, defiantly silent. She was not at all certain herself that she was doing the right thing— or even why she was doing it when *he* was not there to see.

'My dear Miss France!' Lady Billington threw up her hands. 'Enchanting! How very well that simpler style becomes you. I declare you will be the toast of the ball.'

'But her hair!' Mrs Herrick exclaimed. 'So plain in that severe style without any curls.' She walked around her niece, staring critically. 'Although it is very sophisticated with that complex knot at the back. And your gown—where have the floss and the crystals gone?'

'Extremely tasteful and very elegant,' Lady Billington pronounced. 'And the choice of just your diamond ear drops and the simple diamond necklace: perfect.'

'But you have so many diamonds,' Mrs Herrick lamented.

'I do not have to show them off all at once,' Lily countered, trying to convince herself. 'It feels strange to dress so simply, but I think, now I am used to it, that it does make more of an impact.' After all, everyone knew how rich she was. Perhaps she did not have to flaunt it.

'You look like a lady,' Lady Billington pronounced with satisfaction. 'I do not see how you can fail to make an eligible connection now.'

It was too much to hope that Lily would be considered the belle of the ball at an event that was acknowledged to be the high point of the Season, but her chaperon's hopes were not disappointed. Miss France's new style was causing a stir—and every comment, from the grudgingly approving nods of the matrons to the murmurs of envy from the other young ladies, was favourable.

And the men were definitely impressed. Lily smiled demurely as gentlemen from the most impressionable youths to hardened rakes solicited her hand, and her card rapidly filled up.

Which is all very well, she reflected, promising a country dance to Lord Fanshawe, *and being admired unreservedly for a change is very pleasant. But I don't want any of them!* What she wanted was one obstinate, battered, thoroughly unfashionable, gorgeous man who did not want her and who was not here to see her triumph.

And Adrian Randall *was* here; she had glimpsed him across the dance floor more than once. Sooner or later they were going to come face to face and she had no idea how he was going to act. Lily was convinced he had been smearing her name—Lord Dovercourt's actions were proof enough of that—but how widely? Not widely enough for her to be cut here at any event, not after Lady Jersey's support reinforced by her own efforts at an understated, ladylike appearance.

Even so, Lily took pains to move around the ballroom in a way that kept her on the opposite side from Adrian. It was a wonderful space. Finding herself at the far end of the long rectangle, Lily could admire the gilded and mirrored walls, the painted ceiling and the shallow flight of steps down at the entrance end. They made a dramatic focus, allowing the duchess to receive her guests at the top and for them to descend in full view of the company below. Most of the ladies were taking full advantage of this opportunity to display their finery, and the parade of gowns alone, Lily observed to Lady Billington, made the evening memorable.

The orchestra ceased its programme of light airs and, with a flourish of strings, indicated the start of the dancing. Lily was claimed by Colonel Strangman for the quadrille and she put everything else out of her mind as she concentrated on the steps of the dance.

The colonel was a good dancer and a pleasant companion; Lily enjoyed the dance and was still chatting animatedly to him as he walked her off the floor. It was possible, if one kept busy enough, to behave as though nothing untoward had happened, as if one's heart had not broken. How very strange.

'Miss France!' It was Lady Jersey. The colonel bowed and effaced himself and Lily steeled herself for the patroness's critical appraisal. 'You look charmingly, my dear. Now then, there is someone I wish you to meet.' Lady Jersey steered Lily through the press and arrived in front of a handsome young man. 'Miss France, do allow me to introduce my godson, Lord Gledhill. George, I am sure Miss France must be in need of a glass of lemonade.'

She fluttered off, leaving the two of them regarding each

other with a certain reserve. 'Matchmaking, I am afraid,' Lord Gledhill remarked ruefully. 'Would you care for some refreshment, Miss France?'

'No, nothing at all, I thank you. Why should your god-mama—?'

'She always is,' he replied cheerfully. 'Thinks I should settle down and establish my nursery. Don't pay any attention, I don't.' He must have realised this was a less than flattering remark, for he grinned and added, 'Not that any man would be about in his head if he didn't admire you Miss France, but I'd make a devilish bad husband. Is anything wrong?'

Lily realised she was staring over his left shoulder and hastily recollected herself. 'No, nothing. Only, there is someone I would prefer not to meet and he is coming this way. If you do not mind…'

'Randall, eh?' Lord Gledhill remarked after one glance, confirming her worst fears about how widely her personal troubles were known. 'Chap's a bounder. We'll just head this way, shall we?'

He steered her down the room a little, closer to the entrance staircase. 'I say, that's a frightening turban just come in.'

Lily looked up, saw Lady Philpott in one of her signature purple head dresses and tried not to smile. 'Her ladyship looks very…imposing,' she countered repressively.

'Lord Allerton!' The footman's voice lifted above a lull in the music.

'Who? Never heard of him.' Lord Gledhill glanced at the head of the stairs with mild curiosity. 'Never seen him before either. Not a fellow you'd miss—must have been out of the country.'

Lily, still smiling at the outrageous toque, followed his gaze. Just turning from shaking hands with the duchess was a tall, broad-shouldered man. His linen was immaculate, his dark head ruthlessly barbered into a fashionable Brutus cut. He paused at the head of the stairs, his eyes scanning the crowd below, then began to descend in a leisurely manner. He was heading in her direction.

'Jack?' It couldn't be—unless he had a double.

'Know him, do you, Miss France?'

'Yes. I mean, no. No, absolutely not. I have never heard of Lord Allerton. It must be a coincidental likeness.' But of course it could not be—she could see the red line of the newly healed scar on his temple now, savagely exposed by the severe crop. What was he doing here, pretending to be someone else entirely? How on earth had he bluffed his way past the formidable Duchess of Oldbury? There would be the most dreadful scandal when he was unmasked.

And he was coming directly towards her. With the same ability she had noticed when he had cut his way through the mob outside her house, Jack was finding a path through the fashionable crowd. People were watching him with scarcely veiled interest—it seemed that his assumed title was mystifying most of them, as was his appearance.

'He's been in the wars, our mystery man,' George Gledhill remarked. And now Jack was closer Lily could see a darkening bruise on his cheek and a cut near the corner of his mouth. He looked dangerous in the midst of this elegant throng, for all his formal attire and scrupulous grooming.

What am I going to say to him? Why is he here? Who has he been fighting? Her heart was thudding, but through the confusion and the anxiety Lily could feel nothing but happiness at the sight of him. She tried to push the feeling away; there was nothing that could be between them, he had made that very clear. Whatever was about to happen was going to mean nothing but trouble.

'Allerton?' The voice behind her made her turn to see Lord Winstanly frowning in thought. 'Now that's a title I haven't heard for a long while.'

Oh, Lord! Jack, what on earth are you doing? Lily braced herself to confront him, wondering if she could persuade him to leave before his imposture was revealed to everyone. Then she saw he was not making directly for her, but for a group of men standing somewhat to the side of her.

'Adrian.' She must have spoken out loud.

'Miss France?'

'Lord Gledhill, I am very much afraid there is going to be some sort of confrontation.' She began to make her way through the crowd, most of whom had lost their momentary interest in the new face and were making up sets for the first of the country dances. George followed her.

'Look here, Miss France, if there is going to be trouble, don't you think you should stay well away?'

'No.' She sighed as she dodged behind the back of the Marquis of Haverstock. 'No. Whatever it is will be entirely my fault, I cannot run away from it.'

She reached the edge of the circle of friends and sycophants who always surrounded Lord Randall at any social gathering, stopping where she could watch unobserved from behind a potted palm. He was flirting languidly with a pair of giggling young ladies and his attention, and that of his friends, was focused on the girls and not towards the entrance. Adrian seemed quite unaware of who had entered the ballroom and was now almost directly behind him.

'We all thought you were lost to us, Lord Randall.' It was Miss Berwick, a pert blonde who most mamas stigmatised as unbecomingly forward. 'When we heard you were engaged to be married to Miss France, why, hearts were broken all across London!'

'What a terrible rumour to put about,' her friend struck in, eager not to be left out of the contest for his attention. 'As if Lord Randall would have contemplated such a thing.'

'Oh, but I did contemplate it, my dear.' Adrian caressed her with his intense blue gaze and she wriggled like a puppy at the attention. 'We men are weak, you know—that lovely money can make fools of us all.'

Lily's hand clamped down on Lord Gledhill's arm as he exclaimed under his breath and took a step forward. 'No, please!' she whispered.

'But what went wrong?' The little brunette was gazing up into Lord Randall's face with an adoration that made Lily want to slap her.

'Not something one can discuss in front of innocent young ladies such as yourselves, my dear.' He patted her hand as her eyes grew wide. 'Suffice it to say, a gentleman expects certain standard of conduct from the lady he marries.'

There were sniggers around the circle of his cronies and both young ladies blushed with horrified delight. 'Damn it all!' Lord Gledhill tried to turn Lily away and steer her back into the crowd. 'You go back to your chaperon, Miss France—I am going to take this fellow to task.'

'Oh, please, no,' Lily begged. 'The last thing I want is a scene, here of all places.'

'Looks as though you are going to get one anyway,' George remarked, giving up on his efforts to persuade her to move. 'Here is your mystery man.'

'Lord Randall.' It was Jack—there could be absolutely no doubt about it, although she could hardly see him. The calm, chill voice cut through the giggles and chat like a blade of ice.

Adrian turned. 'And who might you be?' His back effectively blocked Lily's view. She ducked sideways between the palm and a pillar and saw Jack. He was regarding Adrian steadily, his expression perfectly pleasant—until one saw the dark, dangerous, flint of his eyes.

'Allerton. It is a long time since we were both at Eton, but we have met twice since then. Quite recently.' *Eton?* What dangerous game was Jack playing? Was he attempting to purloin the entire identity of the unknown Lord Allerton?

'Allerton? Good Lord, yes, I recall now. You were a skinny little wretch then, weren't you?' Adrian's laugh was an insult all in itself. 'And you vanished mid-term one year because your father ruined himself—I remember now. Coal, wasn't it? Or something equally grubby.'

'Yes,' Jack agreed levelly. 'Coal. And after our recent meetings, I find I have the most pressing desire to discuss matters further with you.'

'Recent?' Randall stared at Jack. 'What can you mean?' Lily saw the recognition dawn and Adrian's lips draw back into a snarl. 'You! You were the man in that coffee house— and you were the one in Li—'

'Exactly.' Jack took a step forward. 'And before you start bandying a lady's name around, I suggest we go into the retiring room behind you.'

'Absolutely. Excellent idea.' George Gledhill strode forward, effectively carrying Lord Randall with him. As he went, he caught the arm of a serious-looking gentleman who had been observing the scene with disapproval. 'Mountain out of a molehill—see what you can do to smooth things over out here, Perry, there's a good fellow.'

Ripples of disturbance spread out from the scene, but most of the gentlemen left outside the door turned aside, making conversation, acting as though nothing untoward had taken place. Lily realised what was going on—a matter of honour, a lady involved, bad form to draw attention to it.

Jack had vanished, as had Lord Randall, along with a few of the men who had been close at hand and Lord Gledhill. The door of the retiring room was firmly shut and Lily, unseen behind her sheltering palm, was unobserved.

She found she was shaking and leaned back against the wall to steady herself. Jack had bluffed his way into the ball, apparently set on picking a fight with Adrian. But was he bluffing? Adrian appeared to accept his explanation of who he was. But a title? Trying to pull herself together, she stepped out of her shelter and found herself next to Lord Winstanly.

'What an extraordinary scene,' she said lightly. 'Did you say you knew the gentleman, my lord?'

'Knew his grandfather, the fourth earl—this one's the spitting image. Great family, sadly diminished now, of course. I hadn't realised there were any of them left.'

Earl? Jack was an earl? Emotions chased through Lily, so jumbled she could not distinguish any of them clearly except one. Anger. She looked around; somehow she was going to find out what was going on in that room.

Jack nodded his thanks to the tall man who had so neatly cut them out of the crowded room and into this private chamber. There were six of them, incongruous in a room that had obviously been set aside as a boudoir for ladies to rest in. Flowers decked the little tables, candles shimmered in crystal holders and bowls of dainty sweetmeats stood around. A screen, delicately hand painted, cut off the draught from the door on the far wall.

The six men regarded each other with varying degrees of puzzlement and hostility. Jack held his peace—let Randall blunder himself into a situation where a challenge was inevitable. With any luck it could be achieved without mention of Lily's name.

'Well?' Randall demanded. 'What do you want of me now? Not to chat about the good old times at school, I imagine?' One of the men, apparently his crony, sniggered. Jack let his gaze rest on the man and he subsided.

'No. I came merely to inform you that I consider your presence at any civilised gathering offensive and to request that you remove yourself.'

'*You* find my presence offensive!' The colour was high in Randall's cheeks. 'I find you, sprawled in the arms of—'

'You found me injured in the salon of a lady—whose name you are not going to mention as it is quite irrelevant—and you immediately put upon it a construction that was as deeply offensive to the lady as it was totally inaccurate. When the lady attempted to explain matters to you, you addressed her in terms both immoderate and crude; when I attempted to silence you, you knocked me out with a cowardly blow despite the fact that I was barely conscious.'

There was a murmur around the room. Randall's crony, who had obviously heard his side of the story before, sneered. The other gentlemen looked serious.

'You allege you were wounded and Lord Randall struck you?' It was the tall young man who had taken command outside.

'Yes.' Jack raised his hand to the scar on his temple. 'I had been felled by a thrown cobblestone in the street outside. The lady had me brought into her house to await the doctor. I was barely conscious, blinded with blood. When Randall began to insult the lady, I attempted to stand and was felled to the ground.'

'Rubbish!' Randall snarled. 'I come into the room, find him clutched to the near-naked bosom of the lady who—'

'Careful.' Jack could feel his fingers curling and reined in his temper.

'The scene was one of obvious intimacy. I was outraged.'

'Well, you might be able to make love to a lady when semi-conscious, Randall—' it was the tall man again, his voice contemptuous '—but the rest of us lesser mortals would find it a challenge. Lord Allerton appears to have a justifiable grievance. I would suggest you apologise.'

'Apologise? To that coal-hewer's son? Look at him, he is obviously a brawling drunk—see the bruises on him!'

'You should see the other fellow.' Jack could not resist the cheap jibe. 'Lord Dovercourt's rather ordinary looks have not been improved by the loss of his front teeth.'

'Dovercourt?'

'Indeed. He was foolish enough to repeat some of the offensive remarks you have made about a certain lady.'

'For heaven's sake, Randall, apologise. And I suggest you give your word not to make any further remarks about the lady to boot,' the tall gentleman suggested disdainfully.

'To hell with you and your meddling, Gledhill, I'll do no such thing.'

'Coward,' Jack said softly.

'I'll not be insulted by the likes of you!' Randall was white to the lips now. Even his friends were looking doubtfully at him.

'Well, it certainly appears to be very difficult to achieve.' It was also increasingly difficult to keep his hands off the man's throat. 'I have never attempted to insult a lily-livered coxcomb before. I had no idea it would be such an effort. Apologise or name your friends.'

'I'll not fight a coal merchant. Gentlemen do not duel with riff-raff.'

'You can fight me here and now,' Jack offered, regarding his clenched right fist with its grazed knuckles thoughtfully. 'You can name your friends. Or you can walk out of here leaving five sober witnesses to your cowardice. Which is it to be?'

It seemed to Jack that the four onlookers were holding their breath, then, 'Damn you. Fellthorpe, Dunsford—will you act for me?'

They nodded, muttering their agreement, looking none too happy about it. Jack realised he had landed himself in a fix with no one to ask to second him, then Lord Gledhill stepped forward.

'I'll act for you, my lord. Webster?' The remaining man nodded curtly.

'Aye. Bad business, best kept amongst ourselves. Give Gledhill your direction, my lord, we will call on you tomorrow.'

Randall swept out of the room without looking back, his seconds on his heels. Jack nodded to Gledhill. 'I thank you for that. I am putting up at the Bull and Mouth. May I offer you gentlemen breakfast in the morning?'

'You most certainly may. Noon? I suggest you give us a few moments, Allerton, before you reappear.' He smiled. 'Enjoy the ball.'

'Phew.' Jack looked round the empty room, assessing the various frail pieces of furniture, and sat down on the *chaise*. That had been achieved with less public fuss than he had feared; now all that remained was to attempt to get out of this alive—and without killing Randall either. Putting a period to his lordship's existence might be tempting, but exile abroad most certainly was not.

Jack scooped up a few bonbons and absently put one in his mouth while running through what he now had to do. His will was in order, that was one mercy. Then he must write a letter to his mother to leave with his seconds, just in case.

Then… 'You *bastard*!'

Chapter Thirteen

'Lily.' He was on his feet in a small shower of sweetmeats. 'Lily, what on earth are you doing in here?'

'This.' The slap across his face rocked him back on his heels. 'I could think of all kinds of perfectly good reasons why you should not wish to marry me, but I did at least think you would have the courage to tell me if you did not consider me good enough for you, *my lord.*'

She looked magnificent, her green eyes blazing, her cheeks full of colour, her breast heaving, but Jack was in no mood to admire the effect.

'Lily, for God's sake—'

'Do not blaspheme,' she stormed, putting him squarely in the wrong. 'How you must have laughed up your sleeve when I told you I wanted to marry a lord! Why could you not have told me then, before I made any more of a fool of myself than I already had? Or were you too afraid I would make a dead set at you?'

'I was not using my title in London. I had every hope of remaining undetected. If I found a suitable investor, I would have had to admit who I really was, but do you think I wanted it advertised all around the place that the Earl of Allerton was so poor as to have to seek money in that way?'

'Which way? Asking rich cits and merchants like my family to be investors in your mine? How humiliating for you to even have to speak to that class of person. How lowering to be reduced to propositioning us for our money. How you must have looked down your nose at my trustees. And how high and mighty you are with your tumbledown castle and your out-at-elbow coats, *my lord*. The likes of Lord Randall would marry me.'

'But then I am not the likes of him, I am glad to say.' He wanted to shake her, kiss her, hold her… Infuriating woman, meddling everywhere. 'Lily, how on earth do you come to be here?'

'I was listening from behind the screen.' She gestured angrily at it. 'Do not try and change the subject. You turned me down because you consider me vulgar and underbred. You might at least have told me the truth and then I would not have had to humiliate myself—'

'*You* humiliate *yourself?*' Jack found he was losing his temper and suddenly did not care. He had just put his life on the line for this woman he loved and all she could do was storm at him. 'You make me a patronising offer like Lady Bountiful; you inform me that once your money has turned the situation around I will be able to buy myself a title; you instruct me in how to grovel to a corrupt system to buy favour; you map out my future career in politics for me; and you expect me to accept with gratitude. Well, let me tell you, Lily France, I would never take that from you, not because I am an earl, but because I am a man and I have my pride and I have my honour. I would not be your petticoat pensioner if I was at my last crust.'

She stared at him in fulminating silence, then, 'How did you get in here, to this ball?'

'I wrote to her Grace, reminding her that she was my mother's godmother and begging the privilege of an invitation, as I found myself unexpectedly in town.'

'You *are* well connected, my lord.' Lily made it sound like an insult. 'I am sure her Grace will be delighted to have received a man who looks as though he has just staggered out of a tavern brawl, and who promptly starts another one in her ball room.'

'I did not start a brawl here and I imagined—obviously foolishly—that you would be glad that I floored Lord Dovercourt on your account, even if it *was* in a tavern.'

'What you do in taverns, my lord, is entirely your affair. Good evening. You can leave by that door over there. At least you will not be seen.'

'I have no intention of leaving, Miss France. I came here to enjoy the ball, and I fully intend doing just that. Might I suggest that you take that door yourself? It would not do to appear to be engaging in clandestine assignations, now would it?'

Something very like a growl emerged from Lily's throat, then she turned in a swish of skirts and stalked back towards the screen. An impression that had been niggling at the back of Jack's mind surfaced. 'Lily?'

'What now?'

'Have you changed your hairstyle?'

'Oh! You…you *man,* you!' She seized the nearest weapon, a bowl brimming with bonbons, and threw it with remarkable accuracy at his head. Ducking in a shower of fine sugar, Jack perceived that his innocent question had infuriated her at least as much as anything else that evening.

Women! Or, at least, this one. Damn it, he was proposing to go and risk his life for her honour and what did she do? Treat him to a Cheltenham tragedy, that's what. She had not even mentioned the duel. The door slammed behind her as he brushed himself down.

Well, he had introduced himself to society in his true colours, he had achieved his aim of calling Randall to book and now he was here, dressed up like a damned dandy, he was going to dance at the ball, whatever Rich Miss Moneybags had to say about it. The simmering anger subsided into a stubborn resolution not to let Lily France get the better of him which, given that he loved the woman to distraction, did nothing for his common sense and everything to put a sharp edge of reckless danger into his mood.

He ran a hand through his modish crop, grimacing at the unfamiliar feel of it, and opened the door on to the heat and light of the ballroom.

Lily swept down the corridor and abruptly round a corner only to stop short. The woman approaching her stopped too, then Lily realised that she was looking at her own, almost unrecognizable, reflection. A furious, imperious stranger stared back at her, hair swept up, elegant gown still fluttering from the speed of her steps, colour high. She looked magnificent— there was no point in false modesty. She had utterly altered the way she looked for Jack, and all the insensitive, unobservant beast could think of to say was to ask her if she had changed her hairstyle!

It was much easier to be angry about that than it was to think about anything else: all the reasons why she hurt so much inside, all the hideous images of death or wounding that rose up if she thought about the duel. If she thought about those, about how much she loved Jack—stubborn, pig-headed, beast that he was—she would cry. And he was not worth crying about. She stamped her foot and the troubled green eyes looking back at her seemed to protest silently that he was.

Lily unfurled her fan with a snap and opened the door into the ballroom. Here she was a success. Here she was admired. Doubtless here were dozens of men who would be honoured to marry her.

'Miss France? Our cotillion, I believe.'

'Of course.' She directed a glittering smile at Mr Fancot, tossed her diamond earbobs and allowed herself to be led out to take her place in the set. They had worked through the first set of changes and figures and were just going down the grand chain when Lily caught a glimpse of the set on the other side of the room. There, cheerfully smiling at his partner and executing a rigadoon as though he did it every day of the week, was Jack Lovell. *Lord Allerton.*

Lily lost her place, found she was holding out the wrong hand for the circle and hastily corrected herself. What was he doing here still?

'Are you all right, Miss France?'

'I am sorry, Mr Fancot, merely a moment's inattention.'

The demands of the cotillion were enough to keep her attention focused until it ended, but she was searching the room for him as Mr Fancot led her off. Would Jack approach her? Would he have the intolerable effrontery to ask her for a dance? She would soon deal with him if he did.

Unfortunately, he did not give her that satisfaction. Lily danced every dance, even when her feet were aching and she wanted nothing more than to sit one out and take a little refreshment. And Jack—*Lord Allerton*—danced every one as well. He had no shortage of partners, and no lack of skill either, she observed resentfully.

And then it was the last waltz on the programme, with just the closing cotillion yet to come. Lily watched the approach of her partner, Mr Beresford, second son of the Earl of Standon. He was pompous, he was crashingly boring, but he was also one of the handsomest men in London, and every young lady present felt that to dance with him could only lend them distinction.

Before he reached her, Jack was at her side. 'Miss France, our dance, I believe?'

'It is not, my lord, you are mistaken. I am promised to Mr Beresford.' Lily produced a glittering smile for the gentleman.

'Miss France, how could you forget? I am wounded. You promised me this last dance only the other day.' There was a shadow of emphasis on *last*.

Punctiliously Mr Beresford bowed. 'Lord Allerton, I would naturally not wish to intrude.'

'But—' Lily found her hand firmly possessed and then she was on the dance floor, held in such a way that she could only escape by a very obvious struggle. 'Let me go!'

'Smile, Lily. People will be watching.'

'I will not!' He swept her round as the music started and Lily found she could not dance and quarrel at the same time—not without falling over her own feet, at any rate. She plastered a complaisant smile on her lips and glared at him with her eyes. 'Lout.'

'Cat.'

'Stubborn, pig-headed, snobbish, deceitful, odious man—'

'Meddling, patronising, vulgar, spoilt brat.'

'How dare you speak to me like that!'

'I have absolutely no wish to speak to you at all.' Jack said it so blandly that it took Lily's breath away and she found herself whisked through the terrace doors and out into the open air before she had a chance to protest. 'I just want to do this.'

The kiss was an outrageous, arrogant gesture that rocked her back against his constraining arm. She could feel her heartbeat thundering in her breast, her whole body yearning towards him even as she strained away. Her hands were trapped, one in his grasp, the other pressed against his chest. When he released her she staggered, too shaken to slap him as he so richly deserved.

'Goodbye, Lily, my love. Good luck finding your lord.' He paused on the threshold of the ballroom, outlined in dark elegance for a moment against the rich gold brocade, smiling back at her as she stood panting with fury and arousal on the flags. 'I do like your hair.'

'Well, I do not like yours!' she flung back childishly. But he was gone.

Somehow Lily got herself back into the ballroom, danced the final cotillion with perfect grace and an absolute lack of awareness, made her farewells and thanks to the duchess and, at long last, sank back against the squabs in the carriage.

'You may well sigh,' Lady Billington remarked, settling down opposite her. 'What an evening, I declare I am quite worn out and *I* was not dancing. You must have holes in the soles of your shoes, Lily dear.

'But what a success you were. And, of course, there was that incredible revelation when your Mr Lovell turned out to be an earl. I can recall his father, now I come to think of it— a more classically handsome man than the son. What a surprise that he appeared at the ball tonight.'

'He came to challenge Lord Randall to a duel,' Lily said listlessly. Her temper had ebbed into sick anticlimax, her feet ached and she was filled with the miserable realisation that not only had Jack hurt her abominably, but that she had been cruelly unfair to him. And that he was now in peril of his life. Because of her.

'But why?' Jane Billington dropped her reticule as she sat bolt upright.

'Over Adrian's insults to me.' *Oh, God, Jack is going to die. Or he will kill Adrian and then he will be a fugitive. Or be hanged. And it is all my fault. I love him and I let my wretched pride and my temper rule me and now I have lost him for ever.* 'Lady Billington, what can I do to stop it?'

'Nothing! Good heavens, child, that would be a disaster— a scandal. And in any case, nothing you can do would stop them. A challenge is a matter of honour—they cannot withdraw now, not without one of them apologising.'

'I'll inform on them,' Lily said vehemently, as the carriage lurched round a corner, hitting the kerb and throwing her against the door post. She pushed herself upright without noticing. 'I'll find out where it is and inform at the magistrates' office.'

'They will just go elsewhere. It is a matter of *honour,* Lily.'

'I have to stop it. I love him.'

'Who, Lord Randall? Surely not.'

'No.' Lily's breath escaped in a little, gasping sob. 'Jack Lovell.'

'You mean once you discovered he was an earl?'

'*No,* before then. Days ago. I did not care that he was poor and had no title. I proposed to him and he turned me down.'

'You did *what?* Of all the fast, forward, imprudent things to have done! Why, he might have made any sort of capital out of that, taken any sort of advantage. And he is so ineligible.' She caught herself up, and although Lily could not see her companion's face in the darkness, she could imagine her calculating expression. 'Only he is not ineligible any more, is he?'

'It is too late,' Lily said bitterly. 'He turned me down. After all, he does not love me, I insulted him by the way I handled it and now we have just had a blazing row.'

'But he is fighting over your honour.' Lady Billington sounded thoroughly confused.

'I know. But I think he would do so for any lady of his acquaintance. And he has his own score to settle with Adrian Randall from a long time ago.' Lily stared out blindly into the street. 'I must stop it. I *will* stop it.'

'Impossible, Miss France!' Lord Gledhill stared at her, aghast. Whether it was over her demand that he stop the duel or whether it was her presence in his rooms that shocked him most she was unsure. 'This is all most improper. I cannot discuss a matter of honour with you—'

'Even if it is *my* honour?' she interjected tartly.

'Even so. Especially so. And you should not be here. What if anyone saw you arrive and enter?'

'In an unmarked carriage and veiled? But this is irrelevant. Lord Gledhill, you are Lord Allerton's second—why cannot you stop this nonsense?'

'Because to do so, without Lord Allerton receiving an apology from Lord Randall, would be to acknowledge that my principal's accusations were untrue and would label him a coward and a liar.'

'Oh.' Lily sank down in the nearest chair, her knees suddenly weak. 'What are they fighting with?'

'Pistols, thank goodness.' Lord Gledhill, still looking thoroughly harried, sat down too.

'Why is that a good thing? Would not swords be safer?'

'Lord Allerton, although a reasonable fencer, admits that he is out of practice. He is, however, a very good shot.' He must have noticed her confused expression, for he added, 'Why then should Lord Randall choose pistols, you are wondering? Because he does not know how well Lord Allerton shoots, and I suspect that he would prefer to use pistols at a distance against a man who presents a larger target than he does, and whose physical presence he may well find intimidating at close quarters.'

Larger target. Lily felt quite ill. She swallowed the solid lump in her throat. 'Do you at least have a good surgeon engaged?'

'Naturally. It is up to Lord Randall to provide his own should he wish to, but I have engaged Dr Ord. A most excellent physician.'

'Yes. Yes, that at least is a relief, he is very experienced. When is it to be?'

'Miss France, I must decline to tell you. Duelling is illegal. I have no intention of placing you in a position where you have prior knowledge of such a thing.'

In case I inform on them. Lily assumed an expression of spurious meekness. 'I understand, Lord Gledhill. Please… please take care of Lord Allerton. I would not like to think that any gentleman should be hurt in defence of my honour.'

'Of course, ma'am, let me get the door for you. Your veil ma'am!'

Lily found herself almost bundled out of the bachelor dwelling and into her carriage. She waited until the vehicle had turned the corner, then pulled the check string. 'Dr Ord's house, please, William.'

The doctor was at home, as Lily suspected he would be, for this was his normal time to receive patients who preferred to call rather than to be visited. When his housekeeper showed her in, he rose.

'My dear Miss France! You had but to send for me and I would have attended upon you immediately. Have you been taken ill while out driving?'

'No. I am quite well, thank you.' Lily settled her veil back tidily and sat down. 'Dr Ord, I understand that you have been engaged on a matter of some delicacy by Lord Gledhill.' She could see the denial on his face before he spoke and added, 'I should tell you that I have just come from his lordship.'

'Then, yes, I can confirm that he has requested my presence at a location on Hampstead Heath tomorrow morning. Naturally I do not have certain knowledge of the reason my presence has been requested.'

'Quite.' Lily could be as dry as he. 'But how fortunate that you will be on hand should any accident befall a gentleman. At what time do you intend leaving London?'

The doctor looked startled. 'At five, Miss France. But why do you ask?'

'Because I would like you to collect me on your way, if you please.'

'Certainly not! Miss France, you may not fully comprehend the nature of this business—'

'I most certainly do. A duel is to take place in defence of my honour and I intend to be there. If you do not take me up, I will go alone. I have no intention of intervening, or being seen. I just wish to be there and to find out what happens.'

'Miss France.' He got to his feet and took an agitated stride across the room. 'If you insist, I will tell you upon my return. I will call upon you as soon as I reach London again.'

'No, that is not good enough.' If she was to find herself responsible for a household of women whose son and brother had been killed on her account, she wanted to know at once. Thinking in such brutally practical terms was the only way Lily believed she could get by until this was all over.

'It is most improper. You should not be driving alone in a carriage with a man, and I doubt very much that your chaperon will be with you!'

'If I can be alone in my bedchamber in a state of undress with you, Doctor, I think I can cope with your company in a carriage,' Lily retorted. 'I mean this—if you do not take me, I will go by myself.'

'Very well. You leave me no choice. I will be at your door at five.'

Chapter Fourteen

It was a chilly, slightly misty morning. Lily huddled her black cloak around herself and sat back in the corner of the carriage. Doctor Ord was obviously grievously put out by her having pressured him into taking her up; he regarded her with unveiled disapproval.

'I hardly dare to ask how you left this morning without raising questions amongst your household Miss France.'

'I simply told the footman I was going out.' She shrugged, 'It is not his place to question me.'

'At this time in the morning? He will not think fit to mention the matter to Mrs Herrick?'

'Not if he values his position,' Lily said grimly. The doctor lapsed into frowning silence and stared out of the window. Lily let her eyes flicker over the sinister black case by his side and hastily looked out of the other side.

The traffic out of London was light at that time in the morning and their progress was steady, despite the steep climb up Haverstock Hill. Lily's mouth was uncomfortably dry and she wished she had thought to bring something to drink. What was Jack thinking? Had he been in this position before, or was this new?

How could men do it—go out to kill or be killed in cold blood? She shuddered as the carriage lurched off the road on to a track. They must have reached the Heath. The doctor leaned across and pulled down the blinds. 'You will please stay here with the blinds shut, Miss France.'

She nodded, telling herself she was acknowledging his comment, not agreeing to it. The carriage stopped and she pulled up her hood, curling herself back into her corner as the groom opened the door for Doctor Ord and lifted down the black instrument case.

Silence, then the sound of voices at a distance. Lily eased back the corner of the blind and saw two carriages some way off, standing apart from each other. Jack was by one, looking out over the view towards London. He seemed relaxed, yet watchful. Adrian was by the other, staring at the huddle of men—presumably the seconds—halfway between the two vehicles.

The coachman had stopped the doctor's carriage by a small stand of trees. Lily looked out of the opposite door— under their cover she could circle round and get much closer, especially as the whole group were now making their way down into some sort of depression in the ground below the copse.

Lily slipped out of the door and into the trees.

Jack stood patiently, watching two of the seconds examining the box of duelling pistols that Lord Gledhill had produced. There seemed to be a cold lump where his stomach should be, and his heartbeat was unusually rapid, but he felt he could sustain the appearance of calm. Anything, rather than betray himself as Randall was doing, with his white face and constant fidgeting.

'They appear perfectly satisfactory,' said Randall's second. What was his name? Dunsford? 'No rifling, both well balanced, no difference in the triggers that I can find. I am happy to accept these on behalf of my principal. Shall we load, Webster? It does not look as though either party is offering or accepting an apology.'

Jack's man nodded, with a glance towards Lord Gledhill and Fellthorpe, his opposite number. Both were shaking their heads, their faces grave, while the doctor stood discreetly to one side.

Doctor Ord! Jack bowed slightly and received a frosty bow in return. It seemed the good doctor did not approve of such affairs, or perhaps he simply did not wish to see a man he had recently patched up putting himself at hazard again. Difficult to blame him—if anyone was killed, Ord would have to convince a jury he had not connived in the duel from the start.

Jack was not at all sure he approved of the duel either, but there was nothing to be done about it. It was an affair of honour and he was damned if he was going to leave that sneering lordling unchastised. Lily apart—he was trying very hard not to think about Lily just now—he had a long score to settle with Randall, going right back to his schooldays as the undersized victim of Randall's bullying.

I am not so undersized now, Jack smiled grimly to himself, then was struck by a thought. As Webster and Dunsford took the pistols over to Randall for him to make his choice, Jack shrugged out of his coat and began to untie his neckcloth.

'What are you about?' Lord Gledhill asked, finding coat, neckcloth and finally, shirt, thrust into his hands.

'I've seen bullet wounds with cloth carried into them before now. They fester. I am sure our good doctor would agree with me that this is a sensible precaution.'

'What's the matter, Allerton?' Lord Randall's sneering voice carried across the short distance between them as the remaining pistol was handed to Jack. 'Afraid I am going to hit you?'

'Of course,' Jack replied calmly. 'With unrifled barrels goodness knows where the shot might go—even you might hit something.'

Randall turned an angry shoulder and his seconds began to whisper at him urgently as he began to button his coat right up to the neck, hiding the target of white shirtfront and neck-cloth.

Lord Gledhill grinned at Jack. 'You are a sight to scare anyone with those scars on you. You strip well,' he added with the assessing stare of a sporting aficionado. 'Box, do you?'

'Occasionally. Mostly I wield a pick.' Jack glanced up at the scrub on the edge of the depression. 'Thought I saw something up there.'

'Fox, probably.' Lord Gledhill looked across. 'We are ready.' The sudden, fleeting, pressure of his hand was warm on Jack's bare shoulder as Jack moved the pistol from hand to hand, relaxing the muscles and tendons so that his grip, when he finally took it, was steady.

He spared a final thought for his family and the letter he had handed to Gledhill, then steadied his mind as he walked towards Randall. The man's blue eyes flickered as he met them. The duellists turned and stood back to back, the heat radiating from the other man's body just reaching Jack's chilled skin. Then Gledhill began to count and he paced forward, stopped, turned and waited.

'Take aim.'

Li—

Before Gledhill could continue, Randall's pistol arm came up, there was a bang, the sudden lash like a red hot wire across his left bicep, a puff of smoke, and his opponent was staring at him, white faced, across the damp grass.

'Damn it, Randall, you fired too soon!' The baron's own second was shouting at him, aghast.

The pain was acute, shocking. Jack did not look down. Slowly he raised his own pistol, feeling the sweat break out on his brow with the effort to stand still, to exercise control while his body hurt so. Randall's face swam into focus and he took aim, squarely in the middle of his chest. *Now I have you!*

Time seemed to stand still, sound vanished, the only reality was his opponent's white, terrified face and the weight of the pistol in his hand, the ache of his wrist as he held it steady, the heat of blood on his left arm, the pain. *Lily.* Jack turned the muzzle of the pistol away, out over the deserted heath, insultingly wide of Randall, and pulled the trigger.

Then noise flooded back, and movement. Doctor Ord was at his side, Gledhill was steadying him. 'I am all right.' He glanced down at his arm. The bullet had cut a red raw furrow through the flesh. 'It is merely a flesh wound.'

'Sit on this tree stump and let me bandage it.' The doctor produced an unpleasant black bottle and poured it over the wound.

'Hell and damnation!' Almost deprived of breath by the fiery wash of the spirit, Jack sat down and submitted his arm to be bandaged. 'Where's Randall?' Gledhill's lanky frame was blocking his view. It was beginning to dawn on him that he was alive, relatively unscathed and was neither a murderer nor a fugitive. On balance, even with a wound that stung like hell, that was a better outcome than he had expected at three in the morning when he was lying flat on his back, giving up on sleep as the noise of night coaches reached his high room.

'Slunk off back to his carriage.' His second stood aside, revealing the black coach swaying off across the rough ground. 'That was a bad business, firing early like that. And you deloping simply highlighted how badly he has behaved. *And* he knows there are six witnesses to his behaviour. Randall will not show his face in town for a while, I'd bet.'

'You will do, Lord Allerton.' The doctor straightened up. 'Get your clothes on before you catch the chill—I would not be surprised if you take a fever, even so.'

That was it: score settled. Nothing to stop him taking the next coach north. Home.

As Jack got to his feet and began to shrug on his shirt with Lord Gledhill's assistance, Lily sank back against the bush under which she had been hiding. *I am not going to faint. I am* not!

To have crouched there, silent, through that interminable, formalised ritual had been a nightmare. It had all seemed impossibly unreal at first as the men stood and talked in their little groups, as though they were striking a bargain over the price of something, or solemnly conferring on a matter of law. Then the shock of seeing Jack stripping off, the shame of feeling a thrill run through her at the physical power of him and then the terror of seeing Adrian raise his pistol and fire.

To have seen the bullet strike Jack, tear through skin and muscle, watch him stand there as the blood coursed down his arm—and shake with reaction when she realised he was not killed—then be struck with terror that he would drop Adrian where he stood and become a fugitive… It was worse than she could ever have believed possible.

Swallowing, Lily backed out from her cover and hurried away through the spinney. Before she could reach the doctor's carriage, nausea overtook her and she clung to a sapling, retching miserably until the fit passed.

She climbed into the carriage with legs that trembled and sank into her corner again. Doctor Ord joined her after an interminable wait that had her believing that Jack had collapsed through loss of blood, or that the bullet had pierced some vital organ after all. Twice she had got up and reached for the door handle, twice she had made herself sit down again to try and wait calmly.

'What did you see?' the doctor demanded without ceremony as the coachman cracked his whip. One look at her face must have told him the truth.

'Everything,' Lily admitted. 'Is he all right? Was he badly hurt?'

'He will live. He is young and tough.' The doctor regarded her from under dark brows, sighed, and let the window blinds up. 'Another scar to add to an impressive collection. Don't you go rushing round there disturbing him and weeping all over him—I have told him to get as much sleep as he can: not that that is an easy task at an inn as busy as the Bull and Mouth.'

Lily dropped her gaze to her hands, demurely folded in her lap. So that was where Jack was. Yes, let him rest for a day and a night, then she would go to him and apologise. For everything. Not that she expected much from that, but at least they might part as friends. *I love you…but you do not want me.*

'Thank Heavens Lord Allerton did not kill Lord Randall,' she said, recalling her other great fear.

'Indeed. Although Lord Randall may yet come to wish Allerton had, when word gets out of how he behaved.' Lily looked her surprise. 'Did you not realise? Randall should have waited for the second to call *Fire*. Effectively he cheated and did himself more damage than Allerton could ever hope to.'

'Did Ja…did Lord Allerton deliberately miss? I can see that might be an added insult.' Men were so peculiar, with their mysterious honour and their rituals. What was the point of all this lethal business if, in the end, you did not try and hit your opponent?

'Delope.' The doctor nodded. 'Yes, it is quite common where one duellist wishes to show that he has no wish to harm the other, merely to make a point. Or sometimes two hot-headed friends find themselves in that position and both delope.'

No, it seemed she would never understand this male pride, and somehow that made it all worse, that she could not comprehend such an essential part of the man she loved, and that she had misjudged her dealings with him so totally. Well, she might not understand honour, but she did know how to apologise when she had been wrong, and she was going to end this with dignity.

Attempting to find a single gentleman in the organised chaos that was the Bull and Mouth at nine o'clock on a Thursday morning proved anything but dignified.

Lily had dressed with care in the most sober and restrained of her walking dresses, studied herself in the mirror and removed half of the items of jewellery she had put on, thought again and removed several more, then had Janet take the plumes out of her new hat. She was still wrestling with the concept that consciously failing to demonstrate your wealth was somehow more of a sign of class than flaunting it, but that approach had certainly seemed to win her approval from the society matrons and, to some extent, from Jack. And she wanted him to remember her with approval.

She had deliberately left her footman and her maid with the carriage. It might be highly improper to visit a man in his rooms alone, but she had no intention of having any witnesses to her carefully composed, dignified speech of regret, thanks and farewell.

As a result she had to use her elbows to make her way through the throng, was narrowly missed by a valise thrown from the top of a stage and knew herself to be both flushed and flustered by the time she reached the inside of the hostellery.

'Allerton? No one of that name here, miss.' The harassed man behind the flap-up counter ran a cursory eye down a bulky register, shook his head and began to turn away.

'Lovell, then,' Lily persisted, her voice rising to compete with the racket from the coffee room. 'He was here yesterday.'

'He's not here either.'

Exasperated, Lily took hold of the book and swung it round, running a gloved forefinger down the pot-hooked and blotted writing. 'There! Lovell.'

'That was Tuesday night. He left yesterday afternoon.'

'But—' *But he is wounded! Doctor Ord said he should rest all day and all night.* 'Where? Where did he go?'

'Now how would I know that, miss?' The man removed the ledger from her grip and shut it firmly. 'He paid, he left.'

'You mean you have no record of who catches which coach

here?' Lily demanded. She was not used to being treated in such an offhand manner and was inclined to put it down to the plainness of her dress.

'Of course we have.' The man's expression made her hackles rise still further. 'But that's in the stage booking office, not in here.' He pointed outside. 'Across the yard.'

Lily stalked back outside, was adjured to 'Mind yourself—got a death wish, have yer?' by an ostler leading a pair of horses, and joined the long and noisy queue outside the ticket office.

He has gone. He cannot have gone, he should not be travelling, he is hurt. Where has he gone? Her head was spinning.

Eventually, after a spirited exchange of personalities with a woman with a goose in a rush basket who attempted to push in front of her, Lily reached the desk.

'Where to?'

'I do not know. I don't want a ticket—I want to know where someone went to yesterday.'

'What time?' With a definite air of being put upon, the clerk reached for a bundle of waybills.

'Afternoon.'

'Have you any idea how many coaches leave here of an afternoon, miss?'

'No, and I have not the slightest interest either,' Lily snapped. 'How many go to Newcastle?'

'Under Lyme? Only that's the Manchester coach from the Belle Sauvage.'

'Upon Tyne.' Lily swung round to glare at the woman with the goose, which was pecking at her pelisse now. 'Will you kindly keep that creature under control?'

'Name?'

'Lovell or Allerton.'

The man sucked an inky finger and ran it down the list. 'Yes. Cove name of Lovell. Ticket through to Newcastle upon Tyne on the three thirty. Inside seat.'

'What time does it get there?'

'Half past ten tonight. Fast coach—thirty-one hours,' the man added with pride.

'Thank you.' Lily stepped away from the window and made her way back to her carriage. He was gone. She nodded absent thanks to the footman who helped her in, and tried to work it out. Jack had left at three-thirty in the afternoon, having been up at dawn. He had fought a duel, been wounded, had come back here to this noisy bedlam where he could hardly have hoped to rest and then had set out, jammed into the stage with probably five other persons, to be jolted north for a night and a day.

And it was her fault that he was wounded and probably her fault he had left London without finding an investor. And they had parted in anger and with him thinking her forward, vulgar, interfering and overbearing. Someone who thought they could buy anything, including a man. A husband.

Lily bit her lip. She had thought just that. She realised the footman was still standing patiently holding the door, waiting for her orders.

'Oh! Home, please. At once.'

Well, now she knew better. She *could* buy herself a husband, but she did not want one who would allow her to do so. Which meant that she had better become used to being single, unless she could contrive to fall out of love with Jack and into love with a man at least as wealthy as she was.

But there was something she had to do first, and Aunt Herrick was not going to like it.

Chapter Fifteen

'You are going *where?*' Mrs Herrick sat bolt upright on the chaise, sending a shower of copies of Ackerman's *Repository of Useful Arts* cascading to the floor.

'Newcastle upon Tyne,' Lily repeated. 'I shall want the travelling carriage, John Coachman, two footmen and Janet.'

'But why?'

'I intend looking at that new warehouse Lovington wrote to recommend we purchase. I shall also have a very close look at the books; I am most suspicious about the decline in demand for tea in the north east that he is reporting.'

'Then send for him to come here! And surely an agent can assess this warehouse? Or one of your trustees can go.'

'I want to go. I am tired of London, and I want a holiday, and no one can say I am running away from a scandal now.' Lily sat down and reached for the standish and pen. There were apologies to send for invitations she had already accepted, and Lady Billington to warn that she would not be required until further notice.

'You are running after that man,' Mrs Herrick accused. 'Lily, you cannot do such a thing.'

'I shall certainly call upon Lord Allerton,' Lily replied with dignity. 'I wish to thank him for a number of things.'

'Lord Allerton? Who is he?' Mrs Herrick swung her feet off the *chaise* and groped for her vinaigrette.

'Oh, of course, I forgot, you do not know.' Lily put down the pen. 'Mr Lovell is actually the Earl of Allerton. I only found out at the Duchess's ball on Monday night.'

'Why did you not tell me?' Mrs Herrick demanded. 'Of all the bird-witted girls! We could have invited him to dinner, thrown a party, goodness knows what. We have an earl living at the bottom of the garden and you let him go! Words fail me.'

'We quarrelled.' Lily folded a note and stuck a wafer on it with a thump. 'However, it was my fault. *Largely* my fault,' she corrected, thinking of Jack's numerous infuriating tendencies. 'And I do not like being in the wrong and not admitting it. Besides, I am indebted to him.'

'Then write him a polite note thanking him, child!' Her eyes narrowed. 'For what, exactly, are you indebted?' Mrs Herrick added suspiciously.

'He knocked Lord Dovercourt out and he fought a duel with Adrian Randall, both on account of their insults to me.'

'Oh, my heavens.' Mrs Herrick seized the smelling bottle and subsided back on to the *chaise-longue*. 'A duel! The scandal! Was anyone killed?'

'No, although Lord Allerton was wounded. And there will be no scandal.' Lily reached for another piece of notepaper. 'I shall have my holiday, I will attend to business, and I will call upon Lord Allerton and have a civilised conversation with him.'

Mrs Herrick was fanning herself with a copy of the *Repository*. 'You must take a chaperon.'

'No. I am sorry, Aunt, but Janet will be quite sufficient. Lady Billington will not want to leave London at this time in any case.'

'There never was any use arguing with you, you stubborn girl,' Mrs Herrick moaned faintly. 'Just like your mother. How long will this benighted journey take you?'

'Two or three days, I imagine.' Lily frowned in calculation. 'It takes the stage just over thirty hours, but they do not stop at night. I will go and find an atlas.'

'You cannot travel on a Sunday,' her aunt announced as she returned and laid the book open on the table.

'No, naturally not,' Lily agreed, tracing the road. 'I think if I make an early start tomorrow I should get to Stamford by evening. Then to York the next day, which will be Saturday. I shall stay there on Sunday. Just think, I will be able to attend services in the Minster.' Aunt Herrick brightened at the thought of such an uplifting and unexceptionable experience. 'Then Newcastle on Monday.'

'But where will you stay?'

'Mr Lovington is married; I imagine he will invite me to stay.'

'Then you must write to warn him.'

'And give him time to adjust the books? I may be doing him an injustice and the fall in business is merely a change in local demand. But he might be dishonest, or he might be simply idle. I shall see.' Lily sat down and began to make a list. 'I may even travel over to the Lakes—it would be a pity to go that far north and not take advantage of the sights.'

If one was to become resigned to being a wealthy spinster, one might as well take advantage of the freedom that should accompany that state. For after all, if one was not in the Marriage Mart, one did not have to behave like a meek little ninny. Only, resignation seemed a hard state to achieve just at the moment.

Jack reined in the landlord's cob and sat looking out over the shallow valley that cradled Allerton Castle. Home.

Home almost forty-five hours after he had left the Bull and Mouth, ten since he climbed down into the yard of the Saracen's Head in Newcastle. It had been three in the morning when he arrived, after thirty-five hours on the coach, thanks to a cast shoe just north of Stamford. There had been coffee gulped scalding in a dozen crowded tap rooms, indigestible meals left half-eaten, and the enforced company of five other people, who, however many times they changed at the various halts, always seemed to include one man who snored, two who had never washed in their lives, one woman with a rich head cold and a convivial soul who just wanted to talk.

And despite the discomfort, the distractions, the pain in his arm, there had been far too much time to think.

His wound throbbed sickeningly and he thought he was probably running a low fever despite the few hours of snatched sleep at the Saracen's Head. He had slept like the dead, only to be awoken by a shriek. He opened one eye, saw the door shutting on a flurry of skirts, then glanced down. Ah. Hazily he recalled dragging off all his clothes and falling on to the bed. There had been apologies to be made before he got any breakfast.

Now, with the breeze ruffling the trees and bringing him the soft sound of the Aller running over its bed of stones, he began to feel almost human again. The stark mass of the castle, one corner tumbled into ruin, glowed gently in the morning sun. Home. He shook the reins and the cob responded, taking the light gig down on to the bridge over the long-dry moat and into the courtyard in front of the castle.

'Jack!' It was Penelope, hurling herself down the front steps without a thought for the fact that her hair had gone up, and her hemlines come down, upon her sixteenth birthday two months previously. 'You're home! Grimwade, tell Mama that Jack is back!'

Jack grinned as the butler appeared through the battered oak doors. 'Good morning, my lord.' He fixed a dour, but affectionate, eye on the youngest Miss Lovell. 'Miss Penelope, I believe that her ladyship is well aware of his lordship's arrival, having heard your cries of joy from the turret, as we all did. Wilson, take the gig round to the stables and bring in his lordship's luggage.'

Jack handed the reins over and climbed down, fending off his sister's bear-hug with his good arm. 'Hello, brat. Have you been good while I've been away?'

'Of course. I am a young lady now, after all.' She tipped her head to one side and regarded him critically. 'You look *dreadful*. Have you been carousing? I expect you have. And visiting dens of iniquity, whatever they are.'

'Only one, and that was not so very iniquitous,' he admitted. 'I had a very long and uncomfortable journey back on the stage, that is all. And young ladies know nothing at all about carousing.'

'Pooh,' Penelope retorted inelegantly. 'I think it is all a hum anyway, being a young lady. I mean, my hair is a nuisance, I keep tripping over my skirts, I am supposed to behave all the time, but I don't get any of the fun. No balls, no parties, no flirting.'

'You are in training,' Jack explained, tucking her hand under his elbow and nodding his thanks to the butler, who was standing holding the door. 'How is everyone else?'

'Boring,' Penelope pronounced. 'Mama nags me about my deportment, Caroline is mooning over George Willoughby of all people and Susan is writing poetry and insists on reading it after dinner.'

'Is it any good?'

'Ghastly. It is all about how depressed the moors make her and how the lowering face of nature reflects something or another in the human spirit. I wish she would fall in love like Caro—at least she droops about quietly.'

'No one in this house droops, least of all young ladies. Darling, how are you? You look frightful!' Jack grimaced as his mother swept out of her sitting room and kissed him, then took him by the shoulders and stood back to survey him. 'Are you running a fever, Lovell?'

'Possibly—I was a little under the weather when I left London. Nothing a good night's sleep won't cure. I was just telling Penny that the stage was hideously uncomfortable.'

'Did you have to travel in the basket?' his youngest sister crowed. 'And look at your hair! Is it all the crack?'

'It is very smart and I am sure your brother travelled inside in a perfectly respectable manner,' her mother said bracingly, but the look she shot Jack showed thinly veiled anxiety. He realised she had noticed the scar on his temple. 'Have you had breakfast?'

'I could eat another one.' He grinned at her reassuringly. 'Where are Susan and Caro?'

'Here!' Jack surrendered to being kissed, hugged and questioned and finally, with relief, to being dragged off to the small dining room, where he could take refuge in his own chair to wait for the simple snack he was assured Cook would toss together in a moment. Knowing Cook's views on what constituted 'proper' food suitable for his lordship, he was resigned to a wait of at least half an hour, so he sat back and regarded his family affectionately.

'That is a very fetching cap, Mama. And, Caro—is it possible you were in such looks before I left?' His elder sister, at eighteen, was suddenly growing into a beauty. She blushed, but did not respond to his teasing. Possibly Penny was right— was he going to have to investigate George Willoughby's suitability? He could recall very little about the man, he only hoped he was eligible. Interfering in someone else's love affair would be far from his inclination at the best of times— now the very thought touched raw nerves. 'And, Susan, how does the epic poem progress?'

'Very well.' At seventeen Susan was not yet a beauty like her elder sister, and possibly, with her solemn expression, never would be, but she had a serious charm all of her own. 'I have every expectation of seeing it published.' She spoilt this confident assertion by wrinkling her nose at her younger sister. 'Whatever Penny says.'

The incipient argument was quelled by the arrival of the coffee pot. Lady Allerton poured and the three girls sat round the table, watching him attentively. Despite his tiredness, Jack burst out laughing. 'Are you all going to sit there watching me eat my breakfast?'

'Of course,' Penelope replied with dignity. 'We have missed you.'

'I cannot believe you have missed watching me break my fast.' The coffee was bliss, warming through his veins like strong drink.

'Well, no,' she conceded. 'You are always so silent at breakfast.' All four women watched him, three of them far too well bred to demand of the head of the household a full account of his business in London and news of his success, and the fourth all too aware that to clamour to be told would result in her being sent off to her room forthwith.

What to tell them? How much to say? And should he tell them the decision he had finally reached by mid-afternoon the day before, when the stage had finally reached York?

Jack smiled. 'I will tell you all about my adventures before dinner,' he promised. 'I am going to eat my breakfast and then sleep for hours.'

'Dull,' Penny pronounced, caught her mother's eye and subsided as the platter of ham and eggs was borne in, followed by a steaming sirloin and a trencher of bread and cheese. 'Cook must think you've been starving in London.'

'I have. No one cooks like this.' Jack pulled the sirloin towards him and inhaled. It was a vile slander on Mrs Oakman's kitchen, but it would get back to Cook and please her. 'Tell me all your news while I eat.'

They all joined in, telling of their doings, the local gossip, the good news about the state of the flocks, and Jack ate, half-listening, content simply to be home. He glanced round at the room with pleasure, which turned to unease the longer he looked. Despite the best efforts of his mother and the housekeeper the hangings could hardly be called pleasantly faded any longer—they were looking downright shabby. And the ceiling was blackened from years of log fires, the furniture not so much antique as old.

They had all grown used to the castle, loved it too much to be critical. By going away he had come back with fresh eyes. What would Lily make of it? It was the first time he had allowed himself to think directly about her since he had climbed out of the coach at the Saracen's Head. Would she be fascinated by the age of the place or critical of the state of it? Charmed as he was or appalled? Or worse, amused.

Jack accepted a second cup of coffee with a murmur of thanks and tried to imagine how Lily would redecorate in here. 'What are you smiling about?' Penny demanded.

'I was thinking that a little redecoration might be in order.'

'Did you see many fashionable interiors in London?' Susan put down the pencil with which she had been listing rhymes for 'gloom' in her notebook, and looked up with interest.

'Some. One house in the very forefront of fashion— I was thinking how it would translate here.'

'Describe it, please, dear.' Even his mother sounded interested.

'Well.' Jack closed his eyes, the better to conjure up Lily's best spare bedroom. 'It is in the Egyptian manner—'

'With mummies?'

'No, Penny. No mummies. But the couches were in black and gold upholstered with leopard skins, and instead of legs they were supported by gilded crocodiles. The carpets were woven with borders of papyrus and strange birds and the torchères were made like palm trees. Oh, yes, and some things had camels embossed on them.'

'Gilded crocodiles!' He opened his eyes and saw Penny's fascinated expression. 'Whose house was it? The Prince Regent's?'

'No, it belonged to a very rich and very fashionable lady.' He caught Caro watching him, realised he was still smiling and straightened his face. His sister's eyebrow lifted, just a touch. Caro always could read him better than any of them.

'I do not think crocodiles would be right in here,' Susan said doubtfully. 'And we would have to change all the furniture.'

'I promise, no crocodiles. But new hangings, perhaps?' Everyone looked cheerful at the thought and Jack grimaced inwardly. He had hardly been home an hour and he had given the family the impression that there was money to spare for redecorating the castle. That was what came of being so ill disciplined as to be thinking about Lily when he had promised himself that he would do no such thing.

The trouble was that everything conspired to bring her to mind. He had longed to see her sweeping into the coffee rooms of the inns along the way, demanding fresh coffee and her eggs done just so. He could even imagine her trying to hold up the stage while she finished her meal, blithely confident that even the formidable coachman would sacrifice his sacred schedules if Miss France demanded it.

It was easier to imagine Lily, bossy and demanding, than to recall her face as he had left her on the terrace, flushed and breathless after that cruel kiss, pain and anger in those wide green eyes.

'Shh, he's asleep.' It was Penny, attempting a tactful whisper. Jack opened one eye and found his family regarding him tolerantly.

'I beg your pardon.'

'Go to bed, dear,' his mother said, making him feel eight years old again. 'And do not come down until dinner time!'

Jack made his way slowly upstairs, exchanging greetings with the servants as he went. Up the main staircase, installed by the Tudor baron, through the Long Gallery, modernised by the first earl in the early seventeenth century, then up the spiral staircase, part of the original castle. The weight of his ancestors and their expectations seemed to weigh on his shoulders and he wondered why he had not had the sense to take over his father's comfortable suite on the first floor.

Still, the tower rooms were every boy's dream of what a castle should be and he had been too fond of them to move when he inherited. Lily would doubtless want to add several arrays of armour, a tasteful array of battleaxes and some antlers.

Stamping firmly on the idea of Lily redecorating his bedchamber, Jack pushed open the door and found the room already occupied.

'My lord, welcome home. I have unpacked your luggage already.' It was Denton, his valet. The contents of his bags seemed to have been divided into three unequal piles. The largest Denton was pushing into the arms of a footman, with instructions to have them laundered immediately. Another pile, regrettably torn, was dropped in a corner and the valet was hanging up the meagre remains.

He waited until the footman had closed the door. 'I collect your lordship has been fighting. Unfortunately, I do not believe it will be possible at this late stage to remove the blood, and one does not wish to alarm the ladies, so I will destroy the linen concerned.'

Guiltily Jack remembered throwing his shirt and neckcloth into his bag after his fight in the alehouse. Then there was the shirt that had had all its buttons torn off when he and Lily…and he seemed to recall a neckcloth…and the pile of handkerchiefs, which had been the first thing that came to hand when he knocked over the inkwell one afternoon.

'Yes, well, order me some more shirts and neckcloths, Denton.'

'Fisticuffs, I imagine, my lord.' There was a faint hint of a question.

'Yes. I won.'

'Excellent, my lord.' The valet shook out one remaining shirt, revealing a thin brown line across one sleeve. 'This, however…'

'*This,* however, is not something we discuss outside this

room,' Jack said firmly, shrugging off his jacket and beginning to unbutton his shirt. 'And, yes, I could be said to have won that one as well.'

'Darling, you look so much better.' His mother's greeting was as calm and warm as always, but Jack could sense the tension under it. He had not come home with a broad smile and a banker's draft in his wallet and now she, and no doubt Caro as well, were braced for the worst.

'Six hours' sleep and a bath works wonders.' He smiled at them and went to stand by the fireplace, empty now save for a massive arrangement of foliage and flowers. And the carefully applied dressing on his arm, which Denton had contrived to fit under his evening coat, completed the transformation from dishevelled coach traveller to English nobleman in his own castle.

'I like your hair,' Susan pronounced. 'But how did you get that scar?'

'I found myself in the middle of the most incredible event—a hoax of some sort, and a near riot as it turned out.' He began to tell them about it as Grimwade announced dinner, and the tale took them through almost to the dessert.

'Three undertakers and a bear!' Penelope's eyes were like saucers. 'How I would have liked to see that.'

'It was in the newspapers. To think we read about it and with no idea you were involved,' Susan marvelled.

'I do hope that Miss France sent for a good doctor,' Lady Allerton remarked. 'Poor lady. What a shock at her age.'

'Yes, Doctor Ord was excellent. Her age?'

'I assume she is an elderly spinster, living alone like that.'

'Oh. Ah. Yes, a spinster.' Both Caro's eyebrows were raised now. She gave him a quizzical glance and resumed her dinner. Jack could feel himself colouring. 'I attended a ball given by the Duchess of Oldbury just before I left London.'

As a diversionary tactic it worked marvellously and Jack was still being bombarded with questions when they all retired back to the panelled drawing room, Jack bringing the decanter with him. He could not put it off any longer.

'I did not succeed in finding an investor for the mine,' he said baldly. 'I am sorry, but it seems we are too far north and too far from any canals.'

'Oh.' His mother folded her hands neatly in her lap and was silent for a moment. 'I am sure you did what you could, dearest.'

Jack took a gulp of port. Oh, yes, he had done everything he could. Everything except swallow his damned pride and bring them home a fortune beyond their wildest dreams and with it security, dowries, comfort and no more worries.

'It is too bad!' it was Penny, on her feet, hands clenched, tears in her eyes. 'Why are we so poor? Why cannot Jack make the mine create money? Mr Roper in the next valley does—he is sinking new shafts and he inherited at almost the same time as Jack did. Everything was all right when Papa was alive!'

'Penelope!' Caroline jumped to her feet and shook her sister by the shoulder. 'Apologise to Jack this minute!'

'That was very unfair, Penelope.' Lady Allerton got up, her face white. 'I think I will retire, if you will all excuse me.'

'And you too, Penelope,' Susan added angrily into the shocked silence as the door closed behind their mother. 'I am ashamed of you!'

Jack stood where he was, feeling sick. He had enough on his conscience as it was; the injustice of Penny's attack somehow seemed deserved.

'No.' Caroline rounded on her sisters. 'Sit down, both of

you. It is about time you knew the truth.' Jack held up a hand to try to stop her, but she shook her head. '*I* know about Papa, and I think it is about time the others did too. I will not have them blaming you for what is not your fault.'

Chapter Sixteen

Lily regarded the excellent dinner set out in the best private parlour in the Blue Boar in Stamford for her delectation. She felt decidedly queasy and she was too honest with herself to put it down to travel sickness. No, it was nerves and the strong conviction that she had bitten off more than she could chew.

It was not too late to turn back, of course. All she would suffer would be some lost pride and Aunt Herrick saying 'I told you so' for at least a week . And she would have to live with herself afterwards, knowing she had not got the backbone to do what was right.

But what if Jack did not understand? What if he thought she was pursuing him? She had already demonstrated just how fast and shameless she was by proposing marriage to him. And he could only have deduced from her willingness to yield to his caresses that she was positively wanton, she concluded, mentally flagellating herself for her shortcomings.

Lily pushed a fritter around her plate. *I am pursuing him.* But only to apologise. *I could write.* That would be cowardly. One should face up to things when one made a mistake.

He would be home by now, after that interminable stage-coach journey. She was feeling tired and frazzled and she had been in her own comfortable carriage for just one day, able to stop whenever she wanted and without a bullet wound in her arm. Stubborn man. Stupid, proud, stubborn man. Brave, proud, stubborn man. *I love you. I ought to go home. I am not brave enough to do this. I will go home in the morning.*

'A mistress?' Penelope stared at her eldest sister in horror. 'Papa?'

'Several mistresses. Very expensive ones, by all accounts,' Caroline said grimly. 'Oh, stop frowning at me, Jack! She ought to know, she is old enough.'

'Well, I think men are beastly. All of them,' Penny blurted out.

'I haven't got any expensive mistresses,' Jack protested, only to be glared at by all three girls. 'Nor cheap ones either!'

'Do you mean to say…' Penelope was set on getting to the bottom of the entire sordid matter now '…do you mean that when Papa was away so much in London, he wasn't sitting in the Lords, or looking after business at all?'

'He was gambling and wenching and spending money,' Caroline said ruthlessly, ignoring Jack's attempts to silence her. 'And all Jack inherited were debts. Piles of them. It is entirely due to Jack that we are not all in a debtors' prison now.'

'Poor Mama,' Susan lamented.

'Does she know?'

'Of course she knows, she knew all the time. And when you attack your poor brother, who works and worries to keep a roof over your head, how do you think it makes her feel?'

'I couldn't help it, I didn't know,' Penelope said indignantly. 'I am sorry Jack, I shouldn't have said it, even if it were true. But how horrible for Mama. I do not think I ought to get married—I think I should stay unmarried and be a Comfort to her.'

Despite everything, Jack felt a bubble of laughter rising in his chest. Desperately keeping from making eye contact with Caroline, he said seriously, 'I would much rather you did get married, Penny. It would be less of a financial burden to me if you did.'

'Oh. Well, if it would help, I will try and find a rich husband as soon as possible. Is it all right to ask them first about mistresses? After all, I think I should check.'

'No!' Susan and Caroline chorused.

'If you say so,' she said doubtfully. 'And Caro can marry Mr Willoughby.' She ignored her sister's blushes and explained, 'He is very nice, but rather *dull,* and not very rich. And quite old.' Caroline rolled her eyes at Jack, who shrugged sympathetically, then felt the humour drain out of his veins as Penelope added brightly, 'And Jack is very handsome, as well as being an earl, so he can find a rich wife easily. You should have looked for one in London, but I expect you did not think of it, being so tied up with more important things.' She frowned over the problem. 'I think you should go straight back there—it must be the best place to find them. And we should all contribute our dress allowances so you can buy some fashionable clothes.'

Jack fought to keep the mildly amused smile on his face. 'That is a very noble offer, Penny, but I am afraid none of the rich ladies would want me. I met lots in London and they all want dukes and rich men. Poor earls are quite out of fashion.

'Anyway, I have a plan. I had hoped to find investors, because that seemed the least risky option, but I will borrow from the bank instead, so you can be quite comfortable and keep your dress allowance. And you will not have to interrogate rich bachelors about their mistresses either.'

'Well, that is a relief,' Caro said brightly. 'I think you had better go to bed now, Penny.'

'All right.' Penelope kissed Jack goodnight, then looked her surprise when Susan joined her. 'You too?' The door remained ajar after they went out and Penny's whisper came back clearly. 'I expect you are just being tactful, aren't you? I expect Caro wants to talk to Jack about Mr Willoughby…'

'Impossible child!' Caro laughed and for a moment Jack thought he had got away with it. Then his sister's wide grey gaze became solemn. 'Tell me about her. There is someone, isn't there? Is it the rich spinster with the riot outside her house? Miss France?'

Could he talk about it, even to Caro? Why not? His damned pride again, he supposed.

'Yes. Miss France. Lily.'

'How pretty. Not an elderly spinster, then, whatever Mama thinks?'

'No. She is twenty-five or -six. Tall, red-headed, very lovely. Very, very rich. A tea merchant's daughter and heiress. She is spoilt, stubborn, interfering, opinionated, bossy, insensitive, has absolutely no taste…'

'And you love her?' Caro was smiling at his outburst.

'Yes I love her.' It was like a liberation, being able to talk about it. 'Under it all she is brave and honest and clever and kind. But I do not know why I love her. I would never in a thousand years have imagined loving a woman like that.'

'Well, George Willoughby is thirty-five, and not very good looking, and only moderately well off and very decent and a little dull. And if he does not ask me to marry him soon, I am going to go into a decline,' Caroline pronounced. 'So you see, there is no accounting for love. In fact, they both sound so improbable for us that it proves it *is* love, don't you think?'

'Probably.' Jack crossed his legs and stared at the polished tip of his evening shoe. 'Do you want me to ask Willoughby his intentions?'

'Goodness, no! Poor George—you will scare him halfway to Alnwick. I can manage him. But what about your Lily? Did she turn you down?' Caroline reached over and squeezed his hand consolingly.

'No. I turned her down.'

'What?' Caro gasped. '*She* asked *you* to marry *her*?'

'Yes. She wants to marry a title.'

'But you told us you were going to London incognito.'

'I was, and I did, and she did not know. But she had it all worked out. I would become a rich mine owner, enter Parliament, be ennobled—and we would all live happily ever after.'

'Oh, my goodness,' Caro said weakly. 'I can quite see why you turned her down.'

'You can?' Jack found himself bristling in Lily's defence. His sister's reaction should have justified his original feelings. Now, illogically, it placed him on Lily's side.

'Well, especially if you were not in love with her then…'

'I was. It was just my damned pride and her confounded desire to organise everything just how she wants it. I lost my temper, said things I shouldn't, then later she found out that I did have a title and she thought I had turned her down because she wasn't good enough for me and we had another row.' It sounded so futile, recounted baldly like that. Why couldn't he have explained to Lily how he felt? Where had all the words gone?

Jack got to his feet and began to pace. Caroline watched

him for a moment, then jumped up and threw her arms around him. 'Poor darling!'

'Ow! Bloody hell, Caro!'

'What have you done?' His sister regarded him narrowly. 'I thought you looked under the weather, more than a sleepless journey could account for. Have you been fighting? Those bruises on your face are too fresh for the riot in the street.'

It was never any good trying to fool her. His mother he had often managed to hoodwink; Caro, since she was about five, never. 'Yes.' There was an appalling desire to swagger; Lily had spurned his attempt to defend her honour, his sister at least would value it. Jack pulled himself together and produced a bald explanation. 'Lily was betrothed. Then she broke it off. The man involved spread unpleasant rumours about her. I called him out.'

'Wonderful! You are so brave—but I am glad we did not know about it before, the suspense would have been dreadful. Did you kill him?'

'Of course not! I would be in Calais by now if I had—or in prison. I deloped.'

'But surely Miss France was thrilled that you had risked your life for her honour?'

'She found out about the duel at the same time as she discovered the truth about who I was. She was too angry, thinking I considered her beneath me, to really take in the duel.'

'Well, go and tell her again that you love her, you idiot!' Caro's glare was uncomfortably reminiscent of Lily in a temper. 'You *have* told her that you love her, haven't you?'

'Er. No.'

'Men!' Caroline took a rapid turn about the room. 'Well, for goodness' sake, get back down there and do it! She is probably as miserable as you are.'

'Why should she be? Lily does not love me. Her pride was hurt, that is all.'

'Give me strength!' His sister sat down in a billow of skirts. 'Who was she betrothed to before?'

'A baron.'

'But she broke it off, and before she knew you had a title?'

'Yes, but she did not know me then, in any guise.'

'That is not what I mean. She is quite capable of throwing away an opportunity to marry a titled husband if she does not like him. And she was prepared to marry you on the off chance that you might have a title one day. In fact, she was so determined that she defied all modesty and convention and proposed to you herself.' Caro regarded him quizzically. 'Call me a fanciful female if you like, but that gives me just the *tiniest* suspicion that she likes you rather more than a little.'

'You are a fanciful female,' Jack responded grouchily. He was not going to admit it, but it felt as though a weight was being lifted off his heart. 'You deduce that through intuition, I presume?'

'No, common sense. Now, tell me all about the latest London fashions so I can give you a shopping list for when you go back again.'

'When are you returning to London?' Caroline demanded over breakfast on Tuesday morning, four days after Jack had arrived back at Allerton.

'I have not said that I am.' He reached for the preserve jar and contemplated the gooseberry jam for a while before pushing it away again.

'Back to London?' Lady Allerton put down her post and regarded him with concern. 'You never said anything about going back to London so soon.' With his father's peccadilloes recalled so recently to his mind, Jack thought he glimpsed a related anxiety in his mother's surprise.

'Caro has a long shopping list she unaccountably forgot to give me before,' he replied, making light of it. 'There is possibly some business I might do—I have not yet decided.'

Caroline's sigh was meant only for his ears and he ignored it. It would be easier if he could make up his mind what he did want to do. Never normally indecisive, Jack found his days filled with busy, purposive activity but his nights sleepless and undecided. And when he did sleep it was to dream about Lily—hectic, erotic dreams that left him tired and frustrated. And unable to make up his mind.

The bank had proved—in the face of his determination and his new research—perfectly obliging in the matter of a loan, which would enable him to expand the existing working, if not open another one. Provided the seams ran true. If they did not and the coal failed, then the only course to repay the loan would be to sell the mine and to give up the castle.

For the mine workers and their families it could mean ruin, unless he could sell the pit. Even then, there would be no guarantee the new master would treat the people as he, Jack, had always tried to do. The loan was the last chance for them, a gamble he was instinctively uneasy about, but one he had to risk.

His own family would have to fall back on the old Dower House, which would be cheaper to run. And then he could content himself with learning to be a farmer and carrying out all those breeding experiments on sheep he had always promised himself he would find time for. It was a less than entrancing prospect, but one which would at least provide for his family in modest comfort.

Mr Roper, his nearest neighbour, was interested in hearing about the latest news on steam engines that Jack had gleaned in London and reciprocated with his own experiences with pumping, admirably concealing his disappointment that Jack had not ridden over to offer him the Allerton shaft to buy.

So, all in all, things were as well as he could expect, and could only be made worse by gallivanting off to London, spending more money and distracting himself with a woman who drove him to distraction and who did not want him, whatever Caroline said.

'I have a shopping list too,' Susan put in. 'I have been looking at those wonderful ladies' journals you brought us, Jack, and I can see we are woefully behind the mode, all of us.'

'Then I am afraid you will just have to make do with what the Newcastle modistes can produce and your dress allowances will stretch to,' Jack said, making up his mind. 'I am staying here for the foreseeable future.' He reached for the preserve jar again and spread jam on his toast. He should feel braced and decisive. Relieved, even. Why, then, could he almost smell the smoke of burning bridges and the crackle as lost hopes went up in flames?

Caroline was silent. He could feel her eyes boring into him and kept his own gaze fixed on his newspaper. She was in love, all she could see was happy endings. She wanted her own lover to act decisively, so she was urging her brother to do the same thing. But she had no responsibilities to consider. No family name to protect. *No pride to weigh her down*, a jeering voice whispered in his ear.

After the meal the family dispersed to their various occupations, and Jack managed to evade Caroline. He should have known better; coming out of his study in search of some estate papers, he found himself cornered.

'Jack! Please reconsider—you are going to regret this all your life if you do not.'

He went back into his study, but, short of shutting the door in her face, had to stand aside to let her in. 'No. I will not discuss it any further, Caroline. I have duties, responsibilities and I am not going to change my mind on this.'

He could see the calculation plain on her face: to pursue the matter and risk a breach between them, or to yield when she felt so passionately that she was right. He loved her for caring and wished her anywhere but here. Eventually, when he had come to terms with the loss, he could consider it more rationally. Now, all he wanted was to never have to think about Lily France again.

The sound of the heavy knocker thudding on oak had both of them turning towards the door. 'Who on earth can that be?' Caro puzzled. 'It is scarcely half past ten. Who could be calling?'

'Your suitor come to place his case before me?' Jack teased, seeing an opportunity to get his own back.

But the voice at the front door was not that of the respectable Mr Willoughby with his slight Northumberland burr. It was female, decidedly southern, clear and carrying.

'No, I have come to see his lordship, not Lady Allerton. His lordship is not expecting me. My card.'

Caroline swung round to stare at him. 'Is that…?'

'Lily.' *It cannot be. I am dreaming. I must be.* Jack felt his fists clench and as they did so his biceps contracted, sending a stab of pain through his wounded arm. Oh, no, this was no dream. This was real.

'Jack.' Caroline was tugging urgently at his sleeve. 'Jack—you didn't…there wasn't anything that might have made her realise she *had* to come…was there?'

His sister was blushing hotly and, as her meaning sank in,

Jack felt his own colour rise too, guiltily. 'No,' he replied bluntly, not even trying to pretend he misunderstood her.

'Well, thank goodness for that.' Caroline flapped a hand in front of her hot face and opened the door. 'Grimwade, his lordship is in the study.'

Lily looked around the great hall with its soaring beamed roof and tried not to gape like a yokel. Allerton Castle should not have been a shock—after all, she had seen the print of it. But from the outside it just seemed unreal, something from a story book. It was only when the great oak doors had swung open to reveal a lugubrious butler and she had forced her shaking legs over the threshold that it all ceased to be a fantasy and became hideously real.

Every morning on the journey following that evening in Stamford she had woken, determined to put the doubts and fears of the night before behind her and press on to do what she had set out for. Now, surrounded by the faded evidence of generations of pride and ancestry, every word of her carefully dignified speech fled.

'I will ascertain whether Lady Allerton is at home, ma'am. Whom may I say is calling?' The butler's livery was ancient, the carpet he was standing on threadbare, but he regarded her with the air, she was convinced, of a man who could spot a cit at one hundred yards.

'No, I have come to see his lordship, not Lady Allerton. His lordship is not expecting me. My card.'

She produced the rectangle of pasteboard from her reticule, suddenly seeing it for the over-ornate piece of design it was. Too much gilt edging, too fancy a script. The butler managed not to sneer at it as he laid it on a silver salver. The centre bore an engraved crest, elusive from years of polishing. 'If you will wait in—'

'Grimwade, his lordship is in the study.' Lily turned and saw a tall, slender young woman emerge from a door between two massive pieces of tapestry. She was plainly dressed, but she had a style that gave the gown its own elegance. As she moved into the light Lily was aware of a pleasing, heart-shaped face, dark hair and a pair of familiar deep grey eyes.

'You have come to see my brother? I am Caroline Lovell, Lord Allerton's sister. Refreshments in the front parlour, please, Grimwade.' Lily found herself swept into a room at least three times the size of anything she would have thought to describe by such a homely term as parlour.

'Please, will you not sit down, Miss France? It is Miss France, is it not?'

'Yes.' Lily felt at a disadvantage in front of this self-assured young woman in her simple gown. She had taken enormous care to select the plainest of her own walking dresses, afraid of giving any offence by appearing ostentatious. Yet she still felt overdressed and awkward. 'How did you know?' She tried not to stare at the tarnished suit of armour in the far corner. Did people really have them in their homes?

'Jack described you to me.' Lily swallowed against the embarrassment. She had obviously not succeeded in muting her regrettable taste in clothes if she was instantly recognisable. This elegant young lady must despise her. But Miss Lovell was still smiling. 'He said you were tall, lovely and red haired.'

'Oh!' Had Jack ever commented on her appearance? Is that truly how he thought of her? Lily shook herself mentally; this was not why she had come here. 'I did not intend to disturb you, Miss Lovell, I simply wished to have a few words with Lord Allerton and leave.'

'But you must have some tea at least before you go!' Miss Lovell turned as the door opened. 'You see, here is Grimwade with the tray, and my mother and other sisters. Mama, this is Miss France, all the way from London, who has called to see Jack. Miss France, this is my mother, Lady Allerton. My sister Susan, and my youngest sister Penelope.'

This is a fairy story! I come here to confront an ogre in a castle and I find myself in a tea party with four ladies. I am trapped now, I can hardly insist upon seeing him...

Lily smiled and curtsied and said everything that was proper and found herself seated while four pairs of dark grey eyes observed her with polite interest.

'Have you come far today, Miss France?' Lady Allerton was pouring tea into cups that seemed to be made of parchment, they were so thin.

'From Newcastle only, Lady Allerton. I stayed at York on Sunday, having travelled up from London. What very lovely china.' It was probably ill bred of her to comment, she realised as soon as the remark was out. The aristocracy took old things for granted.

'Thank you. It is Sèvres, from my grandmother's family.' Lily could hear her own words echoing in her memory from when she had ranted at Jack about the upper classes' obsession with all things old. How he must have laughed inwardly at her ignorant indignation when he owned such exquisite heirlooms himself. 'A long journey, Miss France. How fortunate the weather has been clement. Do you visit family?'

'No. It is a business visit.' There was no point in pretending, even if her ladyship regretted offering hospitality to a cit. 'I trade in tea and I have a branch of the business here. It is a long time since I visited my agent here. I think I may then go into the Lake District to see the sights, if the weather holds fair.'

'Tea, how fascinating. Please, give me your opinion on this blend.'

Surprised, for most ladies seemed not to have any understanding that tea blends might vary at all, Lily took a careful sip and rolled it around her mouth. 'Essentially a green tea, with overtones of Oolong. I think it might be given a little more body with a hint of Nilgiri, but that is very much a personal thing.'

'How clever.' The youngest Miss Lovell—Penelope?—clapped her hands. 'What lovely names and how wonderful of you to know all about it.'

'Miss France *is* very clever, Penny.'

The fragile cup rattled in its saucer and Lily put it down hastily on the side table. Jack came in, a smile on his lips and a decidedly chilly question in his flinty eyes.

Chapter Seventeen

'Lord Allerton.' Lily swallowed the lump in her throat and managed not to squeak. She had last seen him on a damp heath, stripped to the waist with blood pouring down his arm. Now he looked relaxed, well and—surrounded by the thick ancestral walls of his home—formidably unapproachable. He was the same man as he had been in London, yet totally different.

'What a surprise to see you again so soon, Miss France.' He gave no indication whether he found the surprise a pleasant one or not, but Lily thought she could guess.

'Miss France was just telling us about tea.' Lady Allerton appeared not to notice the atmosphere. 'Would you care for a cup, Lovell, or shall I ring for coffee?'

'Neither, thank you, Mama.' He did not sit down either and Lily could see both his younger sisters beginning to look uncertainly at him. He was waiting for her to explain herself, as well he might.

'Another cup, Miss France? A biscuit?'

'No, I thank you, ma'am. I…I must not take any more of your time. I came only to say something to Lord Allerton, then I must go.'

'Really? But will you not stay with us a while? We would be delighted to have you, and you are so far from home.'

Lily smiled distractedly at her hostess. 'Thank you, Lady Allerton...but I must say this, and then—'

'You wish to be alone.' Lady Allerton got to her feet and gestured to her daughters. 'Come along, girls, and let Miss France discuss her business.'

'No! No, please do not go. I should say this in front of all of you.' Now she had begun the words came more easily. Lily made herself meet Jack's eyes, even darker now, his eyebrows raised in what seemed to be disdainful query.

'I came only to apologise—to Lord Allerton for failing to thank him as I should for what he has done for me, and to his family for putting him in such peril.'

'Peril?' Lady Allerton half-rose from her chair, but Miss Lovell's hand on her shoulder pressed her gently back down. Caroline's gaze was fixed on her brother, but she remained standing quietly.

'On three—no, four—occasions Lord Allerton has come to my aid. He rescued me when I was escaping the unwanted attentions of a gentleman. He was injured—you can see the scar on his temple—when a mob surrounded my house. He was struck down by that same man even though he was already hurt, and finally, when he called him to account for his behaviour, Lord Allerton was wounded in the arm.'

'Duelling?' From the expressions on the faces of at least three of the women in front of her, Lily realised they had not known about the duel. 'Duelling?' Lady Allerton repeated. 'What wound?'

'A flesh wound in the left upper arm,' Lily explained, the words tumbling out now. Jack's brows had drawn together thunderously. So, he had managed to conceal it from them.

'But that is not all. I was tactless, insensitive, thoughtless.' There was no denial on his face. She forgot the watching women and began to speak only to Jack. 'I made things in London much more difficult for you than they might have been. I did not help your search for investors as I might have done. We parted in anger because I was too self-centred to see your point of view. And too spoilt to stand being thwarted.' She might as well say it all now, humiliate herself thoroughly while she was about it.

'I was brought up to take responsibility for my mistakes. I do not make many.' There was a sudden glimmer of humour in his eyes and her heart twisted. 'Not many, but when I do, I apologise. I went to the Bull and Mouth, but I was too late, you had gone.'

'You could have written, saved yourself a tedious journey.' Jack sounded as neutral as if she had been discussing a minor matter of business.

'That would have been inadequate. You could have been killed.' Lily turned to Lady Allerton. 'I did try and stop it—'

'You did *what?*' It seemed she had penetrated Jack's chilly calm at last.

'I spoke to Lord Gledhill, and to Doctor Ord, but they both explained that there was nothing I could do. I did think of informing the magistrates, but Lord Gledhill said you would only find another place to fight.'

'Where did you speak to Lord Gledhill?' The very quietness of Jack's tone should have warned her.

'I went to his lodgings—'

'You, an unmarried lady, went to a bachelor's lodgings—without your chaperon, I make no doubt—I wonder why I should trouble to defend your honour when you are so careless of it!'

'Jack!' Out of the corner of her eye Lily was aware of Miss Lovell bending to murmur in her mother's ear. Lady Allerton subsided and her daughter slipped from the room.

'Well, it was my fault you were fighting, I had to do what I could to stop it!'

'No, you did not!' They were both furious now. Lily found she was on her feet, her palm itching to slap him. His face was so white that the faded bruises of his fight with Lord Dovercourt were starkly visible. 'And I suppose you were there, on Hampstead Heath? Which idiot did you persuade to take you? If it was Gledhill, I swear I am going straight back down to London to call him out!'

'It was Doctor Ord. Don't you dare bully the poor man—he is twice your age.'

'Poor man? I imagine he must be senile to have allowed such a thing. Of all the bird-witted, brazen-faced things to have done—'

'*Jack!*'

'I am sorry, Mama.' He sounded anything but sorry, despite lowering his voice. 'But what a totty-headed—'

'You,' Lily pronounced with awful dignity, gathering up her reticule, 'are the rudest, most stubborn, most prideful man I have ever met. Lady Allerton, I apologise for being the cause of your son putting himself in the way of harm, and I am deeply thankful for your sake that nothing worse came of it. Thank you for your hospitality. If your butler could please summon my carriage, I will leave you.'

'Oh, but you are staying, are you not, Miss France?' It was Miss Lovell, coming back into the room without showing the slightest consciousness that she was stepping into the eye of a storm. 'I sent your carriage back to Newcastle quite five minutes ago. They have brought in your luggage. I thought the

White Bedchamber, Mama?' She smiled round at her stony-faced brother, her younger sisters, both wide-eyed with horrified excitement, her astonished mother, and hesitated when she got to Lily.

'Is something wrong, Miss France?'

'I am staying with my agent, Mr Lovington and his wife, in Newcastle.'

'But all your luggage was in the carriage, and your maid said you had stayed at the Queen's Head last night and had paid your shot this morning.'

'I was intending to call upon Mr Lovington as soon as I returned to Newcastle today,' Lily explained with as much calm as she could muster.

'Taking him unawares?' Jack observed. 'Very wise.' Lily tried to ignore him.

'Perhaps a servant could be sent after the carriage, Lady Allerton? I regret appearing ungracious, but as you have no doubt become aware in the last few minutes, it would be highly unsuitable for me to stay here a moment longer.'

'But there are no horses available,' Caroline interjected. 'I am so sorry, Miss France, but the carriage team is down at the Home Farm, er…ploughing. And the smith is here attending to the shoes on all the saddle horses—none of them are fit to be ridden for at least two hours, he always starts by removing all the old shoes. And by the time a rider caught up with your carriage it would be back in Newcastle.' She hesitated, a look of doubt on her face. 'Oh, dear, and I have no idea where they will have gone. Does the coachman have your agent's address?'

'No,' Lily said between clenched teeth. 'Presumably he will go to a livery stable. And no doubt there are numerous such establishments in Newcastle.'

'Dozens.' After a long, cool, look at his sister, Jack had strolled away to lean one arm on the massive carved over-mantel.

'And it is coming on to rain now,' Caroline added. 'Never mind, it can all be sorted out tomorrow, I am sure. Will you not come up and see your chamber, Miss France?'

Lily looked around the room, receiving no help from either Jack's expressionless face or his amiably smiling family.

'Please, do indulge us and stay, Miss France.' It was hard to resist a direct request from Lady Allerton. 'My two eldest children appear between them to have placed you in an uncomfortable situation, but I beg that you will not consider it. I would very much welcome your company for as many days as you are able to spare—it would give us great pleasure to hear all the news from London. Lovell has done his best, but his eye for the latest mode in bonnets is not perhaps the sharpest, and his ear for gossip is positively non-existent.'

All the women started as a sudden vicious burst of rain hit the windows. The room darkened. Lily knew that to insist on sending a servant on horseback into Newcastle to hunt up a carriage at an unknown livery yard in this weather was quite impossible. 'Thank you, Lady Allerton. I would be delighted. You are most kind.'

Miss Lovell opened the door and stood waiting. Yielding to the inevitable, Lily followed her out into the Great Hall, wondering how much she had heard of that furious exchange with Jack. His family appeared to take the situation with amazing calm; gloomily Lily decided this must be a sign of their superior breeding and that her own outburst would have damned her utterly in Lady Allerton's opinion, however polite the countess was being.

'Now, you must not worry if you get lost,' Miss Lovell was saying cheerfully as she led the way up the great stone staircase past several more suits of armour and a vast, almost black, oil painting. 'All our guests do. Just tug a bell pull or keep going down whatever stairs you come to. Sooner or later everything ends up back in the Great Hall.'

'It is a wonderful building.' Lily tried to catch glimpses of the rain-swept grounds outside through narrow lancet windows set deep into the walls.

'It is,' Caroline agreed, flipping aside a tapestry to reveal a door. 'I had better tie this back or you will never find it again. We all adore it, even though it is draughty and inconvenient and far too big. And one turret fell down at the time my father inherited the title. Mind you, it needs structural work all the time, never mind the turret, so goodness knows if Jack could ever manage to get round to rebuilding that on top of everything else. He says running Allerton is like standing in front of a fire throwing on five-pound notes,' she added cheerfully.

'Oh.' Lily followed through the door and up a winding wooden staircase with carved beasts on the finials. *And if I had not blundered so tactlessly...*

'Jack is talking about doing some redecoration, though.' Caroline opened a door at the end of the corridor. 'I believe he got some ideas in London. He was telling us about a house with crocodiles and how it was decorated in the Egyptian style, but I think that can only be a joke. Now, what do you think of this room?'

'Lovely.' Lily pushed the hurtful thought that Jack had been laughing about her to the back of her mind. 'It is just like a princess's room from a fairy tale.'

'That is what I always feel.' Miss Lovell seemed pleased

with her response. 'When I was little, I would climb up into this window seat and watch for my handsome prince to come.'

Lily walked across the room and joined her. The window was cut deep into the thick stone walls and a seat had been formed in the embrasure, heaped with tapestry cushions and framed by brocade curtains, once white, now aged into a deep cream. The bed was draped in the same brocade and the walls had been simply plastered and whitewashed.

As she looked round Janet bustled out of a side door, her arms full of underwear, and a maid was on her hands and knees setting a fire. 'We have to light fires most months,' Miss Lovell explained. 'Thank you, Susan.' The maid gathered up her brushes and bobbed a curtsy. Janet tactfully vanished back into what Lily assumed was a dressing room and pulled the door shut.

'Is my brother being *very* difficult, Miss France?' Lily stiffened, then realised she could not resist the wicked twinkle in the eyes that were so like Jack's.

'Very, but I'm afraid we have both been,' she admitted ruefully. 'I am so sorry to have shocked Lady Allerton by telling her about the duel; I had assumed that everyone would know about it because of Jack's wound.'

'He hid it very well from everyone but me. Stubborn creature,' his loving sister pronounced fondly.

'Oh, isn't he!' Lily clapped her hands to her mouth. 'Miss Lovell, I am *so* sorry. I should never have said that.'

'Nonsense. And please will you not call me Caroline? Do you want to wash or rest? Because if not, do come to my room and tell me all about it.'

Lily let herself be borne off along more confusing corridors and settled on a *chaise* in Caroline's room. 'Now, I must know everything! Has Jack been absolutely impossible?'

'It is just as much my fault, I suppose, although that is difficult to remember when he is being…stubborn,' Lily said with some feeling, trying to decide what she could safely tell her new friend. 'I was engaged to be married to a baron. My family particularly wanted me to marry into the aristocracy. We are trade, of course,' she added baldly, just in case Caroline was in any doubt.

'Yes, you said. Tea. You *are* lucky to be able to escape all the boring ladylike things and use your brain.'

'Only one is expected to do all the boring ladylike things as well—like catching an eligible husband. Anyway, I made a dreadful mistake with the one I chose. I knew he wanted my money, that went without saying, but I did not expect him to be such a…he expected me to sleep with him before we were married,' she said baldly.

'And you did not want to?' Caroline did not appear unduly shocked, more curious.

'I thought I would have to. But when it came to it I could not bring myself to do it, and I ran away and Ja…Lord Allerton rescued me. But I didn't know he was an earl then, and I told him about wanting to marry a titled gentleman, and he still didn't tell me who he was. And I tried to persuade my trustees to invest in the mine, but they wouldn't and he was furious and we had the most dreadful row. And still he fought the men who had been insulting me. Which was dreadful.'

'I should think it was,' Caroline agreed warmly. 'Bad enough that he had gained your confidence when he was deceiving you about who he was, but then to put you under an obligation when all you wanted was to be furious with him— that is *such* a typically male thing to do.'

This was an analysis that had not previously occurred to Lily, but she could not but agree with it. She was warming to Jack's sister. 'You should not sympathise with me,' she said penitently. 'I almost got him killed, and he came away from London with no investors.'

'Do not blame yourself Lily. Jack has borrowed from the bank after all, so that is fine, and he wasn't killed, so there is no need to worry over what might have been.'

Lily bit her lip. He had borrowed from the bank, presumably with the mine itself as security. Which meant that, unlike a limited partnership with an investor where each would bear their own losses, Jack would lose the entire mine if he could not repay the debt.

For a moment the notion of approaching the bank to buy up the debt seemed the obvious solution. Then she pulled herself up. Jack would hate that and she would end up blundering in and hurting his pride, just as she had before. He had made a decision—she owed it to him not to interfere.

'Lily?'

'Yes? I do beg your pardon, my mind wandered for a moment.'

'Lily, would you be very kind and set aside your dislike of Jack enough to stay with us for at least a week? You see, Mama has been rather low and it would do her so much good to have a visitor. London gossip and news would be just the thing—I would so much appreciate it.'

Dislike Jack? If only that were the problem! How can I live in the same house—castle—as him without betraying how much I love him? But I have wronged Lady Allerton and her daughters, and I could have been the cause of him being killed, so how can I refuse to do what I can for his mother?

If it was possible to wring one's hands mentally, Lily realised she was doing it now. 'If Lady Allerton truly would like me to stay, of course, I would be delighted. But I feel it is a dreadful imposition—after all, I arrive unannounced, Jack and

I have a flaming…I mean, Lord Allerton and I have a disagreement in front of the entire family—whatever must she think of me?'

'That you have been much provoked by her son, and providentially kidnapped by her daughter.' Caroline chuckled. 'Now, shall we see if luncheon is ready?'

Jack retreated to the study, away from Penny's wide-eyed interest and his mother and Susan's equally intolerable pose of finding nothing whatever to remark upon, other than that it was a charming diversion to have a house guest. Braced for reproaches about duelling, to say nothing of his unflattering exchange of insults with Lily, he came up against the sweet face of good breeding and a ladylike refusal to acknowledge unpleasantness.

He wanted Lily, he realised. He wanted her so much it hurt. He wanted to apologise to her for the thoughts that had gone through his mind after the first incredulous pleasure of realising she really was standing on his threshold. For one, unforgivable moment he assumed she had decided to pursue him—and his title. Then he had seen her face as she had launched into her apology, seen the effort it took to confess her shortcomings in front of an audience of strangers and seen too the dismay when she realised she was stranded at the castle.

That was not feigned. No, Lily had decided she had an apology to make and with typical single-mindedness had set out to do it properly. Of course, being Lily, she had also combined it neatly with a business trip and a holiday, but that practical streak was one of the things he loved about her.

More pressing was the problem of how to exist under the same roof with Lily without either strangling or ravishing her. Both were appealing, neither were acceptable. Jack glanced at the clock. Time for luncheon. To stay put was uncomfortably like sulking, to go out meant making anodyne conversation with a woman who wished him five hundred miles away.

'There you are! Stop skulking in here and come and have luncheon or Lily will think you are trying to avoid her.' Caroline was looking pleased with herself.

'I am,' Jack growled, then remembered a grievance. 'And what on earth was that nonsense about the carriage team? Ploughing? At this time of year? It's a damn good thing Lily hasn't the slightest idea about country life. And the very idea that I would put my carriage horses to the plough in any case is ridiculous.'

'Lily doesn't know that.' Caro kept a strategic distance between them. 'And for all she knows, you are positively cowhanded and drive a team that may as well be plough horses.'

'You're on first-name terms now, are you?' Reluctantly Jack got to his feet and prepared to follow his sister. 'Best friends, I suppose?'

'Of course.' Caro smiled demurely. 'We have been exchanging confidences. Now, what have I said to make you blush, I wonder?' she added wickedly and danced ahead into the dining room before he could seize her wrist and demand to know what she meant by *confidences*. Surely Lily would never tell anyone… No, impossible. Caro was simply teasing. He realised he was sweating slightly and his heart was beating faster for reasons that had got nothing whatsoever to do with his provoking sister and everything to do with Lily and secrets.

Chapter Eighteen

Lily felt she had survived her first meal at Allerton with reasonable success. She had been exceedingly careful to say nothing that might reveal the gap between her dress allowance and those of the Lovell sisters when they questioned her about gowns, she had changed the subject as soon as possible when Penelope had asked about *chaise-longues* with crocodile legs, and she had entertained her hosts with unexceptional anecdotes about the Duchess of Oldbury's ball without the slightest reference to challenges or quarrels.

'And did you dance with Jack?' Penelope demanded.

'Yes, I have done, once or twice,' Lily conceded. 'Once only at that ball, but before then at another party. Lord Allerton,' she added slyly, sliding a glance at him from under her lashes, 'is a most accomplished dancer.'

Jack's mouth twitched slightly. Susan laughed. 'Is he really? I am not sure I believe you, Miss France. He is all flat feet when he has to dance with us.'

'Dancing with Miss France is a much more inspiring matter than having to take the floor with one's baby sisters,' her put-upon brother retorted. 'An elephant would dance well with Miss France.'

Lily liked the way Jack was with his family. He was obviously fond of all of them, he put up with his sisters' teasing with humour and he was clearly a loving and attentive son. This, she found, was not helpful. The discovery that he was a short-tempered domestic tyrant would have made her feel much better.

'Is it still raining?' Penelope lamented when the meal was over. 'I thought we could all go for a walk and show Lily the countryside.'

'Miss France, Penelope,' her mother corrected. 'Really, our visitor will think you were dragged up with no manners.'

'Please, I would like it if the girls call me Lily, ma'am. It is a pity about the weather, Penelope, for I would love you to show me around. Perhaps you can another day.'

'Why not show Lily the picture gallery, Jack?' Caroline suggested helpfully. 'Penny, you and Susan can help me look through the journals Jack brought us and see how we would like our new muslins made up. And then later Lily can tell us whether we will be bang up to the mode or sadly dowdy.'

Lily would have been more than happy to be curled up looking at the *Ladies' Journal,* but to refuse to go with Jack would have looked too pointed. She smiled politely and accompanied him up the main staircase and off down a passage she had not yet seen.

'It is very confusing, I am lost already,' she remarked as they turned a corner and went up a short flight of steps. *That's right, Lily, prattle away, anything but acknowledge you are alone with him.* 'I expect to have to rise at five in order to arrive at breakfast at a reasonable hour.'

'You will get used to it. For children, of course, it is the most wonderful playground. Mama used to live in dread of one of us vanishing and being found, years later, shut in a mysterious chest or locked in a haunted tower room.'

'She must have disliked Gothic tales then, that sort of thing constantly happens in those,' Lily observed. 'I enjoy them, but I *am* nervous of all these suits of armour. I keep thinking I can see them moving out of the corner of my eye.' She shivered, less out of any fear of the armour than from being so close to Jack, alone.

Here, in his own home, he was almost a stranger. It was as though Jack Lovell had retreated from her behind the front of Lord Allerton. 'Do you think I should have them polished?'

'What? The armour? I have no idea—are they supposed to be?' Lily went close and regarded one suit on its plinth. It had no rust, but it had dulled to an almost pewter shade.

'I was thinking the Great Hall looked a little worn and wondered how you would transform it, Lily. If the armour was polished, we could set more of it about in there. Suits of armour up the stairs and possibly some arrangements of weapons on the wall. What do you think?'

Lily regarded him. There was mischief, carefully repressed, in the curve of his mobile mouth and his lashes were lowered over eyes that he knew would betray him. 'I think that would look like a Great Hall in the medieval style,' she retorted tartly. 'As you already *have* a medieval hall, I can only conclude that you are teasing me by suggesting that you dress it up to be a pastiche of itself.'

With a flounce of skirts Lily marched off down the corridor. In a way, arguing with Jack felt much more comfortable than when he was being frigidly polite.

'I miss your style of interior decoration, Lily,' he remarked plaintively, following her.

'No, you do not, Jack Lovell, you miss being able mock it.' She turned to see where he was and found he was right behind her, trapping her neatly against the wall.

'Did I mock, Lily?' He was so close she could see the laughter lines at the corner of his eyes, the way his skin was paler where his hair had been ruthlessly cropped, the way the dark flint of his eyes had lightened into the grey of pebbles under water.

'You laughed at my crocodiles,' she said, breathless.

'Only a little bit,' he coaxed, resting one hand on the panelled wall, just by her right ear. 'You have to admit that a *chaise-longue* with scaly legs is just a trifle amusing, especially when they emerge from under the ruffles on your hem.'

'Very well, I suppose it is.' Was he going to kiss her, or just tease her all afternoon? And what would she do if he did kiss her? Lily swallowed hard as Jack moved closer, his hand brushing the fabric of her skirts at waist level. She could feel her breathing quickening, her eyelids lowering. He smelt just as she recalled, of—

'Careful, you'll fall.' Jack caught her neatly round the waist as the door she had not seen behind her opened to his touch and Lily found herself in a long gallery, lit on one side with tall windows and hung on the other with what looked like hundreds of pictures.

What a fool, to think that he had been about to kiss her—worse, to want him to. Lily smiled brightly, trying to ignore the all-too-familiar urge to reach out and touch Jack. 'What a lot of pictures.'

Inane! Try to think of something intelligent to say, you fool! All these ancestors…

Jack obviously shared her opinion of her originality. 'Yes, aren't there.' His voice was dry. 'They are of varying interest, but that is not why I brought you here.'

'No?' *And as it obviously is not to make love to me, or to abjectly beg my pardon for calling me totty-headed—really, that hurts more even than bird-witted!—just why are we here?* Lily made a show of studying the nearest canvas. As the rain lashing down outside and the thick cloud rendered the unlit room positively gloomy, she could make out little more than a dead stag.

'No. I want to get to the bottom of exactly what happened about the duel.'

'Why? I told you downstairs.' Lily tossed her head and moved on to the next picture. Now this was better—a pretty girl in an arbour and a lovely baroque frame, all ormolu curlicues.

'As it concerns my honour, I would like to know *exactly* what you did and who you told about it.' Jack was not sounding remotely amused any longer. 'Just how many people did you approach in your attempt to stop it?'

'I asked Lady Billington's advice, and she said it would be impossible to stop. And I asked Lord Gledhill—you know about that—and he almost had conniptions and so I asked Doctor Ord. That is all. Satisfied?' She glared at him over her shoulder, but his face was impossible to read in the gloom.

'No I am not *satisfied*.' Jack took several long strides down the gallery, unpleasantly reminiscent of the paces he had taken on the duelling ground. 'How the devil did you get Ord to take you with him?'

'I tricked him into telling me when and where and then told him I would go in my own carriage if he refused to help me.'

'You are unprincipled, manipulative, domineering…'

'Yes, of course I am. For a woman it is often necessary if one is to get what one wants. We do not have the freedom men have.'

'Thank God for that! I shudder to think what the result would be if you were given free rein.'

'You are just upset because you had successfully hidden the fact you were wounded from your family and I let the cat out of the bag. I am sorry about that, I would not have done it, truly, only I could not imagine how you could hide such a nasty gash.'

'Just how close were you that morning?' Jack asked softly. When he wanted to he could move like a cat, Lily had not realised he had come so near. She turned and cut around him, pretending to be intrigued by a group of smaller pictures hanging together further along the wall.

'I was in the tangled knot of undergrowth on the lip of the depression. Very close.'

'Close enough to be killed by a stray bullet, you little idiot!' The next thing Lily knew, she was flat up against the wall again, this time with Jack's hands one each side of her head, effectively caging her with his arms. Cautiously she ran a hand over the lumpy linen-fold panelling behind her; no convenient door handle this time.

'I never thought about that,' she confessed, shaken. If Adrian's shot had been angled upwards, it would have whistled past her head. If she had been lucky.

'No, of course you did not. Do you *ever* think through consequences, you maddening woman?'

The honest answer was, *Not often enough,* but Jack was perfectly capable of supplying that response for himself. Lily hung her head.

'Did you enjoy it?' Jack asked softly.

'What? Watching the duel?' Lily looked up abruptly. 'I was worried to death before and I was physically sick afterwards.'

'But did you enjoy it?' There was a huskiness in his voice

that stirred something deep and hot inside Lily. She was very aware of his closeness, his warmth, the male scent of him. With a burst of insight she realised that, under his anger with her, and his anxiety for her, he was aroused by the thought that she had been there and had seen him defending her honour.

'I…' She could not tear her eyes away from the heat in his. Their bodies were not touching, but she knew her skirts brushed against his legs, could almost feel the friction of the superfine cloth of his coat where his arms were only inches from her face.

'Did you, Lily?' *Oh, yes.* Looking back, she knew she had been stirred, immodestly, shamefully, stirred by the sight of him, the pistol in his hand, his naked, powerful torso, his control, his courage. The fact that two men fought over her.

'Yes,' she whispered, defeated by his will and her own honesty. 'I am not proud of it, but, yes.'

Jack did not move his hands, only leaned forward into her, bending his head until his mouth covered hers, pinning her between the breadth of his chest and the unyielding wall.

Trapped, Lily did not try to move, or want to. Her hands spread open on the oak and she lifted her face to him. She was learning now, learning the taste of him, the way his lips felt on hers, hot and shocking. And more heated, more shocking, the response of her own body, of her own tongue tangling with his, of her breasts, peaking and thrusting against his chest, of the way her hips arched against him so that she could feel the pressure of his arousal against her belly.

Jack's hands came away from the wall, one cupping the back of her head, holding her against the force of his kiss, as though she needed any restraint, the other moulding the curve of her buttock.

He was growling, deep in his throat, a sound that she felt almost more than she heard, a male anthem of possession. What was he seeing in his mind? What was he feeling? The cold air on his naked skin, the heat of fear in his belly, turned by courage into a steely determination? The weight of the pistol butt in his hand? Had he thought of her as he waited to kill or be killed?

Lily knew what she could see in her mind's eye, what she felt. The movement of hard muscle under bare skin. The strength and breadth of his shoulders, the power of those narrow hips, the unflinching stance, the fear in her stomach and the pride and love in her heart.

She twisted her head against his hand, broke away from his kiss. 'No. Stop it. This is wrong.'

'You want me.' His other hand still cupped her buttock, still held her against his aroused body.

'Yes. I am not proud of it, but, yes, I want you. Are you satisfied now I have admitted it?' Lily was panting with churning emotion; frustration, desire, anger, shame, love, all mixed and spun through her. 'You are very attractive Jack Lovell. Very male. But you do not need me to tell you that, do you? Why should I minister to your self-esteem?'

'Why not minister to it even more?' His teeth gleamed white in the shadowed room. From a great distance she could hear rain against glass. 'Do I need to tell you how much you arouse me, Lily? How much I want you? And you want me. Why fight it?'

Yes, why fight it? It seems so simple—let what we both want to happen, make love with Jack. Lily let her hands spread open on his chest, her head tip back again so she was looking up into his face again. Under her right palm she could feel Jack's heart racing. His face seemed more sharply defined to her, etched into lines of strength and of arrogance. He was watching her like a hawk while he waited for her answer, with all the focus and intensity he had shown on the duelling ground.

And this was a duel. He was bending her to his will with no doubt that she would yield to him. It simply was not in his breeding, in his pride, to believe she would deny him. She could feel her will wavering in the face of his dominance, just as Adrian had trembled as he faced him on the heath.

She could give in to him, and give in to her own desire. But the need to make love to him was not all there was. She *loved* him. She could not tell him, ever, and to be his mistress, for however long that lasted, however wonderful it was, felt like a betrayal of that emotion. She would be lying to both of them.

The force with which Lily launched herself away from the wall broke his hold and sent her several steps clear of him. She could not explain, all she could do was to defend herself with thoughtless, hurtful words.

'Oh, no! Oh, no, I am not going to fall into that trap, let my emotions be dazzled by what I think I want now, only to discover soon after that I was wrong. So wrong. I humiliated myself with Adrian Randall, thinking all I wanted was marriage and a title. I made a fool of myself by proposing to you, thinking that a business arrangement could sit with physical desire. Well, I have learned my lesson the hard way, my lord.

'If I need a stud stallion, if I want a lover, I will find one with no complications, and if I need a husband to be a father to my heirs, I will find one who can bring his own fortune with him. And for none of those roles do I need impoverished aristocrats who cannot even look after their own inheritance.'

For a moment she thought Jack was going to reach out and

yank her back into his arms. It was almost too dark in the room now to see his face, but she could hear his breathing, echoing her own panting breaths. Then he turned on his heel and stalked out, leaving the door to swing back on its hinges.

Jack did not stop until he reached his own chamber. He was breathing heavily as he entered it, but not from the winding flight of stairs he had just taken two at a time.

'Stud stallion!' Lily had a tongue like an adder. And she made him feel ashamed of himself, of what he felt naturally because he was a man, because he desired her. Loved her.

Stallion! Damn it, he could certainly fulfil that role for her. Just now he felt he could service every single doxy at Nell's, Newcastle's most notorious and largest brothel, and still be unsatisfied. When had he last had a woman? God knows, and all he was doing was working himself up into an unsatisfied lather over an acid-tongued little tease. *Impoverished aristocrats* indeed. What had possessed him to demand they become lovers? She excited him almost beyond reason and this was the result. Now, even if he tried to tell her the truth, that he loved her, he doubted she would believe him.

'My lord? Did you say something?' Denton was ordering his dressing table, polishing the silver-backed brushes with a soft cloth.

'My working clothes, if you please. I am going to the mine.'

'But it is pouring with rain, my lord.'

'Not underground it isn't Denton.' And there it was safe from interfering sisters, reproachful mothers—and Lily.

'You will need to take care of that arm, my lord.' Denton, radiating disapproval, opened the chest where he meticulously segregated Jack's working clothes. Jack was well aware that his valet considered it a disgrace that an earl should so much as set foot in a mine. If he did, it should be to view the operation only, at a safe distance and taking the advice of his manager. The fact that Jack was frequently found wielding a pick or puzzling over a problem with the ventilation shutters shocked Denton to the core and he rebelled in the only way he knew how, by insisting that Jack's filthy, torn, clothes were always immaculately laundered, mended and pressed after every wearing.

Jack pulled off his coat, threw down his fine linen shirt on to a chair and accepted a much-patched woollen smock in return. He sat on the edge of the bed and drew on thick stockings, a pair of loose canvas trousers and thrust his feet into the stout studded boots that Denton produced at arm's length.

'I do wish you would stop trying to get a shine on these.' The valet sniffed, not deigning to enter into a long-running wrangle, extracted a crisply ironed red-spotted kerchief from a drawer and placed it on the bed next to a leather waistcoat and a battered tricorne hat.

'You will wear the oiled coat, my lord?'

Jack regarded his transformed figure in the long mirror and grinned, suddenly relaxed, anticipating a long afternoon of down-to-earth, uncomplicated, male company. 'Yes please, Denton. Thank you. I will be returning for dinner, should Lady Allerton ask.'

'Yes my lord. I will ensure that there is plentiful hot water: it would not do to present a begrimed appearance with a guest present.'

Fully aware that Denton was attempting to make him feel like a grubby schoolboy skipping lessons, Jack ran downstairs, whistling between his teeth, to the further scandal of his butler and a footman.

'Jack! For goodness' sake, you are not going to the mine now?' It was Caroline, her arms full of fabric, crossing the landing into the room known to the staff as The Young Ladies' Sitting Room.

'I haven't been below ground since I got back from London. There are things to be done, to be looked at.'

'But where is Lily?'

'In the Long Gallery.' Something in his face must have betrayed him, for Caroline dumped the muslin unceremoniously into the sitting room and came back to glare at him. 'What have you done now?'

It was on the tip of his tongue to say *'I had a damn good try at seducing her'* and see what Caroline would do, but he swallowed the words. 'We argued. I will be back for dinner.'

The rain had stopped, some time during her journey back to her bedchamber. Lily found she could begin to navigate about the castle, more by looking out for distinctive suits of armour, than by anything else. 'Battle axe, sword, pointy thing on top...' she muttered to herself. She located the stairs leading up to her room and hesitated, wondering if she should seek out Caroline. But she rather suspected she was betrayingly flushed and damp-eyed and the thought of curling up in the window seat and having a long brood over the rain-soaked landscape felt safer.

Now what to do? What had possessed Jack just now? On the face of it, that was a foolish question. He had done it out of sheer lust and frustration. The uncomfortable idea that he had done it because of her money obtruded, but she dismissed it. If Jack was cynical enough to decide, after all, that he wanted her wealth, then he would hardly have proposed they become lovers in such a way. He would have kept his temper, and his passion, in check and wooed her in a civilised, if hypocritical, manner. Like Adrian had.

What would she have done if that scene had played out differently, if they had not been angry? What would have happened if he had tried to seduce her with soft words and gentle lovemaking?

What would it be like to be wooed by Jack? The hot pulse still beat distractingly inside her, the aftermath of their violent, angry passion. Lily found the thought of gentle courtship a comforting fantasy as she gazed out from her eyrie. Flowers, hand-kissing, compliments, a little flirtation, murmured sweet nothings. All the time in the world to think about what she should do, what she should say.

'Oh yes,' Lily whispered, a smile curving her lips. Below, a door banged shut and a tall figure strode out across the courtyard, his black greatcoat flapping behind him in the wind. It was unmistakably Jack; his long stride, the width of his shoulders, betrayed him. Lily glimpsed trousers, boots, a battered old hat and realised he must be on his way to the mine.

A *frisson* like the one that had run through her on the duelling ground made her shiver: he was so strong, so masculine. His command had nothing to do with title or class, it was bred in his bones and everything feminine in her responded to it, however hard she tried for control.

'Lily?' It was Caroline, peeping round the door. 'Am I interrupting? Are you resting?'

'I was a little tired,' Lily fibbed. 'It was rather dark in the gallery and difficult to see the pictures. Lord Allerton has gone out.'

'He has gone to the mine,' Caroline said briskly. 'He will be back for dinner.' She sounded a trifle out of spirits—it must be the weather.

'Oh, it wasn't that I was wondering or anything…' Lily could hear she was floundering and made an effort to pull herself together. 'I would love to see the mine one day—could you take me to see it? When it stops raining, of course.'

'Certainly.' Caroline came and perched on the window seat beside Lily. 'But why not ask Jack? I understand quite a lot, at least about the work above ground, but not much about the deep mine.'

'Because he will think I want to interfere again,' Lily replied bleakly. 'But I am very interested. I think I might persuade my trustees to invest in mines in the Midlands, where there are canals. They are so dubious about the transport up here, or the lack of it, that is the trouble. Such old stick-in-the muds about new technologies, bless them.' And she wanted to see the place that obsessed Jack so much, touch him in some way through it. Touch him in the only way that seemed to be safe.

Chapter Nineteen

Lily did not expect to see Jack at dinner, but he strolled into the salon where the ladies were congregating before the meal, looking immaculate. Her surprise must have shown on her face, for he came over to her side, one brow raised quizzically.

'Did you expect to see me with black fingernails and coal dust in my hair? I scrub up reasonably well, I believe.'

Lily had had an afternoon, in the intervals between adjudicating in spirited arguments over fashions, to decide on her future tactics with Jack. She could not make her excuses to Lady Allerton, pack her bags and sweep out, nor could she be thrown into blushing confusion every time she saw him. She was too honest to believe that this was all his fault, so there appeared to be only one tactic: ignore it and play games.

She smiled, lowered her eyelashes and murmured, 'You most certainly do.' She was rewarded by both his brows flying up and a glint of grudging amusement in his eyes.

'Society tricks, Miss France?'

'My aunt always emphasises how important it is to minister to a gentleman's vanity,' she replied sweetly.

'And why is that? You appear to have only just recalled this piece of advice, unless I have been very unobservant.'

'Firstly, because if one does not, then they sulk; secondly, because it is the best way to get what one wants.'

'And have you ever observed me to sulk, Lily?'

'Well…' Lily flirted her fan and was rewarded by a reluctant grin.

'To take your second point, what is it that you want from me?' Jack had lowered his voice and Lily kept her face straight. *Now he thinks I am going to blush and stammer and reveal that I really want him to…that I want him.*

'Why, to let me stay here a little longer and to study this wonderful old building, of course. I do believe that I could bring the Baronial style back into fashion in London if I put my mind to it.'

'What? Crumbling, gloomy and atmospheric?'

'No, romantic, solid—and brightly coloured. I like bright colours.'

'I *had* noticed that—but there are none here.' She had his interest, Lily realised. He was no longer playing games.

'But there were. Look at this tapestry.' She moved to one side and indicated a hanging. It was muted, mostly greens and browns, dull yellows and deep reds. 'See—have you never looked at the back?' She flipped up the corner, revealing the almost unfaded original colours, glowing like jewels. 'Imagine the walls, hung with these when they were new. The armour gleaming silver, the torches in their sconces, the firelight, the banners fluttering.'

'Lily, you are a romantic—I had not realised it.'

'Yes,' she conceded, knowing he was teasing, but choosing to take it seriously. 'I am. But I am also a realist. Sometimes those two things clash and when they do, chasing the romantic dream is usually a foolish thing to do. Sometimes it takes me a little while to realise what is possible and what is not, but I get there in the end.' She made herself hold his gaze steadily, praying that the message she was trying to send showed, and not the love and the yearning under it.

'*Touché*, Lily,' Jack murmured as Lady Allerton came up to them.

'We were just talking about romance,' Lily explained brightly. 'Knights, and battlements and banner waving.'

'That, or we were duelling,' Jack added, earning him a puzzled look from his mother and a sharp glance from Lily. It would never do to underestimate Jack Lovell. 'What have you all been doing this afternoon?' he asked as his sisters joined them.

'Gloating over the lovely dress lengths you brought us, and turning out all the pieces and trimmings we have squirrelled away. Lily looked at the latest fashion plates with us—she had some more in her own luggage as well—and has been making suggestions.' Susan was still overflowing with excitement about the experience.

Lily met Jack's eye and said earnestly, 'I have recommended purchasing considerably more trimmings, a number of sprays of artificial flowers and practising appliqué work, ruching and French pleating for hems. I think padded and quilted hems might be a little difficult to attempt at home, but might be tried.' This provocation appeared to be working, so she added, 'I think the muslins you brought are a little plain, if you do not mind me saying so, all those creams and pastels—I recommend having them dyed. Strong yellows, hotter pinks and bright blues would all be excellent. And, of course, the use of gold and silver lamé.'

'Over my dead body are you parading yourselves—'

Penelope burst into giggles, and the other two girls laughed. 'Jack, Lily is teasing you! She has been making the most lovely sketches for us, showing what the gowns in the fashion plates look like with most of the ornamentation removed,' Caroline explained. 'Lily says that no *lady* would appear hung around and bedizened in that way, they just show them like that for impact.'

Lily, conscious that her evening dress had been pared down to elegant simplicity by Janet's skilful hands, met Jack's eyes with an expression of limpid innocence.

She should have known better. 'I really cannot pretend to understand the rules of female fashion,' Jack confessed, taking his mother's arm as Grimwade announced dinner. He waited until the ladies had settled around the table before taking his place at the head and shaking out his napkin. 'Does this rule about simplicity not apply to riding habits? Because I am sure I recall a most striking garment of yours, Miss France.'

'Indeed.' Lily could feel herself colouring up. 'That was an extreme of fashion, I will admit, and probably an error of judgement in retrospect.'

'I thought it most attractive,' Jack observed blandly, gesturing for Grimwade to start serving. 'But then, what do I know?'

'Do describe it, my dear Miss France,' Lady Allerton interjected.

'It is a deep sea-green superfine, with a very long skirt,' Lily said, not meeting Jack's eyes.

'Go on,' urged Susan.

'Completely plain in the skirt. The bodice fastens with several rows of frogging after the military fashion and there is a little bolero jacket. And the sleeves have epaulettes and more frogging.'

'Do not, whatever you do, omit the hat,' Jack urged.

'It is modelled on a shako,' Lily said repressively. 'With ostrich plumes and a cockade of French lace.'

'It sounds very dramatic,' Caroline observed. 'And I imagine the colour would look wonderful on you. I think I would find all that frogging and the jacket a little heavy in appearance, but perhaps I am not envisioning it correctly. And how do you manage your hair under a shako? I have admired them before, but I cannot see what one can do unless one has a crop.'

'I just bundled it up inside,' Lily admitted, whisked back to the woman-only gossip of the afternoon and forgetting that Jack and the servants were in the room. 'And the bodice is very form-fitting.'

'Ooh!' Penelope sighed. 'How *dashing*.'

'It was. Very.' On the surface Jack's voice held nothing but simple agreement, but Lily's gaze flew to his face and saw the heat in his eyes and the suggestion in his slightly parted lips. He had never commented on that habit—had he? She racked her brains as she accepted the dish of peas from Susan beside her. There had been some recognition in his expression that she was riding out to make a splash that day, but when she had come back to his room and pulled off her hat…

She could almost feel the weight of her hair tumbling free, very improperly. And she could recall that Jack had seemed rather strange, distant perhaps, that afternoon. *Oh, goodness, he thought that outfit provocative and now it is making him think about…about the sort of thing we were doing this afternoon.*

'But not, I think, the sort of habit that would be suitable away from London.' Lady Allerton's pronouncement flattened Penny, who was quite obviously calculating how she would look in it herself. 'But we will need a trip into Newcastle to take the dress lengths and the sketches to the modiste. Presumably we will be able to have the use of the carriage horses tomorrow, Lovell?'

'Certainly you may, Mama.'

'Thank you, dear. I was surprised you wanted them for ploughing, but then, I have never understood agriculture. What exactly are you ploughing?'

Caroline broke into a fit of coughing, the footman hastened to fill her water glass and Jack made a considerable business of ensuring his sister was quite all right. It occurred to Lily that he had not answered his mother's question, but if she did not pursue it, a guest hardly could.

'I hope I will have news tomorrow about my own carriage. I really should call on my agent and there is also a warehouse I want to look at.'

'I am sure we can fit all that in,' Lady Allerton said, nodding to the footman to clear the first remove.

'But we wanted Lily to help us choose things,' Penny protested.

'Miss France has more important things to do,' her mother reproved her.

'My business should not take too much time.' Lily smiled reassurance at the flushed girl. 'I will simply call upon Mr Lovington's office and collect some paperwork and have him arrange a visit to the warehouse later in the week when I return.'

'Do you mean to pore over dusty old ledgers?' Penny asked. 'Jack is bad enough—I did not think ladies had to do such things.'

'I enjoy it,' Lily said lightly. 'I find it satisfying to make things work better than they did before.'

'Miss France is a notable businesswoman, and an example to you to pay attention to your lessons.' Jack sounded infuriatingly pious and earned himself a scowl from his youngest sister and a laugh from everyone else. Lily found herself relaxing into the warmth of this close, loving family.

It was only later, as she climbed into the high, curtained bed, and snuggled down to sleep, that she was conscious of the small ache of envy. What joy to have sisters to share with, how wonderful to grow up with a mother to guide you, what a pleasure to have an elder brother to tease and look after you. All the money in the world could not buy her those treasures.

Lily woke the next morning with the disconcerting feeling that she had been dreaming, but with no recollection of the night at all. She had left strict instructions for Janet to wake her in plenty of time to be down for breakfast.

She had been only half-joking when she had told Jack she was worried about getting lost. She was also distinctly nervous that she did not know how one went on in a castle. Luncheon and dinner had appeared reassuringly normal, but for all she knew, breakfast was different up here in the north. She was sure she had heard something about porridge, which did not sound very appealing. Or perhaps that was Scotland.

To her relief, breakfast at Allerton could have been taking place in any London house containing three lively young ladies. Porridge did not make an appearance and Jack was reassuringly untalkative, remaining immersed in his newspaper and apparently content to allow the chatter about modes and bonnets to wash over his head.

Only when he was drinking his second cup of coffee did he remark, 'You will be uncomfortably tight with five in the carriage, Mama. I need to visit Newcastle. I was going to take my curricle and there would be room for—'

'Me!' Penelope was bouncing up and down in her seat. 'You promised me you would take me in the curricle next time we went into Newcastle.'

'I was going to offer the seat to Miss France. She is our guest, Penny.'

'And a promise is a promise. I am more than happy to travel in the carriage, Lord Allerton. But thank you for the offer.' *Goodness, an hour alone in a curricle with Jack, even with a groom up behind, would be terrifying—in fact, even more so with a groom, when one would have to watch every word one said.*

'As you wish, Miss France.' The twist of his lips told her he knew perfectly well that she was nervous of travelling with him. 'I will take you up on the return journey.' Lily opened her mouth to protest, realised just in time that it would sound most ungracious to do so, and shut it again with a snap. He was smiling now, the exasperating man, although what he hoped to achieve, other than to infuriate her, she had no idea.

Expecting a somewhat workaday team, Lily was surprised at the sight of the four matched bays harnessed to Lady Allerton's rather shabby travelling carriage and the neat pair in the curricle.

Her wonder changed to suspicion as they bowled down the drive and on to the road and they remained surrounded by unbroken grazing and coppices. 'Caroline,' she said, low-voiced, while Lady Allerton was busy discussing a distant cousin's impending wedding with Susan.

'Yes, Lily?'

'Where *exactly* were these horses ploughing yesterday, Caroline?'

'Um…'

'They were nowhere near a plough, were they? And the pair in the curricle did not have new shoes either.'

'Oh, dear, you have caught me out—I am afraid I kidnapped you.'

'But why? I mean, I am a complete stranger, I was obviously at outs with Jack…'

'I liked you. And it seemed so inhospitable to let you drive off all the way back to Newcastle in the rain after Jack had been such a grouch.'

Lily regarded her doubtfully. It appeared to her that there was rather more to it than Caroline was saying. She had recognised Lily from Jack's description of her, and she obviously knew about the duel and his wounded arm, unlike the rest of her family—but that ought to have made her hostile, not welcoming.

But Lily could hardly dispute the point or probe further with the others in the carriage, so all she could do was smile and accept it. It was not until they had driven a further three miles and there was a lull in the conversation that Lily recalled that Jack had said nothing about Caroline's transparent fabrication. Had he really wanted her to stay? Lily watched the passing countryside abstractedly while she wrestled with the problem—and the unanswerable question: *what good will it do me to know?*

'Where is your agent's office, Miss France?' Lady Allerton broke into her thoughts and she realised they were coming into Newcastle.

'I have it written down.' Lily flipped through her notebook

and offered it to Lady Allerton. 'I am afraid I have no idea where it is.'

'Very conveniently placed, as it happens. We can leave the carriages at the Maid's Head, which is what we usually do. I have some calls to make and Lovell can escort you to your agent's. With Caroline, of course.' Lily managed to keep from blushing. What Lady Allerton would think if she knew what had taken place yesterday in her own picture gallery she shuddered to imagine, but now she thought it correct for Lily to be chaperoned in public with Jack. For which one could only be grateful.

'We can meet for an light luncheon and you can all do your shopping after that, while Jack sees to his own business,' Lady Allerton continued, satisfied she had organised everyone's conflicting needs to a nicety.

The agent's office was so commonplace to Lily that she was amused at the well-bred interest Caroline was showing at being in such surroundings. A clerk came forward with a polite enough greeting, which turned to positively obsequious grovelling when he realised with whom he was dealing. They were ushered into an inner office with much ceremony. Lily kept an eye on the clock and was not surprised to see Jack doing exactly the same thing.

'Taking a suspiciously long time,' he observed. 'Do you think they are digging out the second set of books?'

'I sincerely hope not,' Lily said with feeling. 'I really do not want to spend a week going through everything with a fine-tooth comb… Good day, Mr Lovington. I imagine you are surprised to see me.'

As soon as she saw him Lily thought she could see the problem: Lovington was a worrier. Appointed by her trustees several years ago, he had seemed a straightforward, cautious and reliable man, but now he looked ineffectual and indeci-

sive. Unless he was a first-class actor, Lily could not imagine
he had the wit to defraud her.

'Miss France! What an honour! I had no idea! Is something
wrong?'

'Nothing, I am sure, Mr Lovington.' He was not going to
recall his manners without a prompt, so she introduced her
companions. 'Miss Lovell and Lord Allerton accompany me,
as you see; I am staying with them and thought I should not
let the opportunity pass to drop in and see how you go on.'

Now she had met him again, she certainly did not want to
find herself a guest in his house. It had not occurred to her
just how uncomfortable that might be, given that she wished
to scrutinise the books. Could she continue to stay at the castle? Caroline and Lady Allerton had both been most pressing. Lily fought a brisk battle with her conscience and lost.
She wanted to stay at the castle, for several reasons; not least
was the completely unacceptable one that she wanted to be
near Jack. Well, she had spent her entire life doing more or
less what she wanted; while her hostess appeared to enjoy her
presence, she would stay.

Half an hour later, Lily emerged with a clerk and a boy trotting at her heels, both laden with ledgers and the keys to the
warehouse, which Mr Lovington had obviously been dither-
ing about—should he visit it himself? Could he make a decision without further guidance? Lily had firmly removed the
keys and assured him she would assess it.

Her trustees were certain that a location nearer the water-
front would be advantageous, and pointed out that the current
warehouse was too small. Lily was not so sure they were correct, and increasingly certain she could not trust Mr Lovington's judgement in any case.

'I cannot decide whether he is lazy, incompetent or merely lacking in confidence,' she murmured to Jack. 'Something will have to be done about him.' She nodded briskly to the clerk. 'Just run those ledgers along to the Maid's Head and have them placed in Lady Allerton's private parlour,' she instructed. They hurried on ahead, Lily strolling after them until they reached the corner. 'I just want to make sure they actually get there,' she confided.

'What a very suspicious mind you do have, Miss France!' Jack grinned at her and Lily found herself smiling back.

'I do like to make sure.' Something across the street caught her eye as she tucked the warehouse keys in her reticule. 'Caroline, I think that lady is waving at you.'

'Oh, yes. Jack, see, it is Jane Henderson and her sister Kate.' Caroline waved back and the Henderson ladies, their maid on their heels, joined the Allerton party.

'We were just on our way to visit Mrs Hodges,' Jane explained once the introductions had been made. 'You remember her from dancing lessons, Miss Allerton—she was Maria Bates. She has just had her first baby.'

'But of course I remember her! Dear Maria—how wonderful. What a pity I cannot call today, but do give her my warmest wishes.'

'Why can you not visit?' Lily asked. 'Is her house so very far?'

'No, I think only five minutes' walk away, but there are rather a lot of us.'

'I meant alone, with your friends. We can meet you back at the Maid's Head.'

'I will send my maid back with you,' Miss Henderson offered. 'Maria would love to see you.'

Jack regarded Caroline's retreating back as, times to meet up again at the inn agreed, she tripped off happily with the Henderson sisters. 'So much for my Mama's careful provision of a chaperon for you, Miss France.'

'I am sure she was only concerned about me going to a place of business without a female companion, not that she thought I needed chaperoning when in your company,' Lily said repressively, and with a complete disregard for past experience. 'If you would just see me back to the Maid's Head, I will wait for the others.'

'Who, as we agreed, will be another hour and a half at least. You will be bored to tears. Shall we go and look at this warehouse?'

'Have we time?'

'I should think so, if we take a hackney carriage.' Jack hailed one as he spoke, calling up the address Mr Lovington had given Lily before handing her in. 'At least this will eliminate it altogether if it is no good, and if it is promising you can always pay another visit.'

'I suspect that this *is* a situation where Lady Allerton would expect me to have a chaperon,' Lily remarked thoughtfully as the hackney headed down to the quayside, clattering over the cobbles.

'Not the most promising location for attempting to ravish a lady,' Jack murmured, watching her from under hooded lids.

'Adrian did not find it inhibiting, if you recall.' Lily thought back to that foggy night and shuddered.

'That was a private carriage, presumably—quite unexceptionable for seduction, whereas this vehicle is thoroughly inappropriate.' Jack prodded a worn seat disdainfully. 'I can assure you that your virtue is completely safe in this.'

'I have no doubt about that whatsoever,' Lily agreed

doucely, letting her reticule, weighed down by the heavy warehouse keys, thud meaningfully into her palm.

From the glint in Jack's eyes she wondered for a moment whether he would regard that as a challenge, then the coach jolted to a halt. From the window she could see a glimpse of the Tyne, its waters almost obscured by river craft large and small, and the noise and odours of the docks filled the carriage as Jack opened the door.

'Well, Miss France? Armed with your loaded reticule, are you willing to venture into a deserted warehouse with me?'

Chapter Twenty

'**C**ertainly I am.' Lily fished out the keys and her purse. 'If you will open the doors, I will just pay the driver.'

Jack removed the keys firmly and handed up some coins to the jarvey.

'I said I would pay!'

'Do you think I cannot afford the hire of a hack?' He had turned back to the wicket gate in the big wooden doors.

'Of course not, but this is my business…'

'This needs oiling, and the lock requires replacing before you put anything of value in here.' Jack heaved the gate open with a screaming of rusty hinges. 'Very well, you pay me back for the hackney fare, and I will invoice you for my opinion of this door. And, of course, I must work out the proportion of your time spent up here on business and charge you board and lodging for that part of your time spent at Allerton.'

He ducked through the wicket. 'It looks safe enough in here.'

'That is not what I meant, you stiff-rumped idiot!' Lily scrambled through and swung irritably at Jack's back with her reticule. Without the weight of the keys it was like swatting an oak tree with a leaf.

'Language, Miss France!' Jack reproved. 'Is it big enough?' He began to pace off the length. Lily left him to it and, with a dubious glance at the holes in the roof and some rapid mental calculation on the likely costs of repairs, went to explore the rooms at the end of the great empty space.

They had been built within the warehouse like sheds within a barn. Lily poked about inside, deciding they would have to be completely demolished, then saw the stairs in one corner. They must lead to what was effectively a flat roof. She was rapidly coming to the conclusion that this warehouse was going to need too much work to make it useable, but a view from a height might give her a better perspective on it.

The stairs creaked as she climbed, her skirts gathered up in one hand, the other clinging to what remained of a crude handrail attached to the wall. Three-quarters of the way up she was coming to the conclusion that perhaps this was not the best idea she had ever had, by the time she reached the top and stepped out onto a crude platform of worm-eaten planks, she was sure of it.

Lily turned round cautiously and put her foot down onto the top step. Some instinct warned her; she lifted it back, but too late. With a groan the rickety structure parted company with whatever rusting nails had been holding it to the wall and it fell to the stone floor beneath with a crash.

Choking in the cloud of dust and cobwebs that rose from the hole, Lily staggered back, felt the planks creaking ominously and froze where she was.

'Lily!'

'Here! I am all right, but I cannot get down.'

There was a sound of crashing below and Jack appeared, clambering over the ruined remains of the stairs.

'What the hell are you doing up there!' he demanded, craning his neck to look up at her. 'Of all the bloody stupid, damned idiotic...'

'Totty-headed?' Lily supplied faintly, finding a rusted piece of iron sticking out of the wall and taking a firm hold on it.

'What?' he bellowed, making the old building echo.

'Totty-headed. I think you forgot that. You are quite right and please do not shout any more—you are shaking the building and I do not think this floor is going to hold for much longer.'

'You cannot come down this way, the wreckage is too fragile for you to land on or for me to climb up.' The fury had gone from his voice and he sounded reassuringly calm. Lily began to think that she would not, after all, end up a crumpled heap on the flagstones below.

She lost sight of him and instinctively grabbed the ironwork with both hands; it broke away, leaving her with nothing but a fistful of rust. Underfoot the boards creaked ominously. 'Jack?'

'I am here, underneath you. I can just see you through the cracks in the floor. Can you take a big step back? Yes, like that. Now the other foot. Good. There is a bigger beam under there.' The new patch of floor did not sag so alarmingly, that was true. Lily put her arms out and used them to keep her balance. 'Now walk straight forward until you get to the edge.' Like a tightrope walker, Lily teetered forward until she could look over. It seemed a long way down.

Jack appeared, foreshortened from her viewpoint, his shoulders covered with dust, which must have showered down as he moved beneath her. 'Sit down on the edge.'

'What?'

'Sit down, and hang your legs over the edge.'

'I can't!' It was hideously high up.

'Why not? Lily, this is not the time to worry about a man looking up your skirts. Besides, I have seen your legs and very nice they are too.'

'Oh!' Lily sat down with a thump, then remembered that she was scared and shut her eyes.

'Now jump.'

'What!' Her eyes flew open. 'Are you mad? Go and get a ladder or something.'

'There is no time. Lily, believe me, you can jump or you can fall. Jump and I will catch you.'

She stared down, thankful that she was sitting, for her legs were trembling. Jack just stood there like a rock, arms held out. '*Lily!* Jump!'

So she did, pushing off with her hands. It was endless, and yet over in a second. Jack caught her in a tumble of limbs and petticoats and took two long strides back as the beam gave way and the makeshift roof hit the ground with a rumble like thunder.

Was it worth the five minutes of absolute terror to achieve a few moments with Lily in his arms, clinging to his neck and quivering? Probably not, especially as she was presumably quivering with fear and quite patently not with the thrill of being in his embrace.

'Lily? Are you hurt?' A violent shake of her head and a tightening of her arms around his neck were the only responses. Jack easily resisted the thought that perhaps he should set her down and walked instead to the other end of the warehouse.

He found a crate and sat on it, holding Lily on his knee.

She was still shaking, so he insinuated a hand under her chin and pushed up her face. 'Lily?'

She was glowing with colour, her eyes were sparkling with excitement rather than the tears he was expecting and she was quivering, not with fright, but with excitement. 'That was wonderful!'

'It was *what?*' Jack demanded. Ready to comfort, cuddle and possibly caress her, this was like a punch in the stomach.

'Wonderful. Jumping like that. For a moment, a split second, it was like flying. I was so frightened, and then I jumped, and I wasn't scared any more.'

'Possibly because you knew I was going to catch you.'

'Of course. But it was something so exhilarating. Jack, they jump out of balloons, don't they? With things called parachutes?'

'I think so. But ladies do not go up in balloons. Women do not go up in balloons. Full stop. Which means they do not come down from balloons, by any method whatsoever.' Best to flatten that idea before she took it one step further. Too late.

'Only because all the aeronauts are men at the moment— I suppose that all their patrons are too. But it is merely a question of who is paying for the ascent, sponsoring the balloon. Is not that so? If one were paying the aeronauts, they would have to take whomever their patron told them to.'

She was wide-eyed with interest and calculation. One part of him wanted to applaud, one part—most of him—wanted to bundle her up, rush her south and press her into the restraining arms of her trustees with the demand that they shut her up for her own safety. To protest was, he suspected from experience, enough to encourage her. Thankfully Lily appeared to be talking herself out of it.

'But what would one wear? Skirts would be most impractical! To adopt breeches would cause a scandal. I shall have to think about it.'

'Yes, do that,' Jack urged with feeling, provoking a gurgle of amusement from Lily.

'I am sorry to tease you. You were very brave to catch me. I did not hurt you, did I?'

'No, not at all,' Jack lied. Lily's slender body arriving in his arms with such suddenness and force had jolted him back on his heels and his shoulders felt half-wrenched out of their sockets, but he realised he would have died rather than admit it. He mocked himself silently for needing to appear heroic in her eyes: first wanting to preen like a peacock because she had watched him duelling and had admitting being stirred by it, now this.

Jack looked down into the wide green eyes that were smiling up into his with amused concern and felt not just his loins, but his heart, contract. He had made love to Lily, he had fought with her, he had spurned her proposal and here they still were. He wanted her with a force that stunned him. She confessed to finding him desirable and most of the time seemed to like and trust him.

What if he tried wooing her properly, in both senses of the word? Chastely, slowly, with flowers and flirtation? Would she react as she had in the Long Gallery with anger and with words that still burned like acid whenever he thought of them?

She would have her title, he would have the woman he loved and all the money he could possibly need and the lovemaking would be…spectacular. And there could be more than that: he could assist in the business. He was not like Randall, he did not look down on commerce and he had experience that would be valuable. They had been a good partnership today, hadn't they?

For a moment the vision of what life might be like swam in front of his eyes. And what would that make him? A kept man, that is what he would be, however much he could assist. Taking a wife with money was a sensible, practical thing to do, there was no disputing that. Men did it all the time—families allied themselves as a matter of course, with an eye to linking up lands, consolidating fortunes. But this was different, this was too extreme a difference in fortunes to be decent...

Could he do it? Could he buy happiness by selling his soul? Lily sat there, patiently waiting for him to finish his thought, her body warm and confiding against his. He focused on her face and she smiled a little so he caught a glimpse of even white teeth. His need for her must have shown somehow, for as he watched she became very still, so that he was conscious of her breathing. Her lids, heavy with sooty lashes, dropped, shielding her thoughts, but her mouth betrayed her. Her lips parted and she ran the tip of her tongue across the sweet, soft curve of her lower lip. Jack could feel himself bending towards her.

He is going to kiss me. Perhaps, after all, she had not been daydreaming and Jack truly was going to woo her with soft kisses and gentle flirtation.

'Lily.' His voice was husky and seemed to resonate through her. How had she lived for twenty-six years without ever hearing anyone speak her name like that before?

'Yes?' This time he would ask her to marry him, and she would say *yes*. They could work out all the problems, she would learn tact, she would learn good taste, she could even learn economy...

'Lily, we cannot go on like this.'

'I know.'

'We argue a lot.'

'Yes.'

'We both have our fair share of pride.'

'Yes.'

'We seem to have a very strong physical attraction to each other.'

'Oh, yes.' She shut her eyes.

'We cannot go on like this.'

'No. You said that. I agree with you.' *Just kiss me, then ask me!*

'I think we should—'

'Yes!'

'Just avoid being alone together.'

'*What?*' Lily bounced to her feet, eyes wide open.

'Behave in a proper, conventional manner. As we should have been, all along. And I blame myself.' As she was standing, Jack got to his feet courteously. 'We have agreed that marriage is out of the question. It would be most improper to act on the attraction between us in any other way. Your trustees have ruled out a business relationship. But I do not want to lose you Lily.'

Lily found she was regarding her hands, twisting the cords of her reticule and not looking at Jack. How could she look at him, watch his face, while he consigned whatever it was that was between them to the anodyne realms of propriety?

'No,' she agreed slowly, keeping every trace of how she felt out of her voice. 'No, I would not want to lose you either. As an acquaintance.' She looked up. For one moment she thought she saw disappointment on Jack's face; but that was ridiculous, she was agreeing with him, it must have been a trick of the light.

'Good.' He was brisk, obviously relieved by her agreement: she had been mistaken about that fleeting expression of yearning. Then his face changed from serious thoughtfulness to almost laughable horror. 'Oh, my Go…goodness. Look at the state of your clothes.'

'And yours.' Lily could not help laughing. 'You look as though a building has collapsed around you and then a woman fell on top of you!'

'Good manners prevents me from telling you what your appearance resembles,' Jack grinned back. 'So what, exactly, do you suggest we tell my mama we have been doing?'

'First of all we find a hackney carriage and then we do what we can on the journey back to the inn to retrieve matters.' Lily delved into her reticule. 'I do have a hairbrush in here, and some pins.'

Struggling in the confines of a lurching hackney carriage to brush off dust and cobwebs, straighten clothing, pin up Lily's hair and pluck wood splinters out of Jack's, reduced both of them to an unfortunate state of juvenile giggles.

They got out of the carriage in the inn yard, struggling for composure in the face of Jack's assembled family. Lady Allerton swept one comprehensive glance over the pair of them and declared, 'We will go inside for luncheon.'

Trailing up the stairs behind Penelope, Lily whispered, 'I feel as though I am twelve again and have been caught skipping lessons to go out scrumping apples.'

'Me too. What happened to you? I got whipped by my tutor.'

'I had to sit in the corner balancing a grammar primer on my head to teach me the importance of decorum.'

Jack's raised eyebrow made it quite clear that Lily's unfortunate governess had failed in this endeavour.

'What on earth happened to you two?' Penelope demanded, the moment the door was closed.

'The roof fell off a building, very close by, and Jack rescued me,' Lily said promptly. It was true, if misleading, and earned her an admiring look from her fellow adventurer. Her respectable acquaintance. Her lost love.

'Outrageous,' Lady Allerton declared. 'One is not safe in the streets these days. As if beggars and pickpockets were not enough, now we have buildings collapsing!'

The rest of the day passed decorously enough. The combined efforts of the chambermaid and Caroline rendered their appearance respectable enough to complete the day's business, Lily pressing the warehouse keys into Jack's hand with a silent plea to do what he could to explain to the agent what had occurred.

The ladies completed their shopping to their perfect satisfaction and Penelope's day was crowned with glory by being allowed to drive back again with her brother in the curricle. Caroline explained, once they had set off, that she did not feel that some of the childbed details from her visit to Mrs Hodges were quite suitable for Penny's tender ears.

Lily was not at all certain she wanted to hear them either. Remarks such as *seven pounds and eight ounces,* and *in labour for thirty hours* made her feel quite dizzy, although Caroline and even Susan were taking these horrid revelations perfectly calmly.

'I suppose you do not visit many lying-in mothers, Miss French,' Lady Allerton remarked. 'As we have many tenants, naturally the older girls and I do so quite often.'

'Oh, yes, I can imagine you would.' There was an entire world out there, of tenants and one's obligations to them, that Lily knew nothing about. By the time the Lovell sisters mar-

ried they would know just how to manage the domestic duties
of an estate, whereas if she and Jack had been so foolish as
to… Her mind baulked at the thought, then she made herself
follow it through. If they had married. She would have had
to learn all these things about tenants from scratch; as for
childbirth, that would have had to be encountered too, very
personally indeed.

The damp moorlands and solid clumps of windswept
beech trees passed the carriage windows while Caroline and
Susan left the subject of babies and began to bicker gently
over which of the new ribbons would look best with Mama's
second-best muslin.

Lily gazed unseeing out of the window and thought about
children. She had never considered them before, assuming
that babies would come along as a consequence of marriage.
The image of Adrian's children had never entered her imagination, but now she found herself trying to conjure up Jack's.
Her children with Jack. What would they have looked like?
Would they have had her dark red hair, or his black silk?
Green eyes or flint? Her impetuosity and stubbornness or his
pride and courage?

Possibly the poor little things would have had the worst
characteristics of both parents and would have had red hair
and a forceful chin allied to a stubborn nature and a regrettable taste for gold and glitter. She would never know.

'A penny for your thoughts, Lily,' Susan said brightly.
'They must be very interesting, for you were smiling, and now
you look quite melancholy.'

'My thoughts? Only fantasy,' Lily prevaricated. 'I was
thinking about…about a play I saw.'

'And was it a tragedy?'

'I hope not,' she said earnestly, only realising, when the

words were out of her mouth, that they would make no sense to her audience.

The bustle of arrival at the castle saved her from having to explain herself, although Caroline's quizzical glance warned her that perhaps she saw more than Lily found entirely comfortable.

The footman stood patiently while the ladies tumbled out of the carriage, pressing parcels into his hands, issuing instructions on what was to go where and impressing upon him that he must be absolutely certain that Miss Susan's new bonnet did not get crushed.

The curricle had arrived just before them and Jack was on the ground, reaching up his hands to lift Penny down. It made a charming picture: the strong big brother lifting down the pretty girl. One day he would be standing like that, lifting his daughter down, tossing her up just a little to make her squeal as Penny, despite all her pretensions to be almost a young lady, was doing uninhibitedly.

Behind Lily, Caroline laughed. 'Jack spoils that child outrageously.'

'I think it charming,' Lily retorted. 'He will make an excellent father.'

'Indeed he will. Perhaps we should find him a wife,' Caroline said lightly. 'I rely on you to help me, Lily—I am sure between us we can find him a charming bride.'

Chapter Twenty-One

'**Y**ou have managed to tear yourselves away from your purchases, I see.' Jack uncoiled himself from the depths of a wing chair in front of the fireplace in the drawing room as Lily and Caroline came in. 'I was resigned to dining alone this evening.'

'Well, I think we have done very well,' Caroline congratulated herself. 'Both Lily and I resisted the temptation to put on anything new tonight, but Mama purchased a very dashing turban and is trying it out on us before she risks it in company and Susan and Penny are bickering over who is going to wear the gauze shawl they bought jointly.'

'Do turbans take a long time?' Jack enquired with a reasonable pretence of interest.

'This one does,' Caroline chuckled. 'Mama is having doubts about it and Maria must have done her hair about three times already in an attempt to please her. For goodness' sake, admire it lavishly when she finally appears.'

'Very well, I will do my best.' Lily felt Jack's eyes on her and struggled to find a topic for small talk. She had never had the slightest problem in talking to him before. Now, when they were supposedly behaving in a manner that should have put all embarrassments behind them, she felt more awkward than she had ever done.

'Did your business prosper this afternoon?' she enquired, sounding to her own ears just like her prosiest cousin, Frederica.

'Thank you, yes. And I called at your agent's office to return that item you had forgotten.'

'I am grateful, I hope it was not out of your way.' What was the matter with her? After the silliness of trying to make themselves respectable in the hackney carriage had subsided, a pall of stultifying shyness seemed to have fallen on her. Lily kept her gaze on her clasped hands, and after a moment picked up a journal and began to flick through it.

No such constraint had fallen on Caroline. 'Lily and I think we should be finding you a wife, Jack,' she remarked chattily. Lily dropped the journal and scrabbled for it on the floor while she tried to cover her confusion.

'Do you, indeed? How very kind of you both.' Lily did not have to raise her eyes from desperately smoothing out crumpled pages to know exactly what Jack's reaction was. One dark eyebrow would be raised and he would be managing to do that while looking down his nose at the same time.

'Yes,' Caroline said complacently.

'No!' Lily interjected, looking up at last to meet a very sardonic gaze.

'Yes, you did, Lily, you said that Jack would make an excellent father and we both agreed that we should find him a charming bride. Don't you remember? When we were getting out of the carriage when we arrived home?'

In the face of this convincing detail Lily could hardly deny that she had said some of this. 'I might have said something like that,' she agreed feebly, waiting for the explosion.

But Jack was unnaturally calm about it. 'Do tell me, Caro—have you anyone particular in mind? A shortlist, perhaps?'

'Of course,' his sister said, with an expression of smug complacency. 'Miss Willoughby—George's elder sister, if you recall.'

'Dull.'

'But very worthy and industrious, which I am sure is what is needed. Or there is Louisa Carfax.'

'Is that the one with the giggle? Certainly not.'

'Lady Georgiana Foster? Now she does not giggle and she is a most handsome girl.'

'She has the brains of a peahen.'

'But, Jack, we are all agreed you need a wife, and here I am doing my best and you are not being at all helpful! If you are going to be so fussy about our local ladies, then you had better do as we suggested the other evening and go back to London to find a rich wife.'

'*Caroline!*' Jack's snapped warning came too late to stop the tide of colour flooding into Lily's face. How could Caroline be so tactless? But perhaps she had no idea how wealthy Lily was. She felt ready to sink, and had to force herself to speak.

'Perhaps Lord Allerton has scruples about marrying someone simply because of their wealth,' she managed between stiff lips. 'No doubt he is waiting to find someone for whom he can feel regard and affection.'

'I do not see how being wealthy excludes a woman from being those things to him,' Caroline persisted, apparently completely insensitive to her friend writhing miserably beside her and her glowering brother. 'Jack could very well find a rich lady to fall in love with and in that case he would have to be a complete blockhead to let her money stand in his way.'

'Caroline—' It was a warning growl this time. Then Jack was getting to his feet as his mother and younger sisters came in, and Lily found she was dragging air into her lungs as though she had been holding her breath for an hour. 'Mama, what a very dashing confection on your head! You are going to reduce all the local ladies to blatant envy when we next entertain.'

'I think it is not so bad,' Lady Allerton agreed, patting her curls with a touch of complacency. Jack sat again, not in his previous chair, but beside Lily, who found her fingers were clenched on the journal.

'I shall strangle my sister,' he remarked, low-voiced.

'She can have no idea… Please, do not make anything of it.' Lily forced herself to a semblance of composure. 'I do not regard it, I promise you.'

'Do you truly think I would make a good father?' Lily risked a sideways glance and found Jack was frowning over the question.

'I beg your pardon—it was perhaps an impertinent observation. I merely thought that the way you are with Penelope shows a charming affection.'

'Lily, are you all right? You sound so unlike yourself.' She sounded strange to herself—Cousin Frederica appeared to be taking over.

'I am fine.' Lily forced a smile, 'I am trying, for once, to heed my chaperon's strictures and to sound more ladylike.'

'Well, please do not! You do not sound like my Lily at all.'

His Lily? Lily turned abruptly, but Grimwade had just announced dinner and Jack was already getting to his feet. *His friend Lily, with whom he had shared some highly improper adventures, that is all he means by it. It is all he can mean.*

'Peter Coachman tells me it will be a fine day tomorrow,' Lady Allerton remarked. 'He is considered quite a weather prophet,' she added for Lily's benefit.

'How useful. Presumably you consult him before undertaking all kinds of agricultural procedures, such as ploughing?' Lily asked with an innocent smile at Caroline and Jack. Caroline, already caught out in her deceit, merely smiled back, but Jack's cheekbones were just touched with betraying colour. *So, he did know that Caroline was fibbing and yet he said nothing and so I stayed here. Why?*

'Shall we go riding tomorrow?' Susan suggested, happily oblivious to undercurrents. 'Do you have a riding habit, Lily? I expect Caro can lend you one.'

'I would enjoy that, thank you. And I have packed a habit.'

'The sea-green one?' Jack enquired. He had regained his composure and was watching her with an air of innocence she deeply mistrusted.

'No,' Lily replied repressively. 'A black one.'

'No frogging?'

'None. And a very sensible hat,' she added for good measure.

'Miss France might care to borrow Chaffinch,' Lady Allerton offered graciously. 'My own mare, Miss France; I think you will be pleased with her.'

Lily thanked her hostess and the remainder of the meal was taken up in a prolonged, and apparently familiar, argument amongst the Lovell siblings about their destination and route.

'Along the Aller Valley,' Jack said firmly as the dessert plates were removed. 'Lily will not want to look at miles of moorland, however starkly romantic you find it, Susan.' Penelope tried to interject and he added, 'And definitely not to the pit head, Penny. That is no place for ladies.'

'Don't worry, I will take you,' Caroline whispered as the ladies rose to leave Jack to his solitary consideration of the decanter. 'Jack is being very stuffy this evening—look how unreasonable he was about finding a wife. I mean, I am his sister and you are a good friend—why should he object to our efforts?'

'Perhaps he feels pressured? Or embarrassed?' Lily hazarded. 'I do not think we should tease him about it any more, do you?'

'Mmm.' There was a steely glint in Caroline's eyes which Lily recognised with a sinking feeling. 'I think he needs throwing together with some young ladies. I shall organise a dance.'

'Oh. How nice.' *And I will be long gone, thank goodness.*

'By next week will be time enough to get our new dresses finished,' Caroline said confidently. 'Mama! Shall we hold an informal dance for Lily? We all do that around here,' she explained cheerfully. 'It is a small society and we know each other far too well to stand on ceremony. Everyone is always ready for a party. And there's a full moon, so people will not mind the travelling.'

'What a lovely idea, Caroline,' her mother approved. 'And how pleased everyone will be to meet a new acquaintance. Tuesday, I think. I will write invitations tomorrow while you are out riding.'

Lily could only smile and agree with every appearance of delight while her heart sank into her satin slippers.

Jack strolled back into the drawing room and found its occupants deep in plans for a dance. After being comprehensively ignored for five minutes, he enquired mildly when it was to be. 'Next Tuesday. Jack—you won't be tiresome and say you have some prior engagement, now will you?' his eldest sister demanded. Denying any such intention, he beat a strategic retreat to the study.

Why Caro was assuming he would want to avoid the dance was a mystery, as was why she was nagging him about finding a wife. Had Lily said something? But that would presuppose Lily had confided their entire story to Caro—she would hardly tell her that she and Jack had decided to behave with circumspection. That would only make sense if she knew Caroline would understand the background. And if Caroline knew that Lily knew that she knew about... He stopped trying to puzzle it out, it was making his head spin.

He could avoid Caro's clumsy matchmaking schemes easily enough. The real mystery was what had happened to Lily. She had become stiff, subdued and formal ever since his suggestion in the warehouse. He had expected her to relax; it seemed it had had the opposite effect and she had become a conformable unmarried young lady.

And he did not want a prim and proper young lady—he wanted *his* Lily back. Jack pulled a face at his distorted reflection in the battered pewter inkpot on his desk. 'You want to have your cake and eat it too,' he informed himself wryly. He wanted to ride with Lily over the estate and hear her views on the landscape. Was she as much of a town mouse as he suspected, or would she find the wide open spaces irresistible? He was looking forward to her observations on sheep; he suspected they would be forthright. He had plans to tease her with extravagant schemes for redecorating the Great Hall in full baronial splendour and he wanted her to rivet the assembled guests at the dance by appearing in one of her completely outrageous evening *ensembles*.

But she had made all her gowns simple and elegant. And now it seemed he had made her so self-conscious that not just her gowns had become conventional, but she had submerged her entire personality. *Oh, Lily, my love, where have you gone?*

Lily appeared next day for their ride in a rigorously tailored black riding habit that drew a covetous gasp from Jack's two elder sisters and a long, unreadable look from under his lashes from Jack.

Lily made friends with Chaffinch, a pretty strawberry-roan mare, and was boosted into the saddle by one of the grooms while Jack was helping his sisters. He strode over, with a curt nod of thanks to the man, and took over checking Chaffinch's girth. 'Are you comfortable? She is not such a spirited ride as you are used to, I am afraid.'

He stood looking up at her, his hand resting on the mare's neck, so close to hers that she could have extended her little finger and touched his. Why did she want to? Wasn't this all supposed to be simple now they were merely acquaintances? Why could she not just stop loving him?

Instead she found herself studying the way his hair was beginning to curl as the crop grew out, the way the laughter lines at the corners of his eyes crinkled as he narrowed them to look up at her. 'Jack, this—'

Whatever it was she was about to say was swallowed up by an exclamation of pleasure from Caroline. 'George! What a nice surprise!'

A tall, sober-looking gentleman on a rangy hack rode into the yard, his austere face breaking into a smile as his eyes found Caroline.

'Willoughby.' Jack turned to greet his neighbour. Caroline's beau, Lily realised, gathering her scattered wits. 'We were just on our way out for a ride to introduce our guest, Miss France, to the countryside. Will you join us?'

The sober gentleman was easily persuaded, despite a mild protest that he had only ridden over with a book of sermons he had promised to lend Caroline. Lily bit her lip as Penelope rolled her eyes behind his back: he certainly seemed a strange choice for vivacious Miss Lovell, but then, who chose who they fell in love with? Certainly not her.

As the party rode out over the moat, Lily began to suspect that Caroline had known only too well that George Willoughby was going to call at this time. She manoeuvred her own gelding so that Lily had no choice but to ride beside Jack, while she fell in beside George, and Susan and Penelope were left to bring up the rear. Even more suspiciously, the two younger girls immediately began to dawdle.

Jack grinned. 'Trust Caro to have a plan,' he remarked softly. 'I believe it is our role to draw on ahead a little while the hapless George hands over his heart along with his sermons.'

'Hapless?' Lily queried. 'Does he not love Caroline?'

'I am sure he does, but if she does not take a hand he is going to hesitate in a damnably respectful manner until she goes into a decline.' He turned his big grey hunter down towards the river. 'Shall we canter?'

Lily realised she had not seen Jack on a horse before. The sight did nothing to subdue any of her feelings about him. He rode as though he was part of the animal, with a relaxed natural balance she could only envy, yet she was not deceived that he was astride an easy ride. The big horse curved its neck, fretting at the bit, and she could see Jack's thigh muscles working as he controlled the animal, as much by his balance as by any pressure on its mouth.

He relaxed the rein and it was away, hitting a controlled canter direct from the walk. Lily found she had to give her borrowed mount clear instructions to follow suit. The mare was far too well mannered to take liberties. But once Chaffinch had hit her stride she proved to have a long, easy action and Lily was soon itching to gallop. But, of course, to race a borrowed horse over unknown ground was just not possible.

'Race?' Jack called back over his shoulder. The big grey was working itself up into a lather of sweat where the reins touched its neck.

'I should not, not riding your mother's horse,' Lily called back.

In answer, Jack circled round, came up alongside her and leaned over to slap Chaffinch on the rump. 'Get up!'

'Jack, for goodness' sake!' Lily tightened her grip and pushed her heel down in the stirrup as she urged an already excited mare after the hunter. *I'll give him get up!*

But, despite her best endeavours, the little mare could not catch the grey. Jack had reined in beside the river where it widened into a shallow ford before Lily was close enough to carry on berating him.

'What would I have told your mama if Chaffinch had put her foot in a rabbit hole?' she demanded, jamming her hat down.

'That her undutiful son had led you astray?' *He already has...* 'Anyway, I know there are no hidden dangers along that stretch. If we cross here, I can take you up to the edge of the moors.'

'This is very lovely.' Lily twisted in the saddle to look

around her as the horses picked their way across the river. 'We have left Caroline and Mr Willoughby behind.'

'The girls can chaperon her—at a safe distance.' Jack chuckled. 'I'd bet ten corves of coal that I'll be greeting a future brother-in-law by lunch time.'

'What is a corve?'

'Corves are the containers coal is moved in underground,' Jack explained. Lily nodded encouragingly; she was actually getting him to talk about mining at long last. 'A miner has his own, moved by members of his own family, so we can keep tally on who has mined what.'

'And how much would that be in a day?' She should have known better. Jack shrugged.

'All depends. There, what do you make of the moors?'

The sharp slope of sheep-nibbled grassland flattened out into rolling, open moors, patched green and brown and punctuated by occasional clumps of trees or thickets of scrub. Dotted across the vastness were flocks of sheep, like so many clouds on a green sky.

'Um.' Lily stared. 'There is an awful lot of it. I was expecting fields—how do you keep the sheep in?'

'We do not have to; they know where they live.' It all seemed very odd to Lily. Jack grinned at her. 'You really are a town creature, aren't you, Lily?'

'I suppose I am…I never thought about it. We have never owned land, you see, so countryside is just something one drives through. How do you know where your land stops? I cannot see any fences.'

'There are none, and everything you can see is mine.'

'All this?' Lily turned in the saddle, looking back over the wide valley and the rising land on the other side. 'And that way?'

'Yes, as far as you can see.'

'But that must be thousands of acres!' Jack nodded and pressed his heels into the hunter's sides so that they began to approach a flock of sheep. Lily eyed them nervously as they came closer. 'Then why do you not sell some land to raise money for the mine?' It seemed so obvious.

'Sell? Sell Allerton land?' Now what had she said wrong? Jack was staring at her as though she had suggested he walk naked down Piccadilly. It was obviously not just a bad idea, but an impossible concept.

'Well, yes. Or is it all entailed?' Lily was not quite certain what a entail was, but she knew it was some sort of legal device to prevent one generation from selling their descendents' inheritance.

'Some of it is.' He was still treating the suggestion as ludicrous. 'But I could not sell land.'

'Why not? Is it not worth much?' Lily had gone beyond any attempt at tactfulness in her need to understand.

'An acre here is not worth as much as an acre of, say, Suffolk, grazing, but it has a reasonable monetary value all the same. But this is not about money. You do not understand, Lily.'

'No. I do not. Explain it to me.'

'I do not know if I can. The land is what we are, where we came from. Blood and bone. I sell this land over my dead body.' That was plain enough, if still incomprehensible. Was land not just another asset? If she wanted to sell parts of the business to improve another section, then she would do it happily, even if it was something her father had bought and built up; that was how it worked.

Lily caught her lower lip between her teeth to stop herself saying as much. To do so would be to blunder, she could tell that. She had come up hard against the heart-deep source of that pride that was so blatantly displayed by Adrian and which ran, like a seam of coal, through Jack. He had all this land, but the mine had his intense interest, took most of his time and energy. Yet he would not sacrifice an acre to save the mine. She shook her head. This, then, was the gulf between the landed classes and the new rich: no amount of money could purchase the elusive *cachet* of ancestral lands.

'Given up trying to understand me, Lily?' Jack was smiling at her; at least she had not blundered too much.

'I did that almost as soon as I met you,' she retorted with an attempt at lightness. 'My goodness—Lady Philpott!'

'Where?' Jack stood in his stirrups and stared round. 'And who the devil is Lady Philpott?'

Lily pointed with her whip at the Roman-nosed sheep that was regarding her stolidly. 'The nose, and that ridiculous clump of curls on top of its head! Lady Philpott is very much given to turbans.'

Jack snorted with laughter and urged his mount closer, scattering the sheep. 'One hopes she is not as dim-witted as a sheep, or one must be deeply sorry for her husband.' Despite his words, Lily could see he was checking the animals, running a knowledgeable eye over them. 'They're in good fettle this year.'

'What is that?' Lily pointed to a plume of grey smoke rising over the edge of the moor.

'The smoke from the engine house at the pit head.' Jack wheeled round and began to head back towards the valley. 'And, no, Lily, before you ask, we are not going to look at it.'

'Why not?' *Because you do not want me interfering in your precious mine. Because I blundered once and I have not been forgiven.*

'Because it is dirty, rough and dangerous and no place for a lady.'

Lily urged Chaffinch up beside the grey. 'I have ridden through Indian hill country and camped out in dacoit territory. I have sailed halfway round the world. I have been in more factories than I can count. I am not one of your conventional ladies, Jack!'

'No?' He twisted in the saddle to look at her, his expression bleak. 'Then I think it will be safer all round if you become one.'

Chapter Twenty-Two

Lily and Jack arrived back at the castle to find that the informal dance had become the ideal opportunity to announce Caroline's betrothal to the world. Caroline was looking radiant, Susan and Penelope were hugging themselves with glee, Lady Allerton was viewing the happy couple tolerantly and only the prospective bridegroom appeared to be suffering any apprehension.

'Caroline, I really feel I should have spoken to Lord Allerton before we announced this.' His earnest face was anxious and did not lighten when Jack swung down from his horse and came over.

'I imagine you had every intention of doing so before you said anything to my sister,' he said, shaking Willoughby by the hand. 'But ten minutes alone with her and she had undermined every very proper resolution you had formed.' He added, straight-faced, 'The girl is obviously a minx—I am amazed you are prepared to take her on.'

Ignoring his betrothed's highly vocal protests, Willoughby cleared his throat and responded earnestly, 'I will not have it so! I am afraid that the merest suggestion that Miss Lovell was not indifferent to my suit was enough to undermine every principle on my part and I most improperly spoke my mind.'

Trying hard not to catch Jack's eye, and pretending she could not hear Penny's stifled giggles, Lily followed the family party into the castle. All very mysterious, the attraction of one human being to another! At least one could be sure that the worthy Mr Willoughby was unlikely to be making love to his betrothed on the drawing-room carpet.

She felt the colour mount in her cheeks at the memory of Jack's lovemaking on that wonderful evening. Was it better to have tasted such passion and then to have lost it, or never to have known it at all?

'You are looking very thoughtful.' Jack was watching her steadily, the dark gaze seeming to touch her skin like a whisper.

'I was thinking what a momentous step it was for them, and hoping they will be happy.'

'So was I.' Jack lifted her hand in his, frowning down at it as it lay within his open fingers. His thumb rubbed idly across her palm and Lily shivered, but made no move away. 'She has a knack of knowing what will make her happy, my sister, I have rarely found her mistaken. I only wish I had the same talent.'

Lily was still brooding over Jack's dark mood the next morning when Caroline caught her after breakfast. 'Would you like to go to the pit head today?'

'That is kind, but surely you will be spending the day with Mr Willoughby?'

'Jack has ridden over to see George so they can discuss tiresome things like settlements and endowments and reversions and goodness knows what else.' Caroline smiled wistfully. 'George will not even discuss the date for the wedding until all that is settled; he is mortified that I cajoled him into proposing before he had spoken to Jack. George,' she added, with a hint of pride, 'is very concerned for good form.'

'Er, yes. I can tell.' Lily could think of nothing to say to that.

Caroline's eyes twinkled wickedly. 'You are thinking that he is unlikely to prove very passionate?' Lily stumbled into a hasty denial, but Caroline simply smiled. 'I think part of the attraction for me is the thought of breaching those walls of propriety.'

'Forgive me, but perhaps underneath the propriety Mr Willoughby really is not…er..is not very passionate.'

'Oh, yes, he is,' Caroline whispered as they entered Lily's bedchamber. 'Very.' She looked around to make sure none of the maids were within earshot. 'I pretended I had to dismount because my stirrup leather was twisted, so he helped me down and so we were standing very close together—and he kissed me!'

'That was all?'

'Well, yes. But it was *wonderful,* my toes tingled.'

Lily rang for Janet and changed into stout boots, reflecting that it was a very good thing that the sheltered Miss Lovell had no idea of what her guest had been doing with her brother. Kissing Jack led to rather more than tingling toes. Lily gave herself a brisk shake and, picking up her heaviest cloak, ran to join Caroline, who had taken the reins of a sturdy cob in the shafts of a gig.

'Have you ever been below ground?' Lily asked, watching the plume of smoke come closer.

'Goodness, no,' Caroline forked off the main track and took a smaller one over the shoulder of the hill.

'But women work down the pit, do they not?'

'Yes, but it is rough, dirty work. There is no safe, clean way to view a mine, I am afraid. Here it is.'

They had come little more than a mile and entered a different world. Great piles of slag formed a wall around the area, like black battlements. Stone huts and bigger buildings were scattered, seemingly haphazardly, and what appeared to Lily's fascinated eye to be a hoard of figures went about their business in the midst of mud, straining wagon-teams, trucks on rails, groups of weary, filthy men and gaggles of children.

Near the centre of the chaos—which, as she watched, she realised was in fact perfectly orderly in its way—the stone chimney rose over the engine house and from it cables snaked out and over a structure with a great wheel laid sideways at the top of it.

'Winding gear.' Caroline pointed. 'It takes the workers up and down and also the corves of coal. Not both at once, of course—if that happens there is a dreadful coming-together and people get hurt. The miners call it a wedding!'

She flicked the reins and the cob made its way through the outskirts of the area to where a sturdy building stood. 'We will see if William Sykes, the manager, is in,' Caroline explained. 'He will show us around.'

The manager obviously kept a sharp eye on his kingdom, for he was at the door before they reached it, doffing his hat when he saw who it was. 'Miss Lovell, good day to you, ma'am. What can I do for you?'

Lily found she had to concentrate to understand him, for his accent had a strong burr to it, and he rolled his r's like a Frenchman.

'This is Miss France, a visitor from London, who is interested in mining, Mr Sykes. I was hoping you might have time to show her around.'

'Be glad to, ma'am. If you'll drive a little closer, that would be better, the ground's that clarty, you'll not want to be walking on it.'

'Muddy,' Caroline translated as they followed Mr Sykes. 'We all used to know a lot of dialect words, but Mama would discourage us from using them and I have forgotten most of the less common ones. Jack now, if you hear him talking to one of the miners, you would think it a foreign language.'

Mr Sykes found them a patch of flagged yard to stand on, away from the worst of the mud. Lily studied the miners with their loose canvas trousers and thick woollen shirts and smocks. They were short of stature—she supposed height would be a serious disadvantage underground—but under the black-grimed faces she thought they looked fit and well fed.

'Is the money good?' she asked the manager.

'Three shillings a day for a collier,' he replied, his eyes fixed on a disturbance nearer the pit head. 'Compares well with a labourer around here. Excuse me a minute, ladies.' He strode off to sort the problem out.

'And the families have free coal and wages when the father is off sick,' Caroline added. 'The miners look down on the agricultural workers, believe me! And most of the family will work here; it all adds up.' She gestured towards a group who were walking towards them and Lily realised that they were girls and young women, coarse skirts kirtled up to reveal trouser legs below.

'What do they do?' The women were as black with coal dust as the men.

'Load and pull corves underground,' Caroline explained. 'The young lads do it too, or work the ventilation shutters. There's Jinny Armstrong—her elder sister works at the castle. They're a nice family.' Caroline waved and the young woman came across.

'I dinnet look to see yous here, Miss Caroline. Our Lizzy says yous to be wed to Master Willoughby.'

'So I am, Jinny. I am showing the mine to Miss France, who is staying with us. Oh, excuse me, Lily, there is Mrs Sykes, come with her husband's luncheon, I expect; I must just go and see how she does.'

Left alone with the girl, Lily found she was being regarded politely, but without deference, by a pair of intelligent brown eyes. An idea was lurking in the back of her mind—could she risk it without placing Jinny in a difficult situation?

'Lord Allerton and his family have been very kind in explaining all about the mine to me,' she remarked. 'I am going to be investing some money in mines further south, and it is important I understand as much as possible.'

Jinny nodded. 'I can see that you'd need to. Yous dinna want to be throwing your brass about.'

'His lordship has been very helpful…' Lily left the sentence trailing.

'Aye, he's a canny mon.' Goodness knows what that meant, but it appeared to be approval.

'The thing is, I need to see underground as well, only I don't feel quite comfortable going down the mine with a man. But I can hardly say that to Mr Sykes, can I? It might hurt his feelings.'

Jinny appeared to accept this. Lily crossed her fingers and pressed on. 'And then Miss Caroline pointed you out. Would you be able to take me down? I would pay you, of course, I understand it would reduce the amount you could be earning. Miss Caroline explained all that. Would five shillings be about right?' It was more than the family would make in the day, and could be explained by Lily's ignorance about mining, but it was not so much that it might make Jinny suspicious that she was being bribed to do something wrong.

'Tha's more than generous, miss. I'll do it gladly, but yous canna be goin doon in those clothes.'

Lily was beginning to get her ear in now. 'No, of course not. And Miss Caroline does not have anything suitable. Could you lend me something?'

'Aye, I can that. I'll send them up to castle by wor Lizzie. When would you be wanting to go down, miss?'

'Would Monday be convenient for you? I don't know what time—Miss Caroline hadn't explained that.'

'About four in the afternoon, miss. I fetch my da's dinner then. If yous wait over yonder...' she pointed to a small hut near the edge of the pithead area '...None of the men go over there.'

Caroline was walking back towards them, chatting happily to Mr Sykes. 'Goodbye until Monday then, Jinny, and thank you.'

'That's a nice young woman,' she commented to the manager.

'Aye, Miss France. A God-fearing, hard-working family, the Armstrongs.'

He took them over to see the winding gear, and, despite his obvious misgivings, let Lily peep into the engine house. She was transfixed by the throbbing engine, the power of the great beams and the gush of water. 'It is so much quieter than I imagined,' she marvelled to Caroline as they drove back. 'Like a great beast, breathing heavily.'

'An expensive beast.' Her friend sighed. 'Jack says he wants two more if he is to open another pit, or go deeper with this one.'

'Just how deep is the current pit?' Lily asked. For some reason that had never occurred to her before. Being underground, the dirt, the thought of mixing with dozens of strange men—none of that concerned her. But why had she not thought about the depth? If she was frightened of anything, it was heights, and Lily had a sinking feeling that gazing down a deep hole in the ground would be no different to looking over the edge of a cliff. Terrifying.

'I have no idea,' Caroline said cheerfully. 'I just know it takes several minutes when they go down on the rope, so it must be a long way.'

'On the rope?' Lily asked faintly. 'You mean, there are baskets, or a cage or something hanging from a rope?'

'No, I don't think so. They make loops in the rope and the adults put one foot in that and hang on. The lads stand on their fathers' feet, or ride on their backs. It's called a bant, a group all going down together. It looks like a big bunch of grapes.'

'Oh.' Lily swallowed. Just what had she let herself in for?

Jack sat back in his chair at the head of the long oak table and regarded the scene before him with a certain benevolence. Negotiations with George Willoughby had proved highly satisfactory and he could congratulate himself that his sister was going to be well provided for in a marriage to a husband who seemed to adore her.

Jack smiled in self-mockery. He was becoming positively patriarchal, taking credit for an alliance that had been entirely of Caroline's own making, and earlier he had caught himself thinking seriously about managing Susan's come-out to her best advantage. Yet he could not even achieve a suitable match for himself and ensure the future of the title.

He moved his attention to Lily, producing a brooding expression that had Grimshaw nervously sniffing the Bordeaux decanter for signs of deterioration.

Lily, to his increasingly experienced and concerned eye, seemed nervous. Her reserve had become even more extreme, her complexion paler, and several times she had appeared to be on the point of asking him something. Jack was not at all certain he wanted to know what it was that was troubling her; he suspected it would be all his fault. But that was what you did when you cared for someone, was it not? However uncomfortable the results of trying to help were.

He chose his moment when they were in the drawing room and his family were poring over the fashion journals in search of wedding outfits. 'Lily? Is something wrong?'

She started, blinked at him and then smiled, suddenly so much like his old Lily that he smiled back. 'No, nothing at all. I was just making lists in my head and worrying about things I need to do. Very foolish at this time of night—I will dream about it now. Jack…'

'Yes?' He recognised the tone. It was the universal feminine tone he had come to dread and usually preceded remarks such as 'I have been thinking…' or 'You know my allowance…'

'There is no need to sound so wary! I was only going to say that Caroline took me to see the mine yesterday—no, do not frown at me! We were escorted by your manager, and did not go very close to the activity at all. And there were some things I wanted to ask, but did not think of until we left. How deep is the shaft?'

'Nigh on two hundred feet. We will not go any deeper.'

'Two hundred. Fancy that,' Lily said faintly. 'Why no deeper?'

'Pumping out water is one problem, but ventilation is the other. There are all sorts of tricks one can use to force air through, but there comes a point when nothing will work.'

'Is it just that you cannot get fresh air in, or is there gas? I had heard about new safety lamps.' Lily was looking brighter again. Trust her to know about something he did not expect his own family to have heard about.

'We do not get choke damp here, the soils are wrong and the shaft too deep, but we do get fire damp, and that is the one that causes explosions. I will buy the new lamps when they have been tested a little more, but even they will not help if there is a stray spark.'

'So what can you do?' She was curled up on the sofa now, facing him. Jack could feel himself sinking into the depths of those intelligent green eyes and had to stop himself reaching out and taking her hand. On the far side of the room the low voices of his family discussing Tuesday's dance seemed a hundred miles away. He just wanted to be alone with Lily; if talking about mining was a safely neutral way to free her from her façade of polite reserve, then so be it.

'We test for it and then create our own controlled explosions.'

'Dangerous!'

'Alarming, but not hazardous if one knows what one is doing. Which reminds me, I must talk to Sykes about seeing it is done again soon.'

Lily had gone pale. Jack yielded to temptation and gave her hand a comforting squeeze. 'Truly, it is not dangerous.'

'Oh, good,' she responded earnestly. 'That is a relief.'

Chapter Twenty-Three

Lily resisted casting a guilty look back at the castle and urged the cob into a trot. The waters of the Aller glinted in the afternoon sunshine and had made her request to borrow the gig, so that she could go along the valley a little with her sketchbook, perfectly understandable. Lady Allerton and the girls were busy with preparations for the dance which they were adamant their guest should not be helping with, so permission was gladly granted and the cob was soon trotting towards the mine, the bundle of clothes Lizzie Armstrong had delivered in a bag on the seat beside Lily.

The other day she had seen an old shed, just the other side of the rise from the pit head and she tied the cob up there on a long rein so it could crop the grass and reach the water trough. When she slipped out of the door again and set off up the slope, Lily was confident that even her aunt would not recognise her.

Her own stout boots protruded from a pair of flapping canvas trousers, a skirt apparently made of sacking was kirtled up to what seemed indecent heights and was supported by the same broad leather belt that pulled in a woollen smock over a worn shirt. She had knotted her betraying hair into a kerchief and clapped the battered billycock hat Jinny had provided on top. Her hands, protruding from the frayed sleeves, were far too white so she stopped by a spring and dabbled them in muddy water, splashing her face while she was at it.

Jinny Armstrong's face when they met at their rendezvous confirmed Lily's assumption that, however bizarre she appeared, she most certainly did not look like the rich heiress from London town.

'Now then,' Jinny cautioned as she pocketed the promised coins, swung the pack she was carrying on to her shoulder and they began to walk towards the shaft head, 'yous stay behind me and do just what I does—and listen out for the banksman, he's there to stop any accidents, so what he says goes.'

'Right.' *What is a banksman? How deep did Jack say?*

'Use your free hand and free foot to push off from th'walls. I'll find yous a candle when we get down there.'

Then they were there, approaching a wooden platform under the great wheel, joining a group of women and boys. If she was going to back out, it had to be now. 'Out the way, you daft bairns.' Jinny administered a mild cuff round the head to a couple of boys who were scuffling. 'Clarting about—don't think I willna tell your ma on you.'

Distracted, Lily realised too late that they were next for the rope. Loops were knotted into it at intervals and here and there someone had thrust a stout stick through. 'Like this.' Jinny stuck her foot in a loop, wrapped her arm around the rope and began to sink into the hole. 'Come on!'

Think of it like a stirrup... Lily grabbed hold, pushed in her foot and found herself hanging in space, the hairy rope clutched to her bosom and rasping against her face. The rope jerked, swung her towards the sides, already darkening as they descended. Lily stuck out her free foot, found the wall, swung back.

How much longer? How deep are we? The descent seemed endless, the darkness impenetrable. Her arm was aching and her leg, braced to support her, was beginning to tremble with the stress. What would Jack say if she tumbled to her death? What would he feel?

Then light began to flicker on the walls, noise began to reach her ears and Jinny was grabbing her ankle. 'Here you go, kick your foot free.' And she was standing on roughly level, solid ground. The girl pulled her back, out of the way as the boy on the rope above her jumped down. 'Take this.' A tallow dip was pressed into her hand and she began to follow Jinny, her eyes straining in the dim, wavering light.

'This be the main heading. A bit like the pike road. Watch out!' A pair of boys pulling a great, laden wicker basket on runners passed them. 'Stick to the sides is favourite,' Jinny advised. 'We've a way to go; me da's working his bord in a gallery right up t'end.'

Lily stumbled after the girl, trying to stop her tallow dip blowing out, fighting to keep her footing, her eyes wide in the gloom. She was no longer afraid, more awed by this alien, subterranean world full of men, women and children, all of whom seemed to know their business and to be perfectly at home in this hostile environment.

'This be wor bord,' Jinny announced suddenly, diving off down a side gallery. Men were working here with picks, shovels, crowbars, hacking the lumps of coal out of the face by brute force. Lily tried to slow down to watch, but Jinny tugged her wrist. 'Don't go getting underfoot now. Here's Da.'

Lily found herself tucked into an alcove out of the way

while Jinny went to speak to the dark figure ahead. The man put down his pick and straightened up as much as he was able in the undercut he was working on.

'Good lass. I'm clamming for a drink.' His accent was even thicker than Jinny's, but had the attractive burr and lilt Lily was coming to like. 'Load up for me, will yer? Tom's gone to fetch more dips.'

'Aye.' The girl came back. 'I've to help me da a while until me little brother gets back. You'd best go back to the foot of the shaft and wait there, 'tis the safest place. Yous canna get lost, just to the end of the gallery and then left, back aways.'

'I will do that, but I will not wait.' Lily did not want the family to suffer any loss of work on her behalf. 'I will go up with the next group of women who come along. Thank you very much for your trouble.'

Lily made her way back to the main heading, dodging the pickaxe-wielding men and flattening herself against the side as the boys came through with their loads of coal. *Corves, that was it.*

She was almost at the point where the gallery reached the heading when a familiar deep voice had her flattening herself back into the deep shadow. *Jack.*

He passed her without a glance, another man at his side carrying a long pole and a bundle and William Sykes bringing up the rear. Jack was stooping, unable to stand erect, even in the main passageway. Lily hesitated, then turned to follow. It was a wonderful opportunity to watch Jack, see what it was about his precious mine that engaged him so much, try to understand him. She could hardly get lost, she reasoned, so long as she did not turn off the heading, and her eyes were beginning to accustom themselves to the gloom.

They passed more galleries, the passage began to curve and

Sykes started to call warnings down the galleries as they passed them. What it was about Lily could not make out, but answering shouts echoed back.

Finally they stopped. The heading stretched ahead into blackness with no glimmers of lights to be seen. The man with the long pole bent and began to tie the bundle to the head of it and William Sykes lit a candle, long, white and of fine wax

Oddly he appeared to be lifting and lowering it slowly. Lily crept closer. It still did not make sense. Now he was conferring with Jack, walking forward again, going through the same process, raising the candle from waist height to above his eye line. Lily inched nearer until she could have reached out and touched the skirts of Jack's greatcoat.

'Aye, there it is.' All three men were gazing at the flame, held near the roof now. 'See the ghost?'

And sure enough, at the top of the flame, a cap of eerie blue light danced.

'I'll light up, shall I, guv'nor?' the man with the pole queried.

'Do that.' Lily could make out Jack's nod of approval. 'And be careful, Sam, I think this one is going to be big.'

Jack reached out a hand and braced himself more comfortably against the wall of the heading while Will set down the candle on the floor and Sam finished securing the bundle of cloth and kindling on the end of the pole. It would be a few more minutes yet—both men were experienced at this and knew it was foolhardy to rush things.

The rock felt warm under his hand and he flexed his fingers, feeling the fissures and nodules. Almost he could believe he could detect a heartbeat, slow and deep.

His land, reaching down into the depths of the earth. He

smiled in the near-darkness, recalling his instinctive recoil when Lily had suggested selling some of it the other day. Practical, sensible Lily. He had not explained his revulsion to her at all well, but then how could he, when it was something he had never articulated to himself?

'Got any twine, sir?' It was Will, clasp knife in hand. 'This stuff's right rubbish.'

'Yes, here.' Jack fished in his pocket and went back to brooding. But talking to Lily had made him realise how blessed he was in owning all that land, in possessing it down to the very roots of the earth. How rich.

Gazing into the blackness until spots of light began to swim in front of his eyes, Jack probed that thought. Rich. Rich in land and in minerals and in history. Rich enough to match Lily's cash wealth, as an equal. Rich enough for them to discount both her money and his title.

Neither meant anything any more, he realised, not when it came to loving Lily. Not his pride, his land, her money, her stubbornness. He was a man, she was a woman and he loved her. Could she love him, after all that had passed between them? There was only one way to find out and that was to talk to her and court her.

'That'll do it, Sam lad.' Will's voice cut through his thoughts, jerking him back into the present and its dangers. 'You moving back, sir?'

'No, I'll stay here.'

Sam bent, set light to the bundle and began to push the blazing ball forward along the ground on the end of its pole. The flames began to change colour, closer and closer to the ghost blue. 'Here we go, I reckon.' He set his foot on the end of the pole and levered it up so the fire lifted towards the ceiling.

Braced, like the others, to throw himself down, Jack half-turned, some instinct warning him they were not alone. At the edge of the light, just behind him, there was an indistinct figure. 'Get back, you bloody fo—'

The gas exploded with a roar and time slowed. Jack threw himself back, hitting the figure, landing on top of it on the hard ground even as the flames ripped past over their heads, filling his vision with fire and his lungs with heat. He burrowed his head down, wrapping the wings of his greatcoat over both of them. The figure was slight, he realised as his senses recovered from the blast. A lad, silly young idiot. Or a woman.

The smell of fire and burning gases and dust subsided. The singing in his ears cleared. Face down, he could see nothing, but he could smell, and he could hear.

Smell not coal, not dirt and sweat as he expected, but jasmine and soap and the haunting scent of feminine skin. And hear someone gasping for breath under the weight of him, and a familiar voice muttering, 'Ouch! You great lummock, what did you have to do that for?'

'Lily? *Lily?*'

Chapter Twenty-Four

'You all right, sir? Did the trick all right, that did.' Half-convinced he was dreaming, Jack got to his feet, trying not to tread on the struggling figure underneath him.

'Yes, I am fine. Sam all right? Good lad, there'll be a bonus for you—you're as good as your father, and you can tell him that for me.' His head was spinning—with shock and anger, he realised. The men must not find out that Lily was here. No one must. 'This foolish wench here has got a bit of a bruising. I will just walk her back to the shaft, make sure she gets back up all right. I'll speak to you tomorrow, Will.'

Lily had struggled up on her elbows and was making undignified whooping noises. 'Quiet,' he hissed, hauling her to her feet and beginning to march her back down the heading. 'Have you hit your head?'

'No.' She had enough breath back to snap at him, and enough sense to keep her voice to a furious hiss. 'No, my head is fine. The rest of me has just been used as a mattress by some idiot man with delusions of chivalry. Or possibly he was just looking for a comfortable landing.'

'You had no business to be here. You might have been

killed.' For endless seconds he had not known whether she was alive or dead or seriously injured as she lay crushed under him. His stomach still churned with reaction.

He should escort her to the surface, he should remonstrate with her in a quiet and dignified manner until she saw the error of her ways. What he wanted to do was to shout at her and shake her until her teeth rattled for scaring him more than he had ever been frightened in his life before.

But it was impossible to do that in the middle of a working mine, as impossible as it would be on the dance floor at Almack's. Jack set his teeth and half-dragged, half-carried Lily to the foot of the shaft.

Her hat was gone. A bedraggled bandana hung down in the midst of a tangle of red curls. With an oath he took off his own hat, bundled her hair under it and jammed it on her head. It came down to her nose.

'Ow!'

'Quiet.' Jack opened his coat. 'Put your arms around me, stand on my right foot. Stand, I said, not stamp! Hold on.'

He crushed her close, the brim of his own hat knocking against his face as he tried to shield her as much as possible. He was shaking, he realised. Just a little. Just enough to be conscious of the tremor running through his arms and legs. She could have been killed, wandering around down there by herself. How the hell had she got there? *Oh, God, Lily. I love you. I am going to strangle you…*

They emerged into the daylight, unnoticed in the usual milling crowd at the top. Jack took Lily's arm above the elbow and walked her fast, straight across the open space to the hovel where he had hitched his horse under the sloping roof. He plucked his hat off her head, clapped it on his own and lifted her, before she could do more than yelp in protest, tossing her over the horse's neck.

'Stay still.' He swung up behind her and kicked the big grey into a canter, away from the mine, over the crest of the hill, down towards a copse of trees that lay a mile distant. A favourite picnic place, it would be deserted now. Deserted and just the place for the blazing row he was aching for. Lily was struggling. He fetched her a light slap on the rump. 'Quiet! You will fall off.' She retaliated by sinking her teeth into his thigh.

'Bloody hell!' Her teeth, however sharp, made little impact through the thick canvas trousers he was wearing. Jack snarled in exasperation as she continued to struggle. When the grey plunged into the clearing in the middle of the copse he let her go immediately, so she slid down on to her feet, glaring up at him. The tracks of tears had cut through the dirt and dust on her cheeks. His heart contracted as though a hand had squeezed it.

'Bully!'

Jack swung down, dropping the reins. 'Have you got windmills in your head? How the hell did you get down there?'

'I shall not tell you. I tricked them into thinking you approved, but I do not trust you not to sack them, so I will not tell you.'

'I can well believe you tricked them, you hellion. Do you think I don't know that? Anyone you deceived has my deepest sympathy. Will you stop at nothing to get what you want?'

'I cannot have what I want.' She said it starkly, stopping him in his tracks. 'I wanted to see the mine because it is so important to you. I wanted to understand. That is all.'

'And do you understand?' Jack knew his voice was harsh. He cleared his throat against the obstruction that seemed to be filling it.

'Yes.' Lily said it quietly. 'It is the land again, isn't it? You love all of it, rock deep. You have to be born to it, I think, so it is difficult for someone who is not, but I do think I understand now.'

'Why do you need to?' He began to move towards her again, not realising just how threatening he must look with his black-grimed face and the heavy coat swirling around him until she took several steps backwards. A tree stopped her. She shook her head, watching him silently.

'I cannot be indifferent to you, Lily. I tried to be just a friend, but I cannot.' He was right in front of her now. Jack rested both hands on the thick oak trunk, trapping her as he had in the Long Gallery. He had mishandled that spectacularly. Now he had frightened her so that she wanted to run away from him.

'I am sorry. It was kind of you to try. I realise I make you very angry.'

Finesse deserted him—he just said what he felt. 'Do you realise I love you more than I have ever loved anything or anyone, Lily? Do you realise that?'

He did not know what to expect. A slapped face. Anger. Chilly rejection. Instead she went white under the dirt and closed her eyes.

He thought he stopped breathing. The wide, glorious green eyes opened again, slowly. 'No. I had not realised that. *Oh, Jack!*' Her arms went round his neck and she was pulling his head down, lifting her face for his kiss. He braced his shoulders, holding her back just an inch from his lips.

'Do you mean you love me? Lily?'

'Of course I love you, you thick-skulled aristocrat! Do you think I go around proposing to men I do not love?'

'I have no idea,' Jack said, finding his mouth was curving into a smile. 'I find I have no idea whatsoever what you might do, Lily, my love.'

'If you don't kiss me soon, I think I might just faint.' Lily thought she would anyway. Things seemed to be spinning, she had no idea if it were possible to be this happy and live, her back felt as though she had been beaten all over with meat-tenderising hammers and every cell in her body wanted Jack. 'I *love* you.'

Jack's mouth on hers was hot, hard, as desperate as hers as she strained into him, her fingers frantic as they clung to his shoulders. He was like a rock, her rock. His tongue was relentless, plunging, plundering, claiming her, as though she might have any intention of resisting. She could feel his anger still, it must be burning through his veins, just as her own fear, transmuted into desire, burned through hers.

His fingers were at her waist, struggling with the buckle of the heavy leather belt. It fell away. 'What the devil are you wearing?'

'Trousers.' Lily tugged at the fastenings, her fingers tangling with Jack's in their mutual urgency.

'Well, you are never going to wear them again. Of all the improper—' He broke off, on a gasp of laughter that answered hers. 'Yes, well, never mind that now.' The trousers dropped away, Jack was doing something to the fall of his own and then Lily found herself lifted, braced against the tree trunk solid at her back. Jack shrugged out of his greatcoat. 'Damn these clothes. Lily—'

Acting on instinct, she wrapped her legs around his waist, panting a little. One hand cupped her bare bottom while the other stroked down, found the warm tangle of curls, slid between their locked bodies. Found her. *'Jack.'*

He shifted her slightly and she felt him, aroused, already brushing against her. 'Lily, sweetheart…'

'Yes, oh, yes, yes…' He moved, just a little, nudging against her, entering her a fraction. Lily stiffened. It was almost like it had been when he had made love to her in London. Almost. This was different, this was…more.

She searched his face for reassurance, found it in the grey eyes steady on hers, in the taut tendons of his neck. He was fighting for control, fighting not to frighten or hurt her. Lily felt the trust wash through her, only to be swept away by a jolt of desire so intense she almost cried out. 'Yes. I love you.'

He lowered her a little, watching her, filling her with love as he filled her with his body. Waves of arousal rippled through her belly, lower, lower, then suddenly it was as though he had hit a barrier. Lily caught back a little cry, tightened her arms around Jack's neck for reassurance.

'Love, I can go slowly, or I can go fast. Beyond this, I promise it will not hurt any more.'

'Fast.' She locked her lips on his, let her cry be swallowed in his kiss as he plunged, took her in one long thrust that turned pain into pleasure, sent her over the edge, down, falling into delight so intense she thought she must die of it.

Somewhere, beyond the swirling blackness, the stars, the liquid delight that turned her limbs to water so that she could hardly cling to him, she was aware of the hard, virile body, sheathed in hers, the final thrust as he joined her in ecstasy. *I have done this,* she thought hazily as he collapsed against her.

Lily came to herself to find they were still in the same position, only Jack was nuzzling gently at the angle where her neck met her shoulder. 'So soft,' he murmured.

'I do not think I have any bones left,' Lily confessed. 'Jack, that was so wonderful. I do love you so much.'

'I love you. I had no idea how much.' He straightened up, gingerly. 'I will try not to drop you.' Unsteadily Lily regained her feet, looked down at herself, then regarded her lover.

'Jack, look at us! We look like the cross between a carriage accident and an orgy!'

'What do you know about orgies?' He was buttoning his trousers and stuffing his shirt back in.

'Nothing,' Lily retorted demurely. 'Although I hope to learn, providing one can have them with only two participants.' She held up her borrowed trousers. 'I do not think I can bear to put those on again.'

'No.' Jack regarded her, his expression a cross between desire and amusement. 'How did you get to the mine?'

Lily explained, and was left to regain what composure she could while Jack rode off to get the gig. He drove her back, wrapped in his greatcoat, the grey hunter trotting along behind.

'Miss France fell in the river,' he explained blandly to the concerned grooms who hurried to greet them. 'I must get her inside as soon as possible before she catches a chill. Give that bundle…' he nodded towards the filthy clothes she had been wearing '…to my valet.'

The Great Hall was mercifully empty. Jack carried Lily through, and up the stairs. 'Where are we going?'

'To my room.'

'But…'

'Shh.' Jack shouldered open the door, deposited Lily on the bed, locked the door and went through to what she assumed was the dressing room. There was the sound of voices. Lily scooted down under the greatcoat until Jack came back.

'Who was that?'

'My valet, who regrets that his lordship feels so tired that he must eat in his rooms tonight, and is so dirty that he needs a very large amount of hot water fetched for his bath and who will, of course, pass the message to Miss Lovell that her friend Miss France is so weary that she is retiring to bed and does not wish to be disturbed by anyone, not even her maid.'

'Jack, you are outrageous.'

'I can do what I like in my own castle.' He smiled at her with unrepentant arrogance as he began to undress.

'Jack—how did you overcome your scruples about my money?' Lily sat up, trying not to stare. She had seen Jack stripped to the waist, she had just been as intimate with him as it was possible to be, but she had never seen him naked before—except for that fleeting glimpse when he had scandalised Aunt Herrick. She realised with a gulp that it was a good thing that she had not, because she might have suffered considerable apprehension if she had seen quite how...how *masculine* he was beforehand.

'When you asked me why I could not sell my land, it made me realise just how rich—how *blessed* I was with what I had. That there was no inequality between us that I need consider, any more than you need feel inferior because of your birth. We both bring wealth to this union, but, infinitely more important, we bring love.'

Lily, struggling with the distraction of the powerful naked body so close to hers, smiled. 'I thought my heart was broken when you said we should act as though there had been nothing between us. It was as though someone had snuffed out the light. I had not realised, but I was still hoping you might come to love me.' In answer, he bent and kissed her eyelids, his lips gentle on the soft skin, his breath tickling the fine hairs at her temple. His hands moved down to the shoulders of her shirt. 'Jack, what are you doing?'

'Taking your clothes off. We will then have a bath. A long, hot, very soapy, very wet bath. I intend ensuring that every nook and cranny of your entirely lovely body is free from coal dust.' He ran one hand, flat-palmed, down over the swell of her breast, making them both catch their breath.

'I then mean to make love to you. At length and slowly and as many times as we can manage before daybreak. I have made love to you on the carpet. I have made love to you in a furious temper and I have made love to you against a tree. I think it is time I made love to my future countess in my own bed, in my own castle.

'Lily, my love, is that a proposition which meets with your approval?'

Lily could feel the blush tingling all the way up from her toes. She dropped her eyes to cover the utterly immodest desire in them and murmured, 'I believe so my lord. Naturally, I will be guided by you in such matters.'

'Naturally,' Jack said drily as he slid the straps of her camisole from her shoulders and leaned forward to trace the sensitive line of her collarbone with the tip of his tongue. 'I look forward to seeing just how long this unnatural state of meekness lasts. Let me see now. Did I mention that I will expect my wife to give up all her business activities once we are married? I would not want you to trouble your feminine brain with all those nasty figures.'

'I will do no such thing!' Lily sat up so abruptly that the camisole fell down to her waist, producing a moan of erotic delight from Jack. 'I have every intention— You are teasing me! Wretch!'

Jack caught her hands, raised to box his ears. 'Yes, my love. Just teasing. Now I *know* I have my Lily back!'

* * * * *

MILLS & BOON®

Live the emotion

Look out for next month's Super Historical Romance

THE CAPTAIN'S WOMAN
by Merline Lovelace

She followed her heart…and found her destiny!

Victoria Parker has two passions: her journalism, which has been confined to the society page, and Captain Sam Garrett, whose heart belongs to another woman. But everything is about to change.

As American soldiers take arms against the Spanish, Victoria follows her captain to Cuba. There, instead of a joyous reunion with the man to whom she has surrendered body and soul, she finds chaos and heartache.

As Victoria grows from novice reporter to dedicated journalist, she becomes a proud, courageous woman – unafraid to fight for her country, her ideals, and her heart!

"…a story of great courage, friendship, loyalty, tenacity and hope in the face of the horrors of war."
—*Romantic Times BOOKclub*

On sale 2nd February 2007

Available at WHSmith, Tesco, ASDA, and all good bookshops

www.millsandboon.co.uk

An enchantingly romantic Regency romp from *New York Times* bestselling author Stephanie Laurens

After the death of her father, Georgiana Hartley returns home to England – only to be confronted with the boorish advances of her cousin. Fleeing to the neighbouring estate of Dominic Ridgely, Viscount Alton of Candlewick, Georgiana finds herself sent to London for a Season under the patronage of the Viscount's sister.

Suddenly Georgiana is transformed into a lady, charming the *ton* and cultivating a bevy of suitors. Everything is unfolding according to Dominic's plan... until he realises that he desires Georgiana for his own.

On sale 15th December 2006

Available at WHSmith, Tesco, ASDA, Borders, Eason, Sainsbury's and all good paperback bookshops

2 FREE

BOOKS AND A SURPRISE GIFT!

We would like to take this opportunity to thank you for reading this Mills & Boon® book by offering you the chance to take TWO more specially selected titles from the Historical Romance™ series absolutely FREE! We're also making this offer to introduce you to the benefits of the Milss & Boon® Reader Service™—

- ★ FREE home delivery
- ★ FREE gifts and competitions
- ★ FREE monthly Newsletter
- ★ Exclusive Reader Service offers
- ★ Books available before they're in the shops

Accepting these FREE books and gift places you under no obligation to buy, you may cancel at any time, even after receiving your free shipment. Simply complete your details below and return the entire page to the address below. You don't even need a stamp!

YES! Please send me 2 free Historical Romance books and a surprise gift. I understand that unless you hear from me, I will receive 4 superb new titles every month for just £3.69 each, postage and packing free. I am under no obligation to purchase any books and may cancel my subscription at any time. The free books and gift will be mine to keep in any case.

H7ZED

Ms/Mrs/Miss/Mr .... Initials ....
BLOCK CAPITALS PLEASE

Surname ....

Address ....

....

.... Postcode ....

Send this whole page to:
UK: FREEPOST CN8I, Croydon, CR9 3WZ